ANCIENT SORCERIES
AND OTHER CHILLING TALES

Algernon Henry Blackwood CBE (1869–1951) was an English short story writer and novelist, one of the most prolific writers of ghost stories in the history of the genre. He was also a journalist and a broadcasting narrator.

Anthony Lejeune is an award-winning broadcaster, journalist and author. He read Classics at Balliol College, Oxford. He lives in London.

Ancient Sorceries
And Other Chilling Tales

Algernon Blackwood

FOREWORD BY ANTHONY LEJEUNE

CAPUCHIN CLASSICS
LONDON

Ancient Sorceries
Copyright © by Susan Reeves-Jones

The Willows first published in 1907 in *The Listener and Other Stories*
The Insanity of Jones first published in 1907 in *The Listener and Other Stories*
Ancient Sorceries first published in 1908 in *John Silence: Physician Extraordinary*
The Wendigo first published in 1910 in *The Lost Valley and Other Stories*
The Land of Green Ginger first published in 1927 in *The Radio Times*
The Man Who Lived Backwards first published in 1930 in *World Radio*

This collection published by Capuchin Classics in 2013
Foreword © Anthony Lejeune, 2013

Capuchin Classics
128 Kensington Church Street, London W8 4BH
Telephone: +44 (0)20 7221 7166
Fax: +44 (0)20 7792 9288
E-mail: info@capuchin-classics.co.uk
www.capuchin-classics.co.uk

Châtelaine of Capuchin Classics: Emma Howard

Cover design by Vicky Wharton

ISBN: 978-1-907429-85-9

Printed and bound by TJ International, Cornwall

Contents

Foreword

'Are they all horrid? Are you sure they are all horrid?' one girl asks the other in *Northanger Abbey* as they discuss their reading list. What they had in mind were thrilling Gothic horrors, replete with black veils and skeletons. Such primitive exercises duly gave way in subsequent decades to somewhat more sophisticated 'sensation' novels, to Wilkie Collins and eventually Bram Stoker's *Dracula*. The ghost story as a distinct form arguably reached its epitome in the hands of M.R. James whose genuinely chilling tales would surely have caused Jane Austen's young ladies to faint clear away.

Algernon Blackwood, born in 1869, overlapped with James but lived on, and worked on, into the Post-War television age, where he became the principal exponent of a now lost or forgotten art – the art of telling a story, without a script or autocue, direct to camera. Some people are said to have 'a good face for radio': Blackwood had, as a BBC producer recalls, 'a wonderful face for television, lined like a walnut. And the eyes of a storyteller, eyes that held you while the story was woven'. He was also a natural and habitual raconteur, swapping anecdotes with Compton Mackenzie and Gilbert Harding in the bar of the Savile Club.

Some of his published tales – and he wrote more than three hundred, ranging from brief anecdotes to full-length novels – might still be considered 'horrid' in the sense of frightening but they are much more varied than the work of M.R. James or that of another contemporary in the field, Arthur Machen. Some of his work is even quite sentimental, with happy endings.

It won't do, therefore, to describe him as a writer of ghost stories or even of weird tales, though there are ghosts in them and weirdness of one sort or another in most of them. The closest one can come, perhaps, is to say that Algernon Blackwood wrote strange stories, which can't be squeezed into any single category.

The Blackwoods were a variously distinguished upper-class family; Algernon's father was a Clerk to the Treasury, later became Secretary to the Post Office and was knighted; his mother had previously been married to the Duke of Manchester. The family, or at least his father, became evangelically Christian to an oppressive degree. Young Algernon's remedy was to slip from his room in the middle of the night, launch his boat on to the lake, commune with nature and perform mystical ceremonies.

After studying agriculture at Edinburgh University, he crossed the Atlantic and spent the next few years partly in Toronto and partly in New York, where he ran a bar, worked as a newspaperman, experimented with drugs, mixed with, and was fleeced by, a gallery of scoundrels.

Returning to London, he found that he could write his kind of story easily and that there was a good market for them in the numerous magazines of the day. For some of the best he drew on his experiences in the Canadian forests. He took to spending time in Switzerland, and was there when the First World War broke out.

He expected to make himself useful in the Field Ambulance service but instead was invited to be a spymaster. He took over the job which was previously done by Somerset Maugham (and was the foundation for Maugham's Ashenden stories) and, before him, by Edward Knoblock (who wrote *Kismet*). Based in Switzerland and speaking good French and German, he recruited agents, equipped them with secret inks and passed on messages. He proved his worth but disliked the work, the deception involved and the constant knowledge that he was putting other men's lives in danger.

It drained and depressed him. Back in London after the war, he never quite caught again the full flood of success which he had enjoyed in the Edwardian period, but he renewed an interest in writing for the theatre. An adaptation of his work, *A Prisoner in Fairyland*, entitled *The Starlight Express*, had been adorned with music by Elgar. Now radio offered a new market, for plays, talks and storytelling, which led ultimately to telling stories on television. The working pattern for the rest of his life was effectively set.

He drove producers mad by never telling a story quite as he had rehearsed it, but his professionalism brought him to the closing moment at just the right time. There is an evocative anecdote which describes an evening of thick fog – the 'London Particular' so familiar in those days, almost unimaginable now – with a frantic television producer standing on the steps of Alexandra Palace, wondering if Blackwood could possibly get there. At the very last moment Blackwood's tall figure emerged from the fog. He had climbed the hill, rehearsing the story in his mind, and then went straight to the studio and delivered an immaculate performance.

On another occasion, a very simple camera trick made it appear that he had suddenly vanished. A flood of telephone calls followed from alarmed viewers of this supernatural phenomenon.

So the years passed, pleasantly and fruitfully. His work never made him rich but in 1949 he was pleased to be awarded a CBE, though he wrote in his diary 'Odd to be a Commander of an Empire which the bestowers of the honour have destroyed!'. He died in 1951.

He never married. He was fond of children, sometimes writing for them, often writing about them. Like J.M. Barrie, he thought they possessed the key to a magical world which adults had lost.

They could slip through a 'crack', as it were in a mountainside, a crack into their world, a crack between one place and another, between today and tomorrow.

In his youth he joined The Hermetic Order of the Golden Dawn, to which W.B.Yeats belonged but seems not to have progressed very far up its hieratic ladder. He was drawn too, as were many people after the losses of the First World War, to Madame Blavatsky and her theosophical doctrines, which included reincarnation. Later he explored the ideas of Gurdjeff and Ouspensky.

His own ultimate beliefs are hard to pin down. Insofar as they can be defined at all, they seem to be a worship –sometimes a dread – of Nature as a powerful personalised life-force. What everyone who knew him agrees is that he was charming and courteous, not in the least 'horrid' or lugubrious. He was a life-enhancer, a devotee of the 'supernatural' in a literal sense.

When the Second World War broke out he volunteered for intelligence work but was rejected as too old. He was bombed out from his house in London, losing his papers and memorabilia but escaping injury. He never cared much for possessions anyway, reducing them in the end, he said, to a pair of pyjamas and a typewriter.

He continued to write for print but the days of his greatest fame lay ahead. BBC pay-scales didn't make him rich but broadcasting did make him more widely celebrated than ever before. He revised and re-shaped old stories. His most orthodox, but by no means the least interesting, exercise was the set of stories about a psychic detective, called *John Silence.*

In so large an output, ideas inevitably recur. But always hovering on the mysterious edge of the crack between the known and the unknown, Somewhere and Elsewhere, the commonplace and the very strange.

Anthony Lejeune

The Wendigo

I

A considerable number of hunting parties were out that year without finding so much as a fresh trail; for the moose were uncommonly shy, and the various Nimrods returned to the bosoms of their respective families with the best excuses the facts of their imaginations could suggest. Dr. Cathcart, among others, came back without a trophy; but he brought instead the memory of an experience which he declares was worth all the bull moose that had ever been shot. But then Cathcart, of Aberdeen, was interested in other things besides moose – amongst them the vagaries of the human mind. This particular story, however, found no mention in his book on Collective Hallucination for the simple reason (so he confided once to a fellow colleague) that he himself played too intimate a part in it to form a competent judgment of the affair as a whole . . . .

Besides himself and his guide, Hank Davis, there was young Simpson, his nephew, a divinity student destined for the 'Wee Kirk' (then on his first visit to Canadian backwoods), and the latter's guide, Défago. Joseph Défago was a French 'Canuck,' who had strayed from his native Province of Quebec years before, and had got caught in Rat Portage when the Canadian Pacific Railway was a-building; a man who, in addition to his unparalleled knowledge of woodcraft and bushlore, could also sing the old *voyageur* songs and tell a capital hunting yarn into the bargain. He was deeply susceptible, moreover, to that singular spell which the wilderness lays upon certain lonely natures, and he loved the wild solitudes with a kind of romantic passion that amounted almost to an obsession. The life of the backwoods fascinated him – whence, doubtless, his surpassing efficiency in dealing with their mysteries.

On this particular expedition he was Hank's choice. Hank knew him and swore by him. He also swore at him, 'jest as a pal might,' and since he had a vocabulary of picturesque, if utterly meaningless, oaths, the conversation between the two stalwart and hardy woodsmen was often of a rather lively description. This river of expletives, however, Hank agreed to dam a little out of respect for his old 'hunting boss,' Dr. Cathcart, whom of course he addressed after the fashion of the country as 'Doc,' and also because he understood that young Simpson was already a 'bit of a parson.' He had, however, one objection to Défago, and one only – which was, that the French Canadian sometimes exhibited what Hank described as 'the output of a cursed and dismal mind,' meaning apparently that he sometimes was true to type, Latin type, and suffered fits of a kind of silent moroseness when nothing could induce him to utter speech. Défago, that is to say, was imaginative and melancholy. And, as a rule, it was too long a spell of 'civilisation' that induced the attacks, for a few days of the wilderness invariably cured them.

This, then, was the party of four that found themselves in camp the last week in October of that 'shy moose year' way up in the wilderness north of Rat Portage – a forsaken and desolate country. There was also Punk, an Indian, who had accompanied Dr. Cathcart and Hank on their hunting trips in previous years, and who acted as cook. His duty was merely to stay in camp, catch fish, and prepare venison steaks and coffee at a few minutes' notice. He dressed in the worn-out clothes bequeathed to him by former patrons, and, except for his coarse black hair and dark skin, he looked in these city garments no more like a real redskin than a stage Negro looks like a real African. For all that, however, Punk had in him still the instincts of his dying race; his taciturn silence and his endurance survived; also his superstition.

The party round the blazing fire that night were despondent, for a week had passed without a single sign of recent moose discovering itself. Défago had sung his song and plunged into a story, but Hank, in bad humour, reminded him so often that 'he kep' mussing-up the fac's so, that it was 'most all nothin' but a petered-out lie,' that the Frenchman had finally subsided into a sulky silence which nothing seemed likely to break. Dr. Cathcart and his nephew were fairly done after an exhausting day. Punk was washing up the dishes, grunting to himself under the lean-to of branches, where he later also slept. No one troubled to stir the slowly dying fire. Overhead the stars were brilliant in a sky quite wintry, and there was so little wind that ice was already forming stealthily along the shores of the still lake behind them. The silence of the vast listening forest stole forward and enveloped them.

Hank broke in suddenly with his nasal voice.

'I'm in favour of breaking new ground tomorrow, Doc,' he observed with energy, looking across at his employer. 'We don't stand a dead Dago's chance around here.'

'Agreed,' said Cathcart, always a man of few words. 'Think the idea's good.'

'Sure pop, it's good,' Hank resumed with confidence. 'S'pose, now, you and I strike west, up Garden Lake way for a change! None of us ain't touched that quiet bit o' land yet –'

'I'm with you.'

'And you, Défago, take Mr. Simpson along in the small canoe, skip across the lake, portage over into Fifty Island Water, and take a good squint down that thar southern shore. The moose 'yarded' there like hell last year, and for all we know they may be doin' it agin this year jest to spite us.'

Défago, keeping his eyes on the fire, said nothing by way of reply. He was still offended, possibly, about his interrupted story.

'No one's been up that way this year, an' I'll lay my bottom dollar on *that!*' Hank added with emphasis, as though he had a reason for knowing. He looked over at his partner sharply. 'Better take the little silk tent and stay away a couple o' nights,' he concluded, as though the matter were definitely settled. For Hank was recognised as general organiser of the hunt, and in charge of the party.

It was obvious to anyone that Défago did not jump at the plan, but his silence seemed to convey something more than ordinary disapproval, and across his sensitive dark face there passed a curious expression like a flash of firelight – not so quickly, however, that the three men had not time to catch it.

'He funked for some reason, *I* thought,' Simpson said afterwards in the tent he shared with his uncle. Dr. Cathcart made no immediate reply, although the look had interested him enough at the time for him to make a mental note of it. The expression had caused him a passing uneasiness he could not quite account for at the moment.

But Hank, of course, had been the first to notice it, and the odd thing was that instead of becoming explosive or angry over the other's reluctance, he at once began to humour him a bit.

'But there ain't no *speshul* reason why no one's been up there this year,' he said with a perceptible hush in his tone; 'not the reason you mean, anyway! Las' year it was the fires that kep' folks out, and this year I guess – I guess it jest happened so, that's all!' His manner was clearly meant to be encouraging.

Joseph Défago raised his eyes a moment, then dropped them again. A breath of wind stole out of the forest and stirred the embers into a passing blaze. Dr. Cathcart again noticed the expression in the guide's face, and again he did not like it. But this time the nature of the look betrayed itself. In those eyes, for an instant, he caught the gleam of a man scared in his very soul. It disquieted him more than he cared to admit.

'Bad Indians up that way?' he asked, with a laugh to ease matters a little, while Simpson, too sleepy to notice this subtle by-play, moved off to bed with a prodigious yawn; 'or – or anything wrong with the country?' he added, when his nephew was out of hearing.

Hank met his eye with something less than his usual frankness.

'He's jest skeered,' he replied good-humouredly. 'Skeered stiff about some ole feery tale! That's all, ain't it, ole pard?' And he gave Défago a friendly kick on the moccasined foot that lay nearest the fire.

Défago looked up quickly, as from an interrupted reverie, a reverie, however, that had not prevented his seeing all that went on about him.

'Skeered – *nuthin!*' he answered, with a flush of defiance. 'There's nuthin' in the Bush that can skeer Joseph Défago, and don't you forget it!' And the natural energy with which he spoke made it impossible to know whether he told the whole truth or only a part of it.

Hank turned towards the doctor. He was just going to add something when he stopped abruptly and looked round. A sound close behind them in the darkness made all three start. It was old Punk, who had moved up from his lean-to while they talked and now stood there just beyond the circle of firelight-listening.

''Nother time, Doc!' Hank whispered, with a wink, 'when the gallery ain't stepped down into the stalls!' And, springing to his feet, he slapped the Indian on the back and cried noisily, 'Come up t' the fire an' warm yer dirty red skin a bit.' He dragged him towards the blaze and threw more wood on. 'That was a mighty good feed you give us an hour or two back,' he continued heartily, as though to set the man's thoughts on another scent, 'and it ain't Christian to let you stand out there freezin' yer ole soul to hell while we're gettin' all good an' toasted!' Punk moved in and warmed his feet, smiling darkly at the other's volubility which he only half understood, but saying nothing. And presently Dr. Cathcart, seeing that further conversation was impossible, followed his nephew's example and moved off to the tent, leaving the three men smoking over the now blazing fire.

It is not easy to undress in a small tent without waking one's companion, and Cathcart, hardened and warm-blooded as he was in spite of his fifty odd years, did what Hank would have described as 'considerable of his twilight' in the open. He noticed, during the process, that Punk had meanwhile gone back to his lean-to, and that Hank and Défago were at it hammer and tongs, or, rather, hammer and anvil, the little French Canadian being the anvil. It was all very like the conventional stage picture of Western melodrama: the fire lighting up their faces with patches of alternate red and black; Défago, in slouch hat and moccasins in the part of the 'badlands' villain; Hank, open-faced and hatless, with that reckless fling of his shoulders, the honest and deceived hero; and old Punk, eavesdropping in the background, supplying the atmosphere of mystery. The doctor smiled as he noticed the details; but at the same time something deep within him – he hardly knew what – shrank a little, as though an almost imperceptible breath of warning had touched the surface of his soul and was gone again before he could seize it. Probably it was traceable to that 'scared expression' he had seen in the eyes of Défago; 'probably' – for this hint of fugitive emotion otherwise escaped his usually so keen analysis. Défago, he was vaguely aware, might cause trouble somehow . . . He was not as steady a guide as Hank, for instance . . . Further than that he could not get . . .

He watched the men a moment longer before diving into the stuffy tent where Simpson already slept soundly. Hank, he saw, was swearing like a mad African in a New York nigger saloon; but it was the swearing of 'affection'. The ridiculous oaths flew freely now that the cause of their obstruction was asleep. Presently he put his arm almost tenderly upon his comrade's shoulder, and they moved off together into the shadows where their tent stood faintly glimmering. Punk, too, a moment later followed their example and disappeared between his odorous blankets in the opposite direction.

Dr. Cathcart then likewise turned in, weariness and sleep still fighting in his mind with an obscure curiosity to know what it was that had scared Défago about the country up Fifty Island Water way, – wondering, too, why Punk's presence had prevented the completion of what Hank had to say. Then sleep overtook him. He would know tomorrow. Hank would tell him the story while they trudged after the elusive moose.

Deep silence fell about the little camp, planted there so audaciously in the jaws of the wilderness. The lake gleamed like a sheet of black glass beneath the stars. The cold air pricked. In the draughts of night that poured their silent tide from the depths of the forest, with messages from distant ridges and from lakes just beginning to freeze, there lay already the faint, bleak odours of coming winter. White men, with their dull scent, might never have divined them; the fragrance of the wood fire would have concealed from them these almost electrical hints of moss and bark and hardening swamp a hundred miles away. Even Hank and Défago, subtly in league with the soul of the woods as they were, would probably have spread their delicate nostrils in vain. . . .

But an hour later, when all slept like the dead, old Punk crept from his blankets and went down to the shore of the lake like a shadow – silently, as only Indian blood can move. He raised his head and looked about him. The thick darkness rendered sight of small avail, but, like the animals, he possessed other senses that darkness could not mute. He listened – then sniffed the air. Motionless as a hemlock stem he stood there. After five minutes again he lifted his head and sniffed, and yet once again. A tingling of the wonderful nerves that betrayed itself by no outer sign, ran through him as he tasted the keen air. Then, merging his figure into the surrounding blackness in a way that only wild men and animals understand, he turned, still moving like a shadow, and went stealthily back to his lean-to and his bed.

And soon after he slept, the change of wind he had divined stirred gently the reflection of the stars within the lake. Rising among the far ridges of the country beyond Fifty Island Water, it came from the direction in which he had stared, and it passed over the sleeping camp with a faint and sighing murmur through the tops of the big trees that was almost too delicate to be audible. With it, down the desert paths of night, though too faint, too high even for the Indian's hair-like nerves, there passed a curious, thin odour, strangely disquieting, an odour of something that seemed unfamiliar – utterly unknown.

The French Canadian and the man of Indian blood each stirred uneasily in his sleep just about this time, though neither of them woke. Then the ghost of that unforgettably strange odour passed away and was lost among the leagues of tenantless forest beyond.

II

I n the morning the camp was astir before the sun. There had been a light fall of snow during the night and the air was sharp. Punk had done his duty betimes, for the odours of coffee and fried bacon reached every tent. All were in good spirits.

'Wind's shifted!' cried Hank vigorously, watching Simpson and his guide already loading the small canoe. 'It's across the lake – dead right for you fellers. And the snow'll make bully trails! If there's any moose mussing around up thar, they'll not get so much as a tail-end scent of you with the wind as it is. Good luck, Monsieur Défago!' he added, facetiously giving the name its French pronunciation for once, *'bonne chance!'*

Défago returned the good wishes, apparently in the best of spirits, the silent mood gone. Before eight o'clock old Punk had the camp to himself, Cathcart and Hank were far along the trail that led westwards, while the canoe that carried Défago and Simpson, with silk tent and grub for two days, was already a dark speck bobbing on the bosom of the lake, going due east.

The wintry sharpness of the air was tempered now by a sun that topped the wooded ridges and blazed with a luxurious warmth upon the world of lake and forest below; loons flew skimming through the sparkling spray that the wind lifted; divers shook their dripping heads to the sun and popped smartly out of sight again; and as far as the eye could reach rose the leagues of endless, crowding Bush, desolate in its lonely sweep and grandeur, untrodden by foot of man, and stretching its mighty and unbroken carpet right up to the frozen shores of Hudson Bay.

Simpson, who saw it all for the first time as he paddled hard in the bows of the dancing canoe, was enchanted by its austere beauty. His heart drank in the sense of freedom and great spaces just as his lungs drank in the cool and perfumed wind. Behind him in the stern seat, singing fragments of his native chanties, Défago steered the craft of birch bark like a thing of life, answering cheerfully all his companion's questions. Both were gay and light-hearted. On such occasions men lose the superficial, worldly distinctions; they become human beings working together for a common end. Simpson, the employer, and Défago the employed, among these primitive forces, were simply two men, the 'guider' and the 'guided.' Superior knowledge, of course, assumed control, and the younger man fell without a second thought into the quasi-subordinate position. He never dreamed of objecting when Défago dropped the 'Mr.,' and addressed him as 'Say, Simpson,' or 'Simpson, boss,' which was invariably the case before they reached the farther shore after a stiff paddle of twelve miles against a head wind. He only laughed, and liked it; then ceased to notice it at all.

For this 'divinity student' was a young man of parts and character, though as yet, of course, untravelled; and on this trip – the first time he had seen any country but his own and little Switzerland – the huge scale of things somewhat bewildered him. It was one thing, he realised, to hear about primeval forests, but quite another to see them. While to dwell in them and seek acquaintance with their wild life was, again, an initiation that no intelligent man could undergo without a certain shifting of personal values hitherto held for permanent and sacred.

Simpson knew the first faint indication of this emotion when he held the new .303 rifle in his hands and looked along its pair of faultless, gleaming barrels. The three days' journey to their headquarters, by lake and portage, had carried the process a stage farther. And now that he was about to plunge beyond even the fringe of wilderness where they were camped into the virgin heart of uninhabited regions as vast as Europe itself, the true nature of the situation stole upon him with an effect of delight and awe that his imagination was fully capable of appreciating. It was himself and Défago against a multitude – at least, against a Titan!

The bleak splendors of these remote and lonely forests rather overwhelmed him with the sense of his own littleness. That stern quality of the tangled backwoods which can only be described as merciless and terrible, rose out of these far blue woods swimming upon the horizon, and revealed itself. He understood the silent warning. He realised his own utter helplessness. Only Défago, as a symbol of a distant civilisation where man was master, stood between him and a pitiless death by exhaustion and starvation.

It was thrilling to him, therefore, to watch Défago turn over the canoe upon the shore, pack the paddles carefully underneath, and then proceed to 'blaze' the spruce stems for some distance on either side of an almost invisible trail, with the careless remark thrown in, 'Say, Simpson, if anything happens to me, you'll find the canoe all correc' by these marks; – then strike doo west into the sun to hit the home camp agin, see?'

It was the most natural thing in the world to say, and he said it without any noticeable inflexion of the voice, only it happened to express the youth's emotions at the moment with an utterance that was symbolic of the situation and of his own helplessness as a factor in it. He was alone with Défago in a primitive world: that was all. The canoe, another symbol of man's ascendancy, was now to be left behind. Those small yellow patches, made on the trees by the axe, were the only indications of its hiding place.

Meanwhile, shouldering the packs between them, each man carrying his own rifle, they followed the slender trail over rocks and fallen trunks and across half-frozen swamps; skirting numerous lakes that fairly gemmed the forest, their borders fringed with mist; and towards five o'clock found themselves suddenly on the edge of the woods, looking out across a large sheet of water in front of them, dotted with pine-clad islands of all describable shapes and sizes.

'Fifty Island Water,' announced Défago wearily, 'and the sun jest goin' to dip his bald old head into it!' he added, with unconscious poetry; and immediately they set about pitching camp for the night.

In a very few minutes, under those skilful hands that never made a movement too much or a movement too little, the silk tent stood taut and cozy, the beds of balsam boughs ready laid, and a brisk cooking fire burned with the minimum of smoke. While the young Scotchman cleaned the fish they had caught trolling behind the canoe, Défago 'guessed' he would 'jest as soon' take a turn through the Bush for indications of moose. '*May* come across a trunk where they bin and rubbed horns,' he said, as he moved off, 'or feedin' on the last of the maple leaves' – and he was gone.

His small figure melted away like a shadow in the dusk, while Simpson noted with a kind of admiration how easily the forest absorbed him into herself. A few steps, it seemed, and he was no longer visible.

Yet there was little underbrush hereabouts; the trees stood somewhat apart, well spaced; and in the clearings grew silver birch and maple, spearlike and slender, against the immense stems of spruce and hemlock. But for occasional prostrate monsters, and the boulders of grey rock that thrust uncouth shoulders here and there out of the ground, it might well have been a bit of park in the Old Country. Almost, one might have seen in it the hand of man. A little to the right, however, began the great burnt section, miles in extent, proclaiming its real character – *brulé*, as it is called, where the fires of the previous year had raged for weeks, and the blackened stumps now rose gaunt and ugly, bereft of branches, like gigantic match heads stuck into the ground, savage and desolate beyond words. The perfume of charcoal and rain-soaked ashes still hung faintly about it.

The dusk rapidly deepened; the glades grew dark; the crackling of the fire and the wash of little waves along the rocky lake shore were the only sounds audible. The wind had dropped with the sun, and in all that vast world of branches nothing stirred. Any moment, it seemed, the woodland gods, who are to be worshipped in silence and loneliness, might stretch their mighty and terrific outlines among the trees. In front, through doorways pillared by huge straight stems, lay the stretch of Fifty Island Water, a crescent-shaped lake some fifteen miles from tip to tip, and perhaps five miles across where they were camped. A sky of rose and saffron, more clear than any atmosphere Simpson had ever known, still dropped its pale streaming fires across the waves, where the islands – a hundred, surely, rather than fifty – floated like the fairy barques of some enchanted fleet. Fringed with pines, whose crests fingered most delicately the sky, they almost seemed to move upwards as the light faded – about to weigh anchor and navigate the pathways of the heavens instead of the currents of their native and desolate lake.

And strips of coloured cloud, like flaunting pennons, signalled their departure to the stars. . . .

The beauty of the scene was strangely uplifting. Simpson smoked the fish and burnt his fingers into the bargain in his efforts to enjoy it and at the same time tend the frying pan and the fire. Yet, ever at the back of his thoughts, lay that other aspect of the wilderness: the indifference to human life, the merciless spirit of desolation which took no note of man. The sense of his utter loneliness, now that even Défago had gone, came close as he looked about him and listened for the sound of his companion's returning footsteps.

There was pleasure in the sensation, yet with it a perfectly comprehensible alarm. And instinctively the thought stirred in him: 'What should I – *could* I, do – if anything happened and he did not come back – ?'

They enjoyed their well-earned supper, eating untold quantities of fish, and drinking unmilked tea strong enough to kill men who had not covered thirty miles of hard 'going,' eating little on the way. And when it was over, they smoked and told stories round the blazing fire, laughing, stretching weary limbs, and discussing plans for the morrow. Défago was in excellent spirits, though disappointed at having no signs of moose to report. But it was dark and he had not gone far. The *brulé*, too, was bad. His clothes and hands were smeared with charcoal. Simpson, watching him, realised with renewed vividness their position – alone together in the wilderness.

'Défago,' he said presently, 'these woods, you know, are a bit too big to feel quite at home in – to feel comfortable in, I mean!. . . Eh?' He merely gave expression to the mood of the moment; he was hardly prepared for the earnestness, the solemnity even, with which the guide took him up.

'You've hit it right, Simpson, boss,' he replied, fixing his searching brown eyes on his face, 'and that's the truth, sure. There's no end to 'em – no end at all.' Then he added in a lowered tone as if to himself, 'There's lots found out *that*, and gone plumb to pieces!'

But the man's gravity of manner was not quite to the other's liking; it was a little too suggestive for this scenery and setting; he was sorry he had broached the subject. He remembered suddenly how his uncle had told him that men were sometimes stricken with a strange fever of the wilderness, when the seduction of the uninhabited wastes caught them so fiercely that they went forth, half fascinated, half deluded, to their death. And he had a shrewd idea that his companion held something in sympathy with that queer type. He led the conversation on to other topics, on to Hank and the doctor, for instance, and the natural rivalry as to who should get the first sight of moose.

'If they went doo west,' observed Défago carelessly, 'there's sixty miles between us now – with ole Punk at halfway house eatin' himself full to bustin' with fish and coffee.' They laughed together over the picture. But the casual mention of those sixty miles again made Simpson realise the prodigious scale of this land where they hunted; sixty miles was a mere step; two hundred little more than a step. Stories of lost hunters rose persistently before his memory. The passion and mystery of homeless and wandering men, seduced by the beauty of great forests, swept his soul in a way too vivid to be quite pleasant. He wondered vaguely whether it was the mood of his companion that invited the unwelcome suggestion with such persistence.

'Sing us a song, Défago, if you're not too tired,' he asked; 'one of those old *voyageur* songs you sang the other night.' He handed his tobacco pouch to the guide and then filled his own pipe, while the Canadian, nothing loth, sent his light voice across the lake in one of those plaintive, almost melancholy chanties with which lumbermen and trappers lessen the burden of their labour. There was an appealing and romantic flavour about it, something that recalled the atmosphere of the old pioneer days when Indians and wilderness were leagued together, battles frequent, and the Old Country farther off than it is today. The sound travelled pleasantly over the water, but the forest at their backs seemed to swallow it down with a single gulp that permitted neither echo nor resonance.

It was in the middle of the third verse that Simpson noticed something unusual – something that brought his thoughts back with a rush from faraway scenes. A curious change had come into the man's voice. Even before he knew what it was, uneasiness caught him, and looking up quickly, he saw that Défago, though still singing, was peering about him into the Bush, as though he heard or saw something. His voice grew fainter – dropped to a hush – then ceased altogether. The same instant, with a movement amazingly alert, he started to his feet and stood upright – *sniffing the air.* Like a dog scenting game, he drew the air into his nostrils in short, sharp breaths, turning quickly as he did so in all directions, and finally 'pointing' down the lake shore, eastwards. It was a performance unpleasantly suggestive and at the same time singularly dramatic. Simpson's heart fluttered disagreeably as he watched it.

'Lord, man! How you made me jump!' he exclaimed, on his feet beside him the same instant, and peering over his shoulder into the sea of darkness. 'What's up? Are you frightened – ?'

Even before the question was out of his mouth he knew it was foolish, for any man with a pair of eyes in his head could see that the Canadian had turned white down to his very gills. Not even sunburn and the glare of the fire could hide that.

The student felt himself trembling a little, weakish in the knees. 'What's up?' he repeated quickly. 'D'you smell moose? Or anything queer, anything – wrong?' He lowered his voice instinctively.

The forest pressed round them with its encircling wall; the nearer tree stems gleamed like bronze in the firelight; beyond that – blackness, and, so far as he could tell, a silence of death. Just behind them a passing puff of wind lifted a single leaf, looked at it, then laid it softly down again without disturbing the rest of the covey. It seemed as if a million invisible causes had combined just to produce that single visible effect. *Other* life pulsed about them – and was gone.

Défago turned abruptly; the livid hue of his face had turned to a dirty grey.

'I never said I heered – or smelt – nuthin',' he said slowly and emphatically, in an oddly altered voice that conveyed somehow a touch of defiance. 'I was only – takin' a look round – so to speak. It's always a mistake to be too previous with yer questions.' Then he added suddenly with obvious effort, in his more natural voice, 'Have you got the matches, Boss Simpson?' and proceeded to light the pipe he had half filled just before he began to sing.

Without speaking another word they sat down again by the fire. Défago changing his side so that he could face the direction the wind came from. For even a tenderfoot could tell that. Défago changed his position in order to hear and smell – all there was to be heard and smelt. And, since he now faced the lake with his back to the trees it was evidently nothing in the forest that had sent so strange and sudden a warning to his marvellously trained nerves.

'Guess now I don't feel like singing any,' he explained presently of his own accord. 'That song kinder brings back memories that's troublesome to me; I never oughter've begun it. It sets me on t' imagining things, see?'

Clearly the man was still fighting with some profoundly moving emotion. He wished to excuse himself in the eyes of the other. But the explanation, in that it was only a part of the truth, was a lie, and he knew perfectly well that Simpson was not deceived by it. For nothing could explain away the livid terror that had dropped over his face while he stood there sniffing the air. And nothing – no amount of blazing fire, or chatting on ordinary subjects – could make that camp exactly as it had been before. The shadow of an unknown horror, naked if unguessed, that had flashed for an instant in the face and gestures of the guide, had also communicated itself, vaguely and therefore more potently, to his companion. The guide's visible efforts to dissemble the truth only made things worse. Moreover, to add to the younger man's uneasiness, was the difficulty, nay, the impossibility he felt of asking questions, and also his complete ignorance as to the cause ... Indians, wild animals, forest fires – all these, he knew, were wholly out of the question. His imagination searched vigorously, but in vain. . . .

Yet, somehow or other, after another long spell of smoking, talking and roasting themselves before the great fire, the shadow that had so suddenly invaded their peaceful camp began to shirt. Perhaps Défago's efforts, or the return of his quiet and normal attitude accomplished this; perhaps Simpson himself had exaggerated the affair out of all proportion to the truth; or possibly the vigorous air of the wilderness brought its own powers of healing. Whatever the cause, the feeling of immediate horror seemed to have passed away as mysteriously as it had come, for nothing occurred to feed it. Simpson began to feel that he had permitted himself the unreasoning terror of a child. He put it down partly to a certain subconscious excitement that this wild and immense scenery generated in his blood, partly to the spell of solitude, and partly to overfatigue. That pallor in the guide's face was, of course, uncommonly hard to explain, yet it *might* have been due in some way to an effect of firelight, or his own imagination . . . He gave it the benefit of the doubt; he was Scotch.

When a somewhat unordinary emotion has disappeared, the mind always finds a dozen ways of explaining away its causes . . . Simpson lit a last pipe and tried to laugh to himself. On getting home to Scotland it would make quite a good story. He did not realise that this laughter was a sign that terror still lurked in the recesses of his soul – that, in fact, it was merely one of the conventional signs by which a man, seriously alarmed, tries to persuade himself that he is *not* so.

Défago, however, heard that low laughter and looked up with surprise on his face. The two men stood, side by side, kicking the embers about before going to bed. It was ten o'clock – a late hour for hunters to be still awake.

'What's ticklin' yer?' he asked in his ordinary tone, yet gravely.

'I – I was thinking of our little toy woods at home, just at that moment,' stammered Simpson, coming back to what really dominated his mind, and startled by the question, 'and comparing them to – to all this,' and he swept his arm round to indicate the Bush.

A pause followed in which neither of them said anything.

'All the same I wouldn't laugh about it, if I was you,' Défago added, looking over Simpson's shoulder into the shadows. 'There's places in there nobody won't never see into – nobody knows what lives in there either.'

'Too big – too far off?' The suggestion in the guide's manner was immense and horrible.

Défago nodded. The expression on his face was dark. He, too, felt uneasy. The younger man understood that in a *hinterland* of this size there might well be depths of wood that would never in the life of the world be known or trodden. The thought was not exactly the sort he welcomed. In a loud voice, cheerfully, he suggested that it was time for bed. But the guide lingered, tinkering with the fire, arranging the stones needlessly, doing a dozen things that did not really need doing. Evidently there was something he wanted to say, yet found it difficult to 'get at.'

'Say, you, Boss Simpson,' he began suddenly, as the last shower of sparks went up into the air, 'you don't – smell nothing, do you – nothing pertickler, I mean?' The commonplace question, Simpson realised, veiled a dreadfully serious thought in his mind. A shiver ran down his back.

'Nothing but burning wood,' he replied firmly, kicking again at the embers. The sound of his own foot made him start.

'And all the evenin' you ain't smelt – nothing?' persisted the guide, peering at him through the gloom; 'nothing extrordiny, and different to anything else you ever smelt before?'

'No, no, man; nothing at all!' he replied aggressively, half angrily.

Défago's face cleared. 'That's good!' he exclaimed with evident relief. 'That's good to hear.' 'Have *you?*' asked Simpson sharply, and the same instant regretted the question.

The Canadian came closer in the darkness. He shook his head. 'I guess not,' he said, though without overwhelming conviction. 'It must've been just that song of mine that did it. It's the song they sing in lumber camps and godforsaken places like that, when they've skeered the Wendigo's somewhere around, doin' a bit of swift travelling. –'

'And what's the Wendigo, pray?' Simpson asked quickly, irritated because again he could not prevent that sudden shiver of the nerves. He knew that he was close upon the man's terror and the cause of it. Yet a rushing passionate curiosity overcame his better judgment, and his fear.

Défago turned swiftly and looked at him as though he were suddenly about to shriek. His eyes shone, but his mouth was wide open. Yet all he said, or whispered rather, for his voice sank very low, was: 'It's nuthin' – nuthin' but what those lousy fellers believe when they've bin hittin' the bottle too long – a sort of great animal that lives up yonder,' he jerked his head northwards, 'quick as lightning in its tracks, an' bigger'n anything else in the Bush, an' ain't supposed to be very good to look at – that's all!'

'A backwoods superstition –' began Simpson, moving hastily toward the tent in order to shake off the hand of the guide that clutched his arm. 'Come, come, hurry up for God's sake, and get the lantern going! It's time we were in bed and asleep if we're going to be up with the sun tomorrow. . . .'

The guide was close on his heels. 'I'm coming,' he answered out of the darkness, 'I'm coming.' And after a slight delay he appeared with the lantern and hung it from a nail in the front pole of the tent. The shadows of a hundred trees shifted their places quickly as he did so, and when he stumbled over the rope, diving swiftly inside, the whole tent trembled as though a gust of wind struck it.

The two men lay down, without undressing, upon their beds of soft balsam boughs, cunningly arranged. Inside, all was warm and cozy, but outside the world of crowding trees pressed close about them, marshalling their million shadows, and smothering the little tent that stood there like a wee white shell facing the ocean of tremendous forest.

Between the two lonely figures within, however, there pressed another shadow that was *not* a shadow from the night. It was the Shadow cast by the strange Fear, never wholly exorcised, that had leaped suddenly upon Défago in the middle of his singing. And Simpson, as he lay there, watching the darkness through the open flap of the tent, ready to plunge into the fragrant abyss of sleep, knew first that unique and profound stillness of a primeval forest when no wind stirs ... and when the night has weight and substance that enters into the soul to bind a veil about it. . . . Then sleep took him. . . . .

III

Thus, it seemed to him, at least. Yet it was true that the lap of the water, just beyond the tent door, still beat time with his lessening pulses when he realised that he was lying with his eyes open and that another sound had recently introduced itself with cunning softness between the splash and murmur of the little waves.

And, long before he understood what this sound was, it had stirred in him the centres of pity and alarm. He listened intently, though at first in vain, for the running blood beat all its drums too noisily in his ears. Did it come, he wondered, from the lake, or from the woods. . . ?

Then, suddenly, with a rush and a flutter of the heart, he knew that it was close beside him in the tent; and, when he turned over for a better hearing, it focused itself unmistakably not two feet away. It was a sound of weeping; Défago upon his bed of branches was sobbing in the darkness as though his heart would break, the blankets evidently stuffed against his mouth to stifle it.

And his first feeling, before he could think or reflect, was the rush of a poignant and searching tenderness. This intimate, human sound, heard amid the desolation about them, woke pity. It was so incongruous, so pitifully incongruous – and so vain! Tears – in this vast and cruel wilderness: of what avail? He thought of a little child crying in mid-Atlantic. . . . Then, of course, with fuller realisation, and the memory of what had gone before, came the descent of the terror upon him, and his blood ran cold.

'Défago,' he whispered quickly, 'what's the matter?' He tried to make his voice very gentle. 'Are you in pain – unhappy – ?' There was no reply, but the sounds ceased abruptly. He stretched his hand out and touched him. The body did not stir.

'Are you awake?' for it occurred to him that the man was crying in his sleep. 'Are you cold?' He noticed that his feet, which were uncovered, projected beyond the mouth of the tent. He spread an extra fold of his own blankets over them. The guide had slipped down in his bed, and the branches seemed to have been dragged with him. He was afraid to pull the body back again, for fear of waking him.

One or two tentative questions he ventured softly, but though he waited for several minutes there came no reply, nor any sign of movement. Presently he heard his regular and quiet breathing, and putting his hand again gently on the breast, felt the steady rise and fall beneath.

'Let me know if anything's wrong,' he whispered, 'or if I can do anything. Wake me at once if you feel – queer.'

He hardly knew what to say. He lay down again, thinking and wondering what it all meant. Défago, of course, had been crying in his sleep. Some dream or other had afflicted him. Yet never in his life would he forget that pitiful sound of sobbing, and the feeling that the whole awful wilderness of woods listened. . . .

His own mind busied itself for a long time with the recent events, of which *this* took its mysterious place as one, and though his reason successfully argued away all unwelcome suggestions, a sensation of uneasiness remained, resisting ejection, very deep-seated – peculiar beyond ordinary.

IV

B ut sleep, in the long run, proves greater than all emotions. His thoughts soon wandered again; he lay there, warm as toast, exceedingly weary; the night soothed and comforted, blunting the edges of memory and alarm. Half an hour later he was oblivious of everything in the outer world about him.

Yet sleep, in this case, was his great enemy, concealing all approaches, smothering the warning of his nerves.

As, sometimes, in a nightmare events crowd upon each other's heels with a conviction of dreadfulest reality, yet some inconsistent detail accuses the whole display of incompleteness and disguise, so the events that now followed, though they actually happened, persuaded the mind somehow that the detail which could explain them had been overlooked in the confusion, and that therefore they were but partly true, the rest delusion. At the back of the sleeper's mind something remains awake, ready to let slip the judgment. 'All this is not *quite* real; when you wake up you'll understand.'

And thus, in a way, it was with Simpson. The events, not wholly inexplicable or incredible in themselves, yet remain for the man who saw and heard them a sequence of separate facts of cold horror, because the little piece that might have made the puzzle clear lay concealed or overlooked.

So far as he can recall, it was a violent movement, running downwards through the tent towards the door, that first woke him and made him aware that his companion was sitting bolt upright beside him – quivering. Hours must have passed, for it was the pale gleam of the dawn that revealed his outline against the canvas. This time the man was not crying; he was quaking like a leaf; the trembling he felt plainly through the blankets down the entire length of his own body. Défago had huddled down against him for protection, shrinking away from something that apparently concealed itself near the door flaps of the little tent.

Simpson thereupon called out in a loud voice some question or other – in the first bewilderment of waking he does not remember exactly what – and the man made no reply. The atmosphere and feeling of true nightmare lay horribly about him, making movement and speech both difficult. At first, indeed, he was not sure where he was – whether in one of the earlier camps, or at home in his bed at Aberdeen. The sense of confusion was very troubling.

And next – almost simultaneous with his waking, it seemed-the profound stillness of the dawn outside was shattered by a most uncommon sound. It came without warning, or audible approach; and it was unspeakably dreadful. It was a voice, Simpson declares, possibly a human voice; hoarse yet plaintive – a soft, roaring voice close outside the tent, overhead rather than upon the ground, of immense volume, while in some strange way most penetratingly and seductively sweet. It rang out, too, in three separate and distinct notes, or cries, that bore in some odd fashion a resemblance, far-fetched yet recognizable, to the name of the guide: *'Dé-fa-go!'*

The student admits he is unable to describe it quite intelligently, for it was unlike any sound he had ever heard in his life, and combined a blending of such contrary qualities. 'A sort of windy, crying voice,' he calls it, 'as of something lonely and untamed, wild and of abominable power. . . .'

And, even before it ceased, dropping back into the great gulfs of silence, the guide beside him had sprung to his feet with an answering though unintelligible cry. He blundered against the tent pole with violence, shaking the whole structure, spreading his arms out frantically for more room, and kicking his legs impetuously free of the clinging blankets. For a second, perhaps two, he stood upright by the door, his outline dark against the pallor of the dawn; then, with a furious, rushing speed, before his companion could move a hand to stop him, he shot with a plunge through the flaps of canvas – and was gone. And as he went – so astonishingly fast that the voice could actually be heard dying in the distance – he called aloud in tones of anguished terror that at the same time held something strangely like the frenzied exultation of delight –

'Oh! oh! My feet of fire! My burning feet of fire! Oh! oh! This height and fiery speed!'

And then the distance quickly buried it, and the deep silence of very early morning descended upon the forest as before.

It had all come about with such rapidity that, but for the evidence of the empty bed beside him, Simpson could almost have believed it to have been the memory of a nightmare carried over from sleep. He still felt the warm pressure of that vanished body against his side; there lay the twisted blankets in a heap; the very tent yet trembled with the vehemence of the impetuous departure. The strange words rang in his ears, as though he still heard them in the distance – wild language of a suddenly stricken mind. Moreover, it was not only the senses of sight and hearing that reported uncommon things to his brain, for even while the man cried and ran, he had become aware that a strange perfume, faint yet pungent, pervaded the interior of the tent. And it was at this point, it seems, brought to himself by the consciousness that his nostrils were taking this distressing odour down into his throat, that he found his courage, sprang quickly to his feet – and went out.

The grey light of dawn that dropped, cold and glimmering, between the trees revealed the scene tolerably well. There stood the tent behind him, soaked with dew; the dark ashes of the fire, still warm; the lake, white beneath a coating of mist, the islands rising darkly out of it like objects packed in wool; and patches of snow beyond among the clearer spaces of the Bush – everything cold, still, waiting for the sun. But nowhere a sign of the vanished guide – still, doubtless, flying at frantic speed through the frozen woods. There was not even the sound of disappearing footsteps, nor the echoes of the dying voice. He had gone – utterly.

There was nothing; nothing but the sense of his recent presence, so strongly left behind about the camp; *and* – this penetrating, all-pervading odour.

And even this was now rapidly disappearing in its turn. In spite of his exceeding mental perturbation, Simpson struggled hard to detect its nature, and define it, but the ascertaining of an elusive scent, not recognised subconsciously and at once, is a very subtle operation of the mind. And he failed. It was gone before he could properly seize or name it. Approximate description, even, seems to have been difficult, for it was unlike any smell he knew. Acrid rather, not unlike the odour of a lion, he thinks, yet softer and not wholly unpleasing, with something almost sweet in it that reminded him of the scent of decaying garden leaves, earth, and the myriad, nameless perfumes that make up the odour of a big forest. Yet the 'odour of lions' is the phrase with which he usually sums it all up.

Then – it was wholly gone, and he found himself standing by the ashes of the fire in a state of amazement and stupid terror that left him the helpless prey of anything that chose to happen. Had a muskrat poked its pointed muzzle over a rock, or a squirrel scuttled in that instant down the bark of a tree, he would most likely have collapsed without more ado and fainted. For he felt about the whole affair the touch somewhere of a great Outer Horror... and his scattered powers had not as yet had time to collect themselves into a definite attitude of fighting self-control.

Nothing did happen, however. A great kiss of wind ran softly through the awakening forest, and a few maple leaves here and there rustled tremblingly to earth. The sky seemed to grow suddenly much lighter. Simpson felt the cool air upon his cheek and uncovered head; realised that he was shivering with the cold; and, making a great effort, realised next that he was alone in the Bush – *and* that he was called upon to take immediate steps to find and succor his vanished companion.

Make an effort, accordingly, he did, though an ill-calculated and futile one. With that wilderness of trees about him, the sheet of water cutting him off behind, and the horror of that wild cry in his blood, he did what any other inexperienced man would have done in similar bewilderment: he ran about, without any sense of direction, like a frantic child, and called loudly without ceasing the name of the guide:

'Défago! Défago! Défago!' he yelled, and the trees gave him back the name as often as he shouted, only a little softened – 'Défago! Défago! Défago!'

He followed the trail that lay a short distance across the patches of snow, and then lost it again where the trees grew too thickly for snow to lie. He shouted till he was hoarse, and till the sound of his own voice in all that unanswering and listening world began to frighten him. His confusion increased in direct ratio to the violence of his efforts. His distress became formidably acute, till at length his exertions defeated their own object, and from sheer exhaustion he headed back to the camp again. It remains a wonder that he ever found his way. It was with great difficulty, and only after numberless false clues, that he at last saw the white tent between the trees, and so reached safety.

Exhaustion then applied its own remedy, and he grew calmer. He made the fire and breakfasted. Hot coffee and bacon put a little sense and judgment into him again, and he realised that he had been behaving like a boy. He now made another, and more successful attempt to face the situation collectedly, and, a nature naturally plucky coming to his assistance, he decided that he must first make as thorough a search as possible, failing success in which, he must find his way into the home camp as best he could and bring help.

And this was what he did. Taking food, matches and rifle with him, and a small axe to blaze the trees against his return journey, he set forth. It was eight o'clock when he started, the sun shining over the tops of the trees in a sky without clouds. Pinned to a stake by the fire he left a note in case Défago returned while he was away.

This time, according to a careful plan, he took a new direction, intending to make a wide sweep that must sooner or later cut into indications of the guide's trail; and, before he had gone a quarter of a mile he came across the tracks of a large animal in the snow, and beside it the light and smaller tracks of what were beyond question human feet – the feet of Défago. The relief he at once experienced was natural, though brief; for at first sight he saw in these tracks a simple explanation of the whole matter: these big marks had surely been left by a bull moose that, wind against it, had blundered upon the camp, and uttered its singular cry of warning and alarm the moment its mistake was apparent. Défago, in whom the hunting instinct was developed to the point of uncanny perfection, had scented the brute coming down the wind hours before. His excitement and disappearance were due, of course, to – to his –

Then the impossible explanation at which he grasped faded, as common sense showed him mercilessly that none of this was true. No guide, much less a guide like Défago, could have acted in so irrational a way, going off even without his rifle . . .! The whole affair demanded a far more complicated elucidation, when he remembered the details of it all – the cry of terror, the amazing language, the grey face of horror when his nostrils first caught the new odour; that muffled sobbing in the darkness, and – for this, too, now came back to him dimly – the man's original aversion for this particular bit of country. . . .

Besides, now that he examined them closer, these were not the tracks of a bull moose at all! Hank had explained to him the outline of a bull's hoofs, of a cow's or calf's, too, for that matter; he had drawn them clearly on a strip of birch bark. And these were wholly different. They were big, round, ample, and with no pointed outline as of sharp hoofs. He wondered for a moment whether bear tracks were like that. There was no other animal he could think of, for caribou did not come so far south at this season, and, even if they did, would leave hoof marks.

They were ominous signs – these mysterious writings left in the snow by the unknown creature that had lured a human being away from safety – and when he coupled them in his imagination with that haunting sound that broke the stillness of the dawn, a momentary dizziness shook his mind, distressing him again beyond belief. He felt the *threatening* aspect of it all. And, stooping down to examine the marks more closely, he caught a faint whiff of that sweet yet pungent odour that made him instantly straighten up again, fighting a sensation almost of nausea.

Then his memory played him another evil trick. He suddenly recalled those uncovered feet projecting beyond the edge of the tent, and the body's appearance of having been dragged towards the opening; the man's shrinking from something by the door when he woke later. The details now beat against his trembling mind with concerted attack. They seemed to gather in those deep spaces of the silent forest about him, where the host of trees stood waiting, listening, watching to see what he would do. The woods were closing round him.

With the persistence of true pluck, however, Simpson went forward, following the tracks as best he could, smothering these ugly emotions that sought to weaken his will. He blazed innumerable trees as he went, ever fearful of being unable to find the way back, and calling aloud at intervals of a few seconds the name of the guide. The dull tapping of the axe upon the massive trunks, and the unnatural accents of his own voice became at length sounds that he even dreaded to make, dreaded to hear. For they drew attention without ceasing to his presence and exact whereabouts, and if it were really the case that something was hunting himself down in the same way that he was hunting down another –

With a strong effort, he crushed the thought out the instant it rose. It was the beginning, he realised, of a bewilderment utterly diabolical in kind that would speedily destroy him.

Although the snow was not continuous, lying merely in shallow flurries over the more open spaces, he found no difficulty in following the tracks for the first few miles. They went straight as a ruled line wherever the trees permitted. The stride soon began to increase in length, till it finally assumed proportions that seemed absolutely impossible for any ordinary animal to have made. Like huge flying leaps they became. One of these he measured, and though he knew that 'stretch' of eighteen feet must be somehow wrong, he was at a complete loss to understand why he found no signs on the snow between the extreme points. But what perplexed him even more, making him feel his vision had gone utterly awry, was that Défago's stride increased in the same manner, and finally covered the same incredible distances. It looked as if the great beast had lifted him with it and carried him across these astonishing intervals. Simpson, who was much longer in the limb, found that he could not compass even half the stretch by taking a running jump.

And the sight of these huge tracks, running side by side, silent evidence of a dreadful journey in which terror or madness had urged to impossible results, was profoundly moving. It shocked him in the secret depths of his soul. It was the most horrible thing his eyes had ever looked upon. He began to follow them mechanically, absentmindedly almost, ever peering over his shoulder to see if he, too, were being followed by something with a gigantic tread. . . . And soon it came about that he no longer quite realised what it was they signified – these impressions left upon the snow by something nameless and untamed, always accompanied by the footmarks of the little French Canadian, his guide, his comrade, the man who had shared his tent a few hours before, chatting, laughing, even singing by his side. . . .

V

For a man of his years and inexperience, only a canny Scot, perhaps, grounded in common sense and established in logic, could have preserved even that measure of balance that this youth somehow or other did manage to preserve through the whole adventure. Otherwise, two things he presently noticed, while forging pluckily ahead, must have sent him headlong back to the comparative safety of his tent, instead of only making his hands close more tightly upon the rifle stock, while his heart, trained for the Wee Kirk, sent a wordless prayer winging its way to heaven. Both tracks, he saw, had undergone a change, and this change, so far as it concerned the footsteps of the man, was in some undecipherable manner – appalling.

It was in the bigger tracks he first noticed this, and for a long time he could not quite believe his eyes. Was it the blown leaves that produced odd effects of light and shade, or that the dry snow, drifting like finely ground rice about the edges, cast shadows and high lights? Or was it actually the fact that the great marks had become faintly colored? For round about the deep, plunging holes of the animal there now appeared a mysterious, reddish tinge that was more like an effect of light than of anything that dyed the substance of the snow itself. Every mark had it, and had it increasingly – this indistinct fiery tinge that painted a new touch of ghastliness into the picture.

But when, wholly unable to explain or to credit it, he turned his attention to the other tracks to discover if they, too, bore similar witness, he noticed that these had meanwhile undergone a change that was infinitely worse, and charged with far more horrible suggestion. For, in the last hundred yards or so, he saw that they had grown gradually into the semblance of the parent tread. Imperceptibly the change had come about, yet unmistakably. It was hard to see where the change first began. The result, however, was beyond question. Smaller, neater, more cleanly modelled, they formed now an exact and careful duplicate of the larger tracks beside them. The feet that produced them had, therefore, also changed. And something in his mind reared up with loathing and with terror as he saw it.

Simpson, for the first time, hesitated; then, ashamed of his alarm and indecision, took a few hurried steps ahead; the next instant stopped dead in his tracks. Immediately in front of him all signs of the trail ceased; both tracks came to an abrupt end. On all sides, for a hundred yards and more, he searched in vain for the least indication of their continuance. There was – nothing.

The trees were very thick just there, big trees all of them, spruce, cedar, hemlock; there was no underbrush. He stood, looking about him, all distraught; bereft of any power of judgment. Then he set to work to search again, and again, and yet again, but always with the same result: *nothing*. The feet that printed the surface of the snow thus far had now, apparently, left the ground!

And it was in that moment of distress and confusion that the whip of terror laid its most nicely calculated lash about his heart. It dropped with deadly effect upon the sorest spot of all, completely unnerving him. He had been secretly dreading all the time that it would come – and come it did.

Far overhead, muted by great height and distance, strangely thinned and wailing, he heard the crying voice of Défago, the guide.

The sound dropped upon him out of that still, wintry sky with an effect of dismay and terror unsurpassed. The rifle fell to his feet. He stood motionless an instant, listening as it were with his whole body, then staggered back against the nearest tree for support, disorganised hopelessly in mind and spirit. To him, in that moment, it seemed the most shattering and dislocating experience he had ever known, so that his heart emptied itself of all feeling whatsoever as by a sudden draught.

'Oh! oh! This fiery height! Oh, my feet of fire! My burning feet of fire . . .!' ran in far, beseeching accents of indescribable appeal this voice of anguish down the sky. Once it called – then silence through all the listening wilderness of trees.

And Simpson, scarcely knowing what he did, presently found himself running wildly to and fro, searching, calling, tripping over roots and boulders, and flinging himself in a frenzy of undirected pursuit after the Caller. Behind the screen of memory and emotion with which experience veils events, he plunged, distracted and half-deranged, picking up false lights like a ship at sea, terror in his eyes and heart and soul. For the Panic of the Wilderness had called to him in that far voice – the Power of untamed Distance – the Enticement of the Desolation that destroys. He knew in that moment all the pains of someone hopelessly and irretrievably lost, suffering the lust and travail of a soul in the final Loneliness. A vision of Défago, eternally hunted, driven and pursued across the skiey vastness of those ancient forests fled like a flame across the dark ruin of his thoughts . . .

It seemed ages before he could find anything in the chaos of his disorganised sensations to which he could anchor himself steady for a moment, and think . . .

The cry was not repeated; his own hoarse calling brought no response; the inscrutable forces of the Wild had summoned their victim beyond recall – and held him fast.

Yet he searched and called, it seems, for hours afterwards, for it was late in the afternoon when at length he decided to abandon a useless pursuit and return to his camp on the shores of Fifty Island Water. Even then he went with reluctance, that crying voice still echoing in his ears. With difficulty he found his rifle and the homeward trail. The concentration necessary to follow the badly blazed trees, and a biting hunger that gnawed, helped to keep his mind steady. Otherwise, he admits, the temporary aberration he had suffered might have been prolonged to the point of positive disaster. Gradually the ballast shifted back again, and he regained something that approached his normal equilibrium.

But for all that the journey through the gathering dusk was miserably haunted. He heard innumerable following footsteps; voices that laughed and whispered; and saw figures crouching behind trees and boulders, making signs to one another for a concerted attack the moment he had passed. The creeping murmur of the wind made him start and listen. He went stealthily, trying to hide where possible, and making as little sound as he could. The shadows of the woods, hitherto protective or covering merely, had now become menacing, challenging; and the pageantry in his frightened mind masked a host of possibilities that were all the more ominous for being obscure. The presentiment of a nameless doom lurked ill-concealed behind every detail of what had happened.

It was really admirable how he emerged victor in the end; men of riper powers and experience might have come through the ordeal with less success. He had himself tolerably well in hand, all things considered, and his plan of action proves it. Sleep being absolutely out of the question and travelling an unknown trail in the darkness equally impracticable, he sat up the whole of that night, rifle in hand, before a fire he never for a single moment allowed to die down. The severity of the haunted vigil marked his soul for life; but it was successfully accomplished; and with the very first signs of dawn he set forth upon the long return journey to the home camp to get help. As before, he left a written note to explain his absence, and to indicate where he had left a plentiful *cache* of food and matches – though he had no expectation that any human hands would find them!

How Simpson found his way alone by the lake and forest might well make a story in itself, for to hear him tell it is to *know* the passionate loneliness of soul that a man can feel when the Wilderness holds him in the hollow of its illimitable hand – and laughs. It is also to admire his indomitable pluck.

He claims no skill, declaring that he followed the almost invisible trail mechanically, and without thinking. And this, doubtless, is the truth. He relied upon the guiding of the unconscious mind, which is instinct. Perhaps, too, some sense of orientation, known to animals and primitive men, may have helped as well, for through all that tangled region he succeeded in reaching the exact spot where Défago had hidden the canoe nearly three days before with the remark, 'Strike doo west across the lake into the sun to find the camp.'

There was not much sun left to guide him, but he used his compass to the best of his ability, embarking in the frail craft for the last twelve miles of his journey with a sensation of immense relief that the forest was at last behind him. And, fortunately, the water was calm; he took his line across the center of the lake instead of coasting round the shores for another twenty miles. Fortunately, too, the other hunters were back. The light of their fires furnished a steering point without which he might have searched all night long for the actual position of the camp.

It was close upon midnight all the same when his canoe grated on the sandy cove, and Hank, Punk and his uncle, disturbed in their sleep by his cries, ran quickly down and helped a very exhausted and broken specimen of Scotch humanity over the rocks toward a dying fire.

VI

The sudden entrance of his prosaic uncle into this world of wizardry and horror that had haunted him without interruption now for two days and two nights, had the immediate effect of giving to the affair an entirely new aspect. The sound of that crisp 'Hulloa, my boy! And what's up *now?*' and the grasp of that dry and vigorous hand introduced another standard of judgment. A revulsion of feeling washed through him. He realised that he had let himself 'go' rather badly. He even felt vaguely ashamed of himself. The native hard-headedness of his race reclaimed him.

And this doubtless explains why he found it so hard to tell that group round the fire – everything. He told enough, however, for the immediate decision to be arrived at that a relief party must start at the earliest possible moment, and that Simpson, in order to guide it capably, must first have food and, above all, sleep. Dr. Cathcart observing the lad's condition more shrewdly than his patient knew, gave him a very slight injection of morphine. For six hours he slept like the dead.

From the description carefully written out afterwards by this student of divinity, it appears that the account he gave to the astonished group omitted sundry vital and important details. He declares that, with his uncle's wholesome, matter-of-fact countenance staring him in the face, he simply had not the courage to mention them. Thus, all the search party gathered, it would seem, was that Défago had suffered in the night an acute and inexplicable attack of mania, had imagined himself 'called' by someone or something, and had plunged into the bush after it without food or rifle, where he must die a horrible and lingering death by cold and starvation unless he could be found and rescued in time. 'In time,' moreover, meant *at once.*

In the course of the following day, however – they were off by seven, leaving Punk in charge with instructions to have food and fire always ready – Simpson found it possible to tell his uncle a good deal more of the story's true inwardness, without divining that it was drawn out of him as a matter of fact by a very subtle form of cross examination. By the time they reached the beginning of the trail, where the canoe was laid up against the return journey, he had mentioned how Défago spoke vaguely of 'something he called a "Wendigo"'; how he cried in his sleep; how he imagined an unusual scent about the camp; and had betrayed other symptoms of mental excitement. He also admitted the bewildering effect of 'that extraordinary odour' upon himself, 'pungent and acrid like the odour of lions.' And by the time they were within an easy hour of Fifty Island Water he had let slip the further fact – a foolish avowal of his own hysterical condition, as he felt afterwards – that he had heard the vanished guide call 'for help.' He omitted the singular phrases used, for he simply could not bring himself to repeat the preposterous language. Also, while describing how the man's footsteps in the snow had gradually assumed an exact miniature likeness of the animal's plunging tracks, he left out the fact that they measured a *wholly* incredible distance. It seemed a question, nicely balanced between individual pride and honesty, what he should reveal and what suppress. He mentioned the fiery tinge in the snow, for instance, yet shrank from telling that body and bed had been partly dragged out of the tent. . . .

With the net result that Dr. Cathcart, adroit psychologist that he fancied himself to be, had assured him clearly enough exactly where his mind, influenced by loneliness, bewilderment and terror, had yielded to the strain and invited delusion.

While praising his conduct, he managed at the same time to point out where, when, and how his mind had gone astray. He made his nephew think himself finer than he was by judicious praise, yet more foolish than he was by minimising the value of the evidence. Like many another materialist, that is, he lied cleverly on the basis of insufficient knowledge, *because* the knowledge supplied seemed to his own particular intelligence inadmissible.

'The spell of these terrible solitudes,' he said, 'cannot leave any mind untouched, any mind, that is, possessed of the higher imaginative qualities. It has worked upon yours exactly as it worked upon my own when I was your age. The animal that haunted your little camp was undoubtedly a moose, for the 'belling' of a moose may have, sometimes, a very peculiar quality of sound. The coloured appearance of the big tracks was obviously a defect of vision in your own eyes produced by excitement. The size and stretch of the tracks we shall prove when we come to them. But the hallucination of an audible voice, of course, is one of the commonest forms of delusion due to mental excitement – an excitement, my dear boy, perfectly excusable, and, let me add, wonderfully controlled by you under the circumstances. For the rest, I am bound to say, you have acted with a splendid courage, for the terror of feeling oneself lost in this wilderness is nothing short of awful, and, had I been in your place, I don't for a moment believe I could have behaved with one quarter of your wisdom and decision. The only thing I find it uncommonly difficult to explain is – that – damned odour.'

'It made me feel sick, I assure you,' declared his nephew, 'positively dizzy!' His uncle's attitude of calm omniscience, merely because he knew more psychological formulae, made him slightly defiant. It was so easy to be wise in the explanation of an experience one has not personally witnessed. 'A kind of desolate and terrible odour is the only way I can describe it,' he concluded, glancing at the features of the quiet, unemotional man beside him.

'I can only marvel,' was the reply, 'that under the circumstances it did not seem to you even worse.' The dry words, Simpson knew, hovered between the truth, and his uncle's interpretation of 'the truth.'

And so at last they came to the little camp and found the tent still standing, the remains of the fire, and the piece of paper pinned to a stake beside it – untouched. The cache, poorly contrived by inexperienced hands, however, had been discovered and opened – by musk rats, mink and squirrel. The matches lay scattered about the opening, but the food had been taken to the last crumb.

'Well, fellers, he ain't here,' exclaimed Hank loudly after his fashion. 'And that's as sartain as the coal supply down below! But whar he's got to by this time is 'bout as unsartain as the trade in crowns in t'other place.' The presence of a divinity student was no barrier to his language at such a time, though for the reader's sake it may be severely edited. 'I propose,' he added, 'that we start out at once an' hunt for'm like hell!'

The gloom of Défago's probable fate oppressed the whole party with a sense of dreadful gravity the moment they saw the familiar signs of recent occupancy. Especially the tent, with the bed of balsam branches still smoothed and flattened by the pressure of his body, seemed to bring his presence near to them. Simpson, feeling vaguely as if his world were somehow at stake, went about explaining particulars in a hushed tone. He was much calmer now, though overwearied with the strain of his many journeys. His uncle's method of explaining – 'explaining away,' rather – the details still fresh in his haunted memory helped, too, to put ice upon his emotions.

'And that's the direction he ran off in,' he said to his two companions, pointing in the direction where the guide had vanished that morning in the grey dawn. 'Straight down there he ran like a deer, in between the birch and the hemlock . . . .'

Hank and Dr. Cathcart exchanged glances.

'And it was about two miles down there, in a straight line,' continued the other, speaking with something of the former terror in his voice, 'that I followed his trail to the place where – it stopped – dead!'

'And where you heered him callin' an' caught the stench, an' all the rest of the wicked entertainment,' cried Hank, with a volubility that betrayed his keen distress.

'And where your excitement overcame you to the point of producing illusions,' added Dr. Cathcart under his breath, yet not so low that his nephew did not hear it.

It was early in the afternoon, for they had travelled quickly, and there were still a good two hours of daylight left. Dr. Cathcart and Hank lost no time in beginning the search, but Simpson was too exhausted to accompany them. They would follow the blazed marks on the trees, and where possible, his footsteps. Meanwhile the best thing he could do was to keep a good fire going, and rest.

But after something like three hours' search, the darkness already down, the two men returned to camp with nothing to report. Fresh snow had covered all signs, and though they had followed the blazed trees to the spot where Simpson had turned back, they had not discovered the smallest indication of a human being – or for that matter, of an animal. There were no fresh tracks of any kind; the snow lay undisturbed.

It was difficult to know what was best to do, though in reality there was nothing more they *could* do. They might stay and search for weeks without much chance of success. The fresh snow destroyed their only hope, and they gathered round the fire for supper, a gloomy and despondent party. The facts, indeed, were sad enough, for Défago had a wife at Rat Portage, and his earnings were the family's sole means of support.

Now that the whole truth in all its ugliness was out, it seemed useless to deal in further disguise or pretense. They talked openly of the facts and probabilities. It was not the first time, even in the experience of Dr. Cathcart, that a man had yielded to the singular seduction of the Solitudes and gone out of his mind; Défago, moreover, was predisposed to something of the sort, for he already had a touch of melancholia in his blood, and his fibre was weakened by bouts of drinking that often lasted for weeks at a time. Something on this trip – one might never know precisely what – had sufficed to push him over the line, that was all. And he had gone, gone off into the great wilderness of trees and lakes to die by starvation and exhaustion. The chances against his finding camp again were overwhelming; the delirium that was upon him would also doubtless have increased, and it was quite likely he might do violence to himself and so hasten his cruel fate. Even while they talked, indeed, the end had probably come. On the suggestion of Hank, his old pal, however, they proposed to wait a little longer and devote the whole of the following day, from dawn to darkness, to the most systematic search they could devise. They would divide the territory between them. They discussed their plan in great detail. All that men could do they would do. And, meanwhile, they talked about the particular form in which the singular Panic of the Wilderness had made its attack upon the mind of the unfortunate guide. Hank, though familiar with the legend in its general outline, obviously did not welcome the turn the conversation had taken. He contributed little, though that little was illuminating. For he admitted that a story ran over all this section of country to the effect that several Indians had 'seen the Wendigo' along the shores of Fifty Island Water in the 'fall' of last year, and that this was the true reason of Défago's disinclination to hunt there. Hank doubtless felt that he had in a sense helped his old pal to death by overpersuading him. 'When an Indian goes crazy,' he explained, talking to himself more than to the others, it seemed, 'it's always put that he's 'seen the Wendigo.' An' pore old Défaygo was superstitious down to he very heels . . .! '

And then Simpson, feeling the atmosphere more sympathetic, told over again the full story of his astonishing tale; he left out no details this time; he mentioned his own sensations and gripping fears. He only omitted the strange language used.

'But Défago surely had already told you all these details of the Wendigo legend, my dear fellow,' insisted the doctor. 'I mean, he had talked about it, and thus put into your mind the ideas which your own excitement afterwards developed?'

Whereupon Simpson again repeated the facts. Défago, he declared, had barely mentioned the beast. He, Simpson, knew nothing of the story, and, so far as he remembered, had never even read about it. Even the word was unfamiliar.

Of course he was telling the truth, and Dr. Cathcart was reluctantly compelled to admit the singular character of the whole affair. He did not do this in words so much as in manner, however. He kept his back against a good, stout tree; he poked the fire into a blaze the moment it showed signs of dying down; he was quicker than any of them to notice the least sound in the night about them – a fish jumping in the lake, a twig snapping in the bush, the dropping of occasional fragments of frozen snow from the branches overhead where the heat loosened them. His voice, too, changed a little in quality, becoming a shade less confident, lower also in tone. Fear, to put it plainly, hovered close about that little camp, and though all three would have been glad to speak of other matters, the only thing they seemed able to discuss was this – the source of their fear. They tried other subjects in vain; there was nothing to say about them. Hank was the most honest of the group; he said next to nothing. He never once, however, turned his back to the darkness. His face was always to the forest, and when wood was needed he didn't go farther than was necessary to get it.

VII

A wall of silence wrapped them in, for the snow, though not thick, was sufficient to deaden any noise, and the frost held things pretty tight besides. No sound but their voices and the soft roar of the flames made itself heard. Only, from time to time, something soft as the flutter of a pine moth's wings went past them through the air. No one seemed anxious to go to bed. The hours slipped towards midnight.

'The legend is picturesque enough,' observed the doctor after one of the longer pauses, speaking to break it rather than because he had anything to say, 'for the Wendigo is simply the Call of the Wild personified, which some natures hear to their own destruction.'

'That's about it,' Hank said presently. 'An' there's no misunderstandin' when you hear it. It calls you by name right 'nough.'

Another pause followed. Then Dr. Cathcart came back to the forbidden subject with a rush that made the others jump.

'The allegory *is* significant,' he remarked, looking about him into the darkness, 'for the Voice, they say, resembles all the minor sounds of the Bush – wind, falling water, cries of the animals, and so forth. And, once the victim hears *that* – he's off for good, of course! His most vulnerable points, moreover, are said to be the feet and the eyes; the feet, you see, for the lust of wandering, and the eyes for the lust of beauty. The poor beggar goes at such a dreadful speed that he bleeds beneath the eyes, and his feet burn.'

Dr. Cathcart, as he spoke, continued to peer uneasily into the surrounding gloom. His voice sank to a hushed tone.

'The Wendigo,' he added, 'is said to burn his feet – owing to the friction, apparently caused by its tremendous velocity – till they drop off, and new ones form exactly like its own.'

Simpson listened in horrified amazement; but it was the pallor on Hank's face that fascinated him most. He would willingly have stopped his ears and closed his eyes, had he dared.

'It don't always keep to the ground neither,' came in Hank's slow, heavy drawl, 'for it goes so high that he thinks the stars have set him all a-fire. An' it'll take great thumpin' jumps sometimes, an' run along the tops of the trees, carrying its partner with it, an' then droppin' him jest as a fish hawk'll drop a pickerel to kill it before eatin'. An' its food, of all the muck in the whole Bush is – moss!' And he laughed a short, unnatural laugh. 'It's a moss-eater, is the Wendigo,' he added, looking up excitedly into the faces of his companions. 'Moss-eater,' he repeated, with a string of the most outlandish oaths he could invent.

But Simpson now understood the true purpose of all this talk. What these two men, each strong and 'experienced' in his own way, dreaded more than anything else was – silence. They were talking against time. They were also talking against darkness, against the invasion of panic, against the admission reflection might bring that they were in an enemy's country – against anything, in fact, rather than allow their inmost thoughts to assume control. He himself, already initiated by the awful vigil with terror, was beyond both of them in this respect. He had reached the stage where he was immune. But these two, the scoffing, analytical doctor, and the honest, dogged backwoodsman, each sat trembling in the depths of his being.

Thus the hours passed; and thus, with lowered voices and a kind of taut inner resistance of spirit, this little group of humanity sat in the jaws of the wilderness and talked foolishly of the terrible and haunting legend. It was an unequal contest, all things considered, for the wilderness had already the advantage of first attack – and of a hostage. The fate of their comrade hung over them with a steadily increasing weight of oppression that finally became insupportable.

It was Hank, after a pause longer than the preceding ones that no one seemed able to break, who first let loose all this pent-up emotion in very unexpected fashion, by springing suddenly to his feet and letting out the most ear-shattering yell imaginable into the night. He could not contain himself any longer, it seemed. To make it carry even beyond an ordinary cry he interrupted its rhythm by shaking the palm of his hand before his mouth.

'That's for Défago,' he said, looking down at the other two with a queer, defiant laugh, 'for it's my belief' – the sandwiched oaths may be omitted – 'that my ole partner's not far from us at this very minute.'

There was a vehemence and recklessness about his performance that made Simpson, too, start to his feet in amazement, and betrayed even the doctor into letting the pipe slip from between his lips. Hank's face was ghastly, but Cathcart's showed a sudden weakness – a loosening of all his faculties, as it were. Then a momentary anger blazed into his eyes, and he too, though with deliberation born of habitual self-control, got upon his feet and faced the excited guide. For this was unpermissible, foolish, dangerous, and he meant to stop it in the bud.

What might have happened in the next minute or two one may speculate about, yet never definitely know, for in the instant of profound silence that followed Hank's roaring voice, and as though in answer to it, something went past through the darkness of the sky overhead at terrific speed – something of necessity very large, for it displaced much air, while down between the trees there fell a faint and windy cry of a human voice, calling in tones of indescribable anguish and appeal –

'Oh, oh! This fiery height! Oh, oh! My feet of fire! My burning feet of fire!'

White to the very edge of his shirt, Hank looked stupidly about him like a child. Dr. Cathcart uttered some kind of unintelligible cry, turning as he did so with an instinctive movement of blind terror towards the protection of the tent, then halting in the act as though frozen. Simpson, alone of the three, retained his presence of mind a little. His own horror was too deep to allow of any immediate reaction. He had heard that cry before.

Turning to his stricken companions, he said almost calmly –

'That's exactly the cry I heard – the very words he used!'

Then, lifting his face to the sky, he cried aloud, 'Défago, Défago! Come down here to us! Come down – !'

And before there was time for anybody to take definite action one way or another, there came the sound of something dropping heavily between the trees, striking the branches on the way down, and landing with a dreadful thud upon the frozen earth below. The crash and thunder of it was really terrific.

'That's him, s'help me the good Gawd!' came from Hank in a whispering cry half choked, his hand going automatically toward the hunting knife in his belt. 'And he's coming! He's coming!' he added, with an irrational laugh of horror, as the sounds of heavy footsteps crunching over the snow became distinctly audible, approaching through the blackness towards the circle of light.

And while the steps, with their stumbling motion, moved nearer and nearer upon them, the three men stood round that fire, motionless and dumb. Dr. Cathcart had the appearance of a man suddenly withered; even his eyes did not move. Hank, suffering shockingly, seemed on the verge again of violent action; yet did nothing. He, too, was hewn of stone.

Like stricken children they seemed. The picture was hideous. And, meanwhile, their owner still invisible, the footsteps came closer, crunching the frozen snow. It was endless – too prolonged to be quite real – this measured and pitiless approach. It was accursed.

VIII

Then at length the darkness, having thus laboriously conceived, brought forth – a figure. It drew forward into the zone of uncertain light where fire and shadows mingled, not ten feet away; then halted, staring at them fixedly. The same instant it started forward again with the spasmodic motion as of a thing moved by wires, and coming up closer to them, full into the glare of the fire, they perceived then that – it was a man; and apparently that this man was – Défago.

Something like a skin of horror almost perceptibly drew down in that moment over every face, and three pairs of eyes shone through it as though they saw across the frontiers of normal vision into the Unknown.

Défago advanced, his tread faltering and uncertain; he made his way straight up to them as a group first, then turned sharply and peered close into the face of Simpson. The sound of a voice issued from his lips –

'Here I am, Boss Simpson. I heered someone calling me.' It was a faint, dried up voice, made wheezy and breathless as by immense exertion. 'I'm havin' a reg'lar hellfire kind of a trip, I am.' And he laughed, thrusting his head forward into the other's face.

But that laugh started the machinery of the group of waxwork figures with the wax-white skins. Hank immediately sprang forward with a stream of oaths so farfetched that Simpson did not recognise them as English at all, but thought he had lapsed into Indian or some other lingo. He only realised that Hank's presence, thrust thus between them, was welcome –

uncommonly welcome. Dr. Cathcart, though more calmly and leisurely, advanced behind him, heavily stumbling.

Simpson seems hazy as to what was actually said and done in those next few seconds, for the eyes of that detestable and blasted visage peering at such close quarters into his own utterly bewildered his senses at first. He merely stood still. He said nothing. He had not the trained will of the older men that forced them into action in defiance of all emotional stress. He watched them moving as behind a glass that half destroyed their reality; it was dreamlike; perverted. Yet, through the torrent of Hank's meaningless phrases, he remembers hearing his uncle's tone of authority – hard and forced – saying several things about food and warmth, blankets, whisky and the rest . . . and, further, that whiffs of that penetrating, unaccustomed odour, vile yet sweetly bewildering, assailed his nostrils during all that followed.

It was no less a person than himself, however – less experienced and adroit than the others though he was – who gave instinctive utterance to the sentence that brought a measure of relief into the ghastly situation by expressing the doubt and thought in each one's heart.

'It *is* – YOU, isn't it, Défago?' he asked under his breath, horror breaking his speech.

And at once Cathcart burst out with the loud answer before the other had time to move his lips. 'Of course it is! Of course it is! Only – can't you see – he's nearly dead with exhaustion, cold and terror! Isn't *that* enough to change a man beyond all recognition?' It was said in order to convince himself as much as to convince the others. The overemphasis alone proved that. And continually, while he spoke and acted, he held a handkerchief to his nose. That odour pervaded the whole camp.

For the 'Défago' who sat huddled by the big fire, wrapped in blankets, drinking hot whisky and holding food in wasted hands, was no more like the guide they had last seen alive than the picture of a man of sixty is like a daguerreotype of his early youth in the costume of another generation. Nothing really can describe that ghastly caricature, that parody, masquerading there in the firelight as Défago. From the ruins of the dark and awful memories he still retains, Simpson declares that the face was more animal than human, the features drawn about into wrong proportions, the skin loose and hanging, as though he had been subjected to extraordinary pressures and tensions. It made him think vaguely of those bladder faces blown up by the hawkers on Ludgate Hill, that change their expression as they swell, and as they collapse emit a faint and wailing imitation of a voice. Both face and voice suggested some such abominable resemblance. But Cathcart long afterwards, seeking to describe the indescribable, asserts that thus might have looked a face and body that had been in air so rarified that, the weight of atmosphere being removed, the entire structure threatened to fly asunder and become – *incoherent. . . .*

It was Hank, though all distraught and shaking with a tearing volume of emotion he could neither handle nor understand, who brought things to a head without much ado. He went off to a little distance from the fire, apparently so that the light should not dazzle him too much, and shading his eyes for a moment with both hands, shouted in a loud voice that held anger and affection dreadfully mingled:

'You ain't Défaygo! You ain't Défaygo at all! I don't give a – damn, but that ain't you, my ole pal of twenty years!' He glared upon the huddled figure as though he would destroy him with his eyes. 'An' if it is I'll swab the floor of hell with a wad of cotton wool on a toothpick, s'help me the good Gawd!' he added, with a violent fling of horror and disgust.

It was impossible to silence him. He stood there shouting like one possessed, horrible to see, horrible to hear – *because it was the truth.* He repeated himself in fifty different ways, each more outlandish than the last. The woods rang with echoes. At one time it looked as if he meant to fling himself upon 'the intruder,' for his hand continually jerked towards the long hunting knife in his belt.

But in the end he did nothing, and the whole tempest completed itself very shortly with tears. Hank's voice suddenly broke, he collapsed on the ground, and Cathcart somehow or other persuaded him at last to go into the tent and lie quiet. The remainder of the affair, indeed, was witnessed by him from behind the canvas, his white and terrified face peeping through the crack of the tent door flap.

Then Dr. Cathcart, closely followed by his nephew who so far had kept his courage better than all of them, went up with a determined air and stood opposite to the figure of Défago huddled over the fire. He looked him squarely in the face and spoke. At first his voice was firm.

'Défago, tell us what's happened – just a little, so that we can know how best to help you?' he asked in a tone of authority, almost of command. And at that point, it *was* command. At once afterwards, however, it changed in quality, for the figure turned up to him a face so piteous, so terrible and so little like humanity, that the doctor shrank back from him as from something spiritually unclean. Simpson, watching close behind him, says he got the impression of a mask that was on the verge of dropping off, and that underneath they would discover something black and diabolical, revealed in utter nakedness. 'Out with it, man, out with it!' Cathcart cried, terror running neck and neck with entreaty. 'None of us can stand this much longer . . . !' It was the cry of instinct over reason.

And then 'Défago,' smiling *whitely,* answered in that thin and fading voice that already seemed passing over into a sound of quite another character –

'I seen that great Wendigo thing,' he whispered, sniffing the air about him exactly like an animal. 'I been with it too –'

Whether the poor devil would have said more, or whether Dr. Cathcart would have continued the impossible cross examination cannot be known, for at that moment the voice of Hank was heard yelling at the top of his voice from behind the canvas that concealed all but his terrified eyes. Such a howling was never heard.

'His feet! Oh, Gawd, his feet! Look at his great changed – feet!'

Défago, shuffling where he sat, had moved in such a way that for the first time his legs were in full light and his feet were visible. Yet Simpson had no time, himself, to see properly what Hank had seen. And Hank has never seen fit to tell. That same instant, with a leap like that of a frightened tiger, Cathcart was upon him, bundling the folds of blanket about his legs with such speed that the young student caught little more than a passing glimpse of something dark and oddly massed where moccasined feet ought to have been, and saw even that but with uncertain vision.

Then, before the doctor had time to do more, or Simpson time to even think a question, much less ask it, Défago was standing upright in front of them, balancing with pain and difficulty, and upon his shapeless and twisted visage an expression so dark and so malicious that it was, in the true sense, monstrous.

'Now *you* seen it too,' he wheezed, 'you seen my fiery, burning feet! And now – that is, unless you kin save me an' prevent – it's 'bout time for –'

His piteous and beseeching voice was interrupted by a sound that was like the roar of wind coming across the lake. The trees overhead shook their tangled branches. The blazing fire bent its flames as before a blast. And something swept with a terrific, rushing noise about the little camp and seemed to surround it entirely in a single moment of time. Défago shook the clinging blankets from his body, turned towards the woods behind, and with the same stumbling motion that had brought him – was gone: gone, before anyone could move muscle to prevent him, gone with an amazing, blundering swiftness that left no time to act. The darkness positively swallowed him; and less than a dozen seconds later, above the roar of the swaying trees and the shout of the sudden wind, all three men, watching and listening with stricken hearts, heard a cry that seemed to drop down upon them from a great height of sky and distance –

'Oh, oh! This fiery height! Oh, oh! My feet of fire! My burning feet of fire . . .!' then died away, into untold space and silence.

Dr. Cathcart – suddenly master of himself, and therefore of the others – was just able to seize Hank violently by the arm as he tried to dash headlong into the Bush.

'But I want ter know, – you!' shrieked the guide. 'I want ter see! That ain't him at all, but some – devil that's shunted into his place . . .!'

Somehow or other – he admits he never quite knew how he accomplished it – he managed to keep him in the tent and pacify him. The doctor, apparently, had reached the stage where reaction had set in and allowed his own innate force to conquer. Certainly he 'managed' Hank admirably. It was his nephew, however, hitherto so wonderfully controlled, who gave him most cause for anxiety, for the cumulative strain had now produced a condition of lachrymose hysteria which made it necessary to isolate him upon a bed of boughs and blankets as far removed from Hank as was possible under the circumstances.

And there he lay, as the watches of that haunted night passed over the lonely camp, crying startled sentences, and fragments of sentences, into the folds of his blanket. A quantity of gibberish about speed and height and fire mingled oddly with biblical memories of the classroom. 'People with broken faces all on fire are coming at a most awful, awful, pace towards the camp!' he would moan one minute; and the next would sit up and stare into the woods, intently listening, and whisper, 'How terrible in the wilderness are – are the feet of them that –' until his uncle came across to change the direction of his thoughts and comfort him.

The hysteria, fortunately, proved but temporary. Sleep cured him, just as it cured Hank.

Till the first signs of daylight came, soon after five o'clock, Dr. Cathcart kept his vigil. His face was the color of chalk, and there were strange flushes beneath the eyes. An appalling terror of the soul battled with his will all through those silent hours. These were some of the outer signs . . .

At dawn he lit the fire himself, made breakfast, and woke the others, and by seven they were well on their way back to the home camp – three perplexed and afflicted men, but each in his own way having reduced his inner turmoil to a condition of more or less systematised order again.

IX

They talked little, and then only of the most wholesome and common things, for their minds were charged with painful thoughts that clamoured for explanation, though no one dared refer to them. Hank, being nearest to primitive conditions, was the first to find himself, for he was also less complex. In Dr. Cathcart 'civilisation' championed his forces against an attack singular enough. To this day, perhaps, he is not *quite* sure of certain things. Anyhow, he took longer to 'find himself.'

Simpson, the student of divinity, it was who arranged his conclusions probably with the best, though not most scientific, appearance of order. Out there, in the heart of unreclaimed wilderness, they had surely witnessed something crudely and essentially primitive. Something that had survived somehow the advance of humanity had emerged terrifically, betraying a scale of life still monstrous and immature. He envisaged it rather as a glimpse into prehistoric ages, when superstitions, gigantic and uncouth, still oppressed the hearts of men; when the forces of nature were still untamed, the Powers that may have haunted a primeval universe not yet withdrawn. To this day he thinks of what he termed years later in a sermon 'savage and formidable Potencies lurking behind the souls of men, not evil perhaps in themselves, yet instinctively hostile to humanity as it exists.'

With his uncle he never discussed the matter in detail, for the barrier between the two types of mind made it difficult. Only once, years later, something led them to the frontier of the subject – of a single detail of the subject, rather –

'Can't you even tell me what – *they* were like?' he asked; and the reply, though conceived in wisdom, was not encouraging,

'It is far better you should not try to know, or to find out.'

'Well – that odour. . .?' persisted the nephew. 'What do you make of that?'

Dr. Cathcart looked at him and raised his eyebrows.

'Odours,' he replied, 'are not so easy as sounds and sights of telepathic communication. I make as much, or as little, probably, as you do yourself.'

He was not quite so glib as usual with his explanations. That was all.

At the fall of day, cold, exhausted, famished, the party came to the end of the long portage and dragged themselves into a camp that at first glimpse seemed empty. Fire there was none, and no Punk came forward to welcome them. The emotional capacity of all three was too over-spent to recognise either surprise or annoyance; but the cry of spontaneous affection that burst from the lips of Hank, as he rushed ahead of them towards the fireplace, came probably as a warning that the end of the amazing affair was not quite yet. And both Cathcart and his nephew confessed afterwards that when they saw him kneel down in his excitement and embrace something that reclined, gently moving, beside the extinguished ashes, they felt in their very bones that this 'something' would prove to be Défago – the true Défago, returned.

And so, indeed, it was.

It is soon told. Exhausted to the point of emaciation, the French Canadian – what was left of him, that is – fumbled among the ashes, trying to make a fire. His body crouched there, the weak fingers obeying feebly the instinctive habit of a lifetime with twigs and matches. But there was no longer any mind to direct the simple operation. The mind had fled beyond recall. And with it, too, had fled memory. Not only recent events, but all previous life was a blank.

This time it was the real man, though incredibly and horribly shrunken. On his face was no expression of any kind whatever – fear, welcome, or recognition. He did not seem to know who it was that embraced him, or who it was that fed, warmed and spoke to him the words of comfort and relief. Forlorn and broken beyond all reach of human aid, the little man did meekly as he was bidden. The 'something' that had constituted him 'individual' had vanished for ever.

In some ways it was more terribly moving than anything they had yet seen – that idiot smile as he drew wads of coarse moss from his swollen cheeks and told them that he was 'a damned moss-eater'; the continued vomiting of even the simplest food; and, worst of all, the piteous and childish voice of complaint in which he told them that his feet pained him – 'burn like fire' – which was natural enough when Dr. Cathcart examined them and found that both were dreadfully frozen. Beneath the eyes there were faint indications of recent bleeding.

The details of how he survived the prolonged exposure, of where he had been, or of how he covered the great distance from one camp to the other, including an immense detour of the lake on foot since he had no canoe – all this remains unknown. His memory had vanished completely. And before the end of the winter whose beginning witnessed this strange occurrence, Défago, bereft of mind, memory and soul, had gone with it. He lingered only a few weeks.

And what Punk was able to contribute to the story throws no further light upon it. He was cleaning fish by the lake shore about five o'clock in the evening – an hour, that is, before the search party returned – when he saw this shadow of the guide picking its way weakly into camp. In advance of him, he declares, came the faint whiff of a certain singular odour.

That same instant old Punk started for home. He covered the entire journey of three days as only Indian blood could have covered it. The terror of a whole race drove him. He knew what it all meant. Défago had 'seen the Wendigo.'

The Insanity of Jones

(A Study in Reincarnation)

I

Adventures come to the adventurous, and mysterious things fall in the way of those who, with wonder and imagination, are on the watch for them; but the majority of people go past the doors that are half ajar, thinking them closed, and fail to notice the faint stirrings of the great curtain that hangs ever in the form of appearances between them and the world of causes behind.

For only to the few whose inner senses have been quickened, perchance by some strange suffering in the depths, or by a natural temperament bequeathed from a remote past, comes the knowledge, not too welcome, that this greater world lies ever at their elbow, and that any moment a chance combination of moods and forces may invite them to cross the shifting frontier.

Some, however, are born with this awful certainty in their hearts, and are called to no apprenticeship, and to this select company Jones undoubtedly belonged.

All his life he had realised that his senses brought to him merely a more or less interesting set of sham appearances; that space, as men measure it, was utterly misleading; that time, as the clock ticked it in a succession of minutes, was arbitrary nonsense; and, in fact, that all his sensory perceptions were but a clumsy representation of *real* things behind the curtain – things he was forever trying to get at, and that sometimes he actually did get at.

He had always been tremblingly aware that he stood on the borderland of another region, a region where time and space were merely forms of thought, where ancient memories lay open to the sight, and where the forces behind each human life stood plainly revealed and he could see the hidden springs at the very heart of the world. Moreover, the fact that he was a clerk in a fire insurance office, and did his work with strict attention, never allowed him to forget for one moment that, just beyond the dingy brick walls where the hundred men scribbled with pointed pens beneath the electric lamps, there existed this glorious region where the important part of himself dwelt and moved and had its being. For in this region he pictured himself playing the part of a spectator to his ordinary workaday life, watching, like a king, the stream of events, but untouched in his own soul by the dirt, the noise, and the vulgar commotion of the outer world.

And this was no poetic dream merely. Jones was not playing prettily with idealism to amuse himself. It was a living, working belief. So convinced was he that the external world was the result of a vast deception practised upon him by the gross senses, that when he stared at a great building like St. Paul's he felt it would not very much surprise him to see it suddenly quiver like a shape of jelly and then melt utterly away, while in its place stood all at once revealed the mass of colour, or the great intricate vibrations, or the splendid sound – the spiritual idea – which it represented in stone.

For something in this way it was that his mind worked.

Yet, to all appearances, and in the satisfaction of all business claims, Jones was normal and unenterprising. He felt nothing but contempt for the wave of modern psychism. He hardly knew the meaning of such words as 'clairvoyance' and 'clairaudience.' He had never felt the least desire to join the Theosophical Society and to speculate in theories of astral-plane life, or elementals. He attended no meetings of the Psychical Research Society, and knew no anxiety as to whether his 'aura' was black or blue; nor was he conscious of the slightest wish to mix in with the revival of cheap occultism which proves so attractive to weak minds of mystical tendencies and unleashed imaginations.

There were certain things he *knew*, but none he cared to argue about; and he shrank instinctively from attempting to put names to the contents of this other region, knowing well that such names could only limit and define things that, according to any standards in use in the ordinary world, were simply undefinable and illusive.

So that, although this was the way his mind worked, there was clearly a very strong leaven of common sense in Jones. In a word, the man the world and the office knew as Jones *was* Jones. The name summed him up and labelled him correctly – John Enderby Jones.

Among the things that he *knew*, and therefore never cared to speak or speculate about, one was that he plainly saw himself as the inheritor of a long series of past lives, the net result of painful evolution, always as himself, of course, but in numerous different bodies each determined by the behaviour of the preceding one. The present John Jones was the last result to date of all the previous thinking, feeling, and doing of John Jones in earlier bodies and in other centuries. He pretended to no details, nor claimed distinguished ancestry, for he realised his past must have been utterly commonplace and insignificant to have produced his present; but he was just as sure he had been at this weary game for ages as that he breathed, and it never occurred to him to argue, to doubt, or to ask questions. And one result of this belief was that his thoughts dwelt upon the past rather than upon the future; that he read much history, and felt specially drawn to certain periods whose spirit he understood instinctively as though he had lived in them; and that he found all religions uninteresting because, almost without exception, they start from the present and speculate ahead as to what men shall become, instead of looking back and speculating why men have got here as they are.

In the insurance office he did his work exceedingly well, but without much personal ambition. Men and women he regarded as the impersonal instruments for inflicting upon him the pain or pleasure he had earned by his past workings, for chance had no place in his scheme of things at all; and while he recognised that the practical world could not get along unless every man did his work thoroughly and conscientiously, he took no interest in the accumulation of fame or money for himself, and simply, therefore, did his plain duty, with indifference as to results.

In common with others who lead a strictly impersonal life, he possessed the quality of utter bravery, and was always ready to face any combination of circumstances, no matter how terrible, because he saw in them the just working-out of past causes he had himself set in motion which could not be dodged or modified. And whereas the majority of people had little meaning for him, either by way of attraction or repulsion, the moment he met someone with whom he felt his past had been *vitally* interwoven his whole inner being leapt up instantly and shouted the fact in his face, and he regulated his life with the utmost skill and caution, like a sentry on watch for an enemy whose feet could already be heard approaching.

Thus, while the great majority of men and women left him uninfluenced – since he regarded them as so many souls merely passing with him along the great stream of evolution – there were, here and there, individuals with whom he recognised that his smallest intercourse was of the gravest importance. These were persons with whom he knew in every fibre of his being he had accounts to settle, pleasant or otherwise, arising out of dealings in past lives; and into his relations with these few, therefore, he concentrated as it were the efforts that most people spread over their intercourse with a far greater number. By what means he picked out these few individuals only those conversant with the startling processes of the subconscious memory may say, but the point was that Jones believed the main purpose, if not quite the entire purpose, of his present incarnation lay in his faithful and thorough settling of these accounts, and that if he sought to evade the least detail of such settling, no matter how unpleasant, he would have lived in vain, and would return to his next incarnation with this added duty to perform. For according to his beliefs there was no Chance, and could be no ultimate shirking, and to avoid a problem was merely to waste time and lose opportunities for development.

And there was one individual with whom Jones had long understood clearly he had a very large account to settle, and towards the accomplishment of which all the main currents of his being seemed to bear him with unswerving purpose. For, when he first entered the insurance office as a junior clerk ten years before, and through a glass door had caught sight of this man seated in an inner room, one of his sudden overwhelming flashes of intuitive memory had burst up into him from the depths, and he had seen, as in a flame of blinding light, a symbolical picture of the future rising out of a dreadful past, and he had, without any act of definite volition, marked down this man for a real account to be settled.

'With *that* man I shall have much to do,' he said to himself, as he noted the big face look up and meet his eye through the glass. 'There is something I cannot shirk – a vital relation out of the past of both of us.'

And he went to his desk trembling a little, and with shaking knees, as though the memory of some terrible pain had suddenly laid its icy hand upon his heart and touched the scar of a great horror. It was a moment of genuine terror when their eyes had met through the glass door, and he was conscious of an inward shrinking and loathing that seized upon him with great violence and convinced him in a single second that the settling of this account would be almost, perhaps, more than he could manage.

The vision passed as swiftly as it came, dropping back again into the submerged region of his consciousness; but he never forgot it, and the whole of his life thereafter became a sort of natural though undeliberate preparation for the fulfilment of the great duty when the time should be ripe.

In those days – ten years ago – this man was the Assistant Manager, but had since been promoted as Manager to one of the company's local branches; and soon afterwards Jones had likewise found himself transferred to this same branch. A little later, again, the branch at Liverpool, one of the most important, had been in peril owing to mismanagement and defalcation, and the man had gone to take charge of it, and again, by mere chance apparently, Jones had been promoted to the same place. And this pursuit of the Assistant Manager had continued for several years, often, too, in the most curious fashion; and though Jones had never exchanged a single word with him, or been so much as noticed indeed by the great man, the clerk understood perfectly well that these moves in the game were all part of a definite purpose. Never for one moment did he doubt that the Invisibles behind the veil were slowly and surely arranging the details of it all so as to lead up suitably to the climax demanded by justice, a climax in which himself and the Manager would play the leading *rôles*.

'It is inevitable,' he said to himself, 'and I feel it may be terrible; but when the moment comes I shall be ready, and I pray God that I may face it properly and act like a man.'

Moreover, as the years passed, and nothing happened, he felt the horror closing in upon him with steady increase, for the fact was Jones hated and loathed the Manager with an intensity of feeling he had never before experienced towards any human being. He shrank from his presence, and from the glance of his eyes, as though he remembered to have suffered nameless cruelties at his hands; and he slowly began to realise, moreover, that the matter to be settled between them was one of very ancient standing, and that the nature of the settlement was a discharge of accumulated punishment which would probably be very dreadful in the manner of its fulfilment.

When, therefore, the chief cashier one day informed him that the man was to be in London again – this time as General Manager of the head office – and said that he was charged to find a private secretary for him from among the best clerks, and further intimated that the selection had fallen upon himself, Jones accepted the promotion quietly, fatalistically, yet with a degree of inward loathing hardly to be described. For he saw in this merely another move in the evolution of the inevitable Nemesis which he simply dared not seek to frustrate by any personal consideration; and at the same time he was conscious of a certain feeling of relief that the suspense of waiting might soon be mitigated. A secret sense of satisfaction, therefore, accompanied the unpleasant change, and Jones was able to hold himself perfectly well in hand when it was carried into effect and he was formally introduced as private secretary to the General Manager.

Now the Manager was a large, fat man, with a very red face and bags beneath his eyes. Being short-sighted, he wore glasses that seemed to magnify his eyes, which were always a little bloodshot. In hot weather a sort of thin slime covered his cheeks, for he perspired easily. His head was almost entirely bald, and over his turn-down collar his great neck folded in two distinct reddish collops of flesh. His hands were big and his fingers almost massive in thickness.

He was an excellent business man, of sane judgment and firm will, without enough imagination to confuse his course of action by showing him possible alternatives; and his integrity and ability caused him to be held in universal respect by the world of business and finance. In the important regions of a man's character, however, and at heart, he was coarse, brutal almost to savagery, without consideration for others, and as a result often cruelly unjust to his helpless subordinates.

In moments of temper, which were not infrequent, his face turned a dull purple, while the top of his bald head shone by contrast like white marble, and the bags under his eyes swelled till it seemed they would presently explode with a pop. And at these times he presented a distinctly repulsive appearance.

But to a private secretary like Jones, who did his duty regardless of whether his employer was beast or angel, and whose mainspring was principle and not emotion, this made little difference. Within the narrow limits in which any one *could* satisfy such a man, he pleased the General Manager; and more than once his piercing intuitive faculty, amounting almost to clairvoyance, assisted the chief in a fashion that served to bring the two closer together than might otherwise have been the case, and caused the man to respect in his assistant a power of which he possessed not even the germ himself. It was a curious relationship that grew up between the two, and the cashier, who enjoyed the credit of having made the selection, profited by it indirectly as much as any one else.

So for some time the work of the office continued normally and very prosperously. John Enderby Jones received a good salary, and in the outward appearance of the two chief characters in this history there was little change noticeable, except that the Manager grew fatter and redder, and the secretary observed that his own hair was beginning to show rather greyish at the temples.

There were, however, two changes in progress, and they both had to do with Jones, and are important to mention.

One was that he began to dream evilly. In the region ofdeep sleep, where the possibility of significant dreaming first develops itself, he was tormented more and more with vivid scenes and pictures in which a tall thin man, dark and sinister of countenance, and with bad eyes, was closely associated with himself. Only the setting was that of a past age, with costumes of centuries gone by, and the scenes had to do with dreadful cruelties that could not belong to modern life as he knew it.

The other change was also significant, but is not so easy to describe, for he had in fact become aware that some new portion of himself, hitherto unawakened, had stirred slowly into life out of the very depths of his consciousness. This new part of himself amounted almost to another personality, and he never observed its least manifestation without a strange thrill at his heart.

For he understood that it had begun to *watch* the Manager!

II

It was the habit of Jones, since he was compelled to work among conditions that were utterly distasteful, to withdraw his mind wholly from business once the day was over. During office hours he kept the strictest possible watch upon himself, and turned the key on all inner dreams, lest any sudden uprush from the deeps should interfere with his duty. But, once the working day was over, the gates flew open, and he began to enjoy himself.

He read no modern books on the subjects that interested him, and, as already said, he followed no course of training, nor belonged to any society that dabbled with half-told mysteries; but, once released from the office desk in the Manager's room, he simply and naturally entered the other region, because he was an old inhabitant, a rightful denizen, and because he belonged there. It was, in fact, really a case of dual personality; and a carefully drawn agreement existed between Jones-of-the-fire-insurance-office and Jones-of-the-mysteries, by the terms of which, under heavy penalties, neither region claimed him out of hours.

For the moment he reached his rooms under the roof in Bloomsbury, and had changed his city coat to another, the iron doors of the office clanged far behind him, and in front, before his very eyes, rolled up the beautiful gates of ivory, and he entered into the places of flowers and singing and wonderful veiled forms. Sometimes he quite lost touch with the outer world, forgetting to eat his dinner or go to bed, and lay in a state of trance, his consciousness working far out of the body.

And on other occasions he walked the streets on air, half-way between the two regions, unable to distinguish between incarnate and discarnate forms, and not very far, probably, beyond the strata where poets, saints, and the greatest artists have moved and thought and found their inspiration. But this was only when some insistent bodily claim prevented his full release, and more often than not he was entirely independent of his physical portion and free of the real region, without let or hindrance.

One evening he reached home utterly exhausted after the burden of the day's work. The Manager had been more than usually brutal, unjust, ill-tempered, and Jones had been almost persuaded out of his settled policy of contempt into answering back. Everything seemed to have gone amiss, and the man's coarse, underbred nature had been in the ascendant all day long: he had thumped the desk with his great fists, abused, found fault unreasonably, uttered outrageous things, and behaved generally as he actually was – beneath the thin veneer of acquired business varnish. He had done and said everything to wound all that was woundable in an ordinary secretary, and though Jones fortunately dwelt in a region from which he looked down upon such a man as he might look down on the blundering of a savage animal, the strain had nevertheless told severely upon him, and he reached home wondering for the first time in his life whether there was perhaps a point beyond which he would be unable to restrain himself any longer.

For something out of the usual had happened. At the close of a passage of great stress between the two, every nerve in the secretary's body tingling from undeserved abuse, the Manager had suddenly turned full upon him, in the corner of the private room where the safes stood, in such a way that the glare of his red eyes, magnified by the glasses, looked straight into his own. And at this very second that other personality in Jones – the one that was ever *watching* – rose up swiftly from the deeps within and held a mirror to his face.

A moment of flame and vision rushed over him, and for one single second – one merciless second of clear sight – he saw the Manager as the tall dark man of his evil dreams, and the knowledge that he had suffered at his hands some awful injury in the past crashed through his mind like the report of a cannon.

It all flashed upon him and was gone, changing him from fire to ice, and then back again to fire; and he left the office with the certain conviction in his heart that the time for his final settlement with the man, the time for the inevitable retribution, was at last drawing very near.

According to his invariable custom, however, he succeeded in putting the memory of all this unpleasantness out of his mind with the changing of his office coat, and after dozing a little in his leather chair before the fire, he started out as usual for dinner in the Soho French restaurant, and began to dream himself away into the region of flowers and singing, and to commune with the Invisibles that were the very sources of his real life and being.

For it was in this way that his mind worked, and the habits of years had crystallised into rigid lines along which it was now necessary and inevitable for him to act.

At the door of the little restaurant he stopped short, a half-remembered appointment in his mind. He had made an engagement with someone, but where, or with whom, had entirely slipped his memory. He thought it was for dinner, or else to meet just after dinner, and for a second it came back to him that it had something to do with the office, but, whatever it was, he was quite unable to recall it, and a reference to his pocket engagement book showed only a blank page. Evidently he had even omitted to enter it; and after standing a moment vainly trying to recall either the time, place, or person, he went in and sat down.

But though the details had escaped him, his subconscious memory seemed to know all about it, for he experienced a sudden sinking of the heart, accompanied by a sense of foreboding anticipation, and felt that beneath his exhaustion there lay a centre of tremendous excitement. The emotion caused by the engagement was at work, and would presently cause the actual details of the appointment to reappear.

Inside the restaurant the feeling increased, instead of passing: someone was waiting for him somewhere – someone whom he had definitely arranged to meet. He was expected by a person that very night and just about that very time. But by whom? Where? A curious inner trembling came over him, and he made a strong effort to hold himself in hand and to be ready for anything that might come.

And then suddenly came the knowledge that the place of appointment was this very restaurant, and, further, that the person he had promised to meet was already here, waiting somewhere quite close beside him.

He looked up nervously and began to examine the faces round him. The majority of the diners were Frenchmen, chattering loudly with much gesticulation and laughter; and there was a fair sprinkling of clerks like himself who came because the prices were low and the food good, but there was no single face that he recognised until his glance fell upon the occupant of the corner seat opposite, generally filled by himself.

'There's the man who's waiting for me!' thought Jones instantly.

He knew it at once. The man, he saw, was sitting well back into the corner, with a thick overcoat buttoned tightly up to the chin. His skin was very white, and a heavy black beard grew far up over his cheeks. At first the secretary took him for a stranger, but when he looked up and their eyes met, a sense of familiarity flashed across him, and for a second or two Jones imagined he was staring at a man he had known years before. For, barring the beard, it was the face of an elderly clerk who had occupied the next desk to his own when he first entered the service of the insurance company, and had shown him the most painstaking kindness and sympathy in the early difficulties of his work. But a moment later the illusion passed, for he remembered that Thorpe had been dead at least five years. The similarity of the eyes was obviously a mere suggestive trick of memory.

The two men stared at one another for several seconds, and then Jones began to act *instinctively*, and because he had to. He crossed over and took the vacant seat at the other's table, facing him; for he felt it was somehow imperative to explain why he was late, and how it was he had almost forgotten the engagement altogether.

No honest excuse, however, came to his assistance, though his mind had begun to work furiously.

'Yes, you *are* late,' said the man quietly, before he could find a single word to utter. 'But it doesn't matter. Also, you had forgotten the appointment, but that makes no difference either.'

'I knew – that there was an engagement,' Jones stammered, passing his hand over his forehead; 'but somehow –'

'You will recall it presently,' continued the other in a gentle voice, and smiling a little. 'It was in deep sleep last night we arranged this, and the unpleasant occurrences of today have for the moment obliterated it.'

A faint memory stirred within him as the man spoke, and a grove of trees with moving forms hovered before his eyes and then vanished again, while for an instant the stranger seemed to be capable of self-distortion and to have assumed vast proportions, with wonderful flaming eyes.

'Oh!' he gasped. 'It was there – in the other region?'

'Of course,' said the other, with a smile that illumined his whole face. 'You will remember presently, all in good time, and meanwhile you have no cause to feel afraid.'

There was a wonderful soothing quality in the man's voice, like the whispering of a great wind, and the clerk felt calmer at once. They sat a little while longer, but he could not remember that they talked much or ate anything. He only recalled afterwards that the head waiter came up and whispered something in his ear, and that he glanced round and saw the other people were looking at him curiously, some of them laughing, and that his companion then got up and led the way out of the restaurant.

They walked hurriedly through the streets, neither of them speaking; and Jones was so intent upon getting back the whole history of the affair from the region of deep sleep, that he barely noticed the way they took. Yet it was clear he knew where they were bound for just as well as his companion, for he crossed the streets often ahead of him, diving down alleys without hesitation, and the other followed always without correction.

The pavements were very full, and the usual night crowds of London were surging to and fro in the glare of the shop lights, but somehow no one impeded their rapid movements, and they seemed to pass through the people as if they were smoke. And, as they went, the pedestrians and traffic grew less and less, and they soon passed the Mansion House and the deserted space in front of the Royal Exchange, and so on down Fenchurch Street and within sight of the Tower of London, rising dim and shadowy in the smoky air.

Jones remembered all this perfectly well, and thought it was his intense preoccupation that made the distance seem so short. But it was when the Tower was left behind and they turned northwards that he began to notice how altered everything was, and saw that they were in a neighbourhood where houses were suddenly scarce, and lanes and fields beginning, and that their only light was the stars overhead. And, as the deeper consciousness more and more asserted itself to the exclusion of the surface happenings of his mere body during the day, the sense of exhaustion vanished, and he realised that he was moving somewhere in the region of causes behind the veil, beyond the gross deceptions of the senses, and released from the clumsy spell of space and time.

Without great surprise, therefore, he turned and saw that his companion had altered, had shed his overcoat and black hat, and was moving beside him absolutely *without sound.* For a brief second he saw him, tall as a tree, extending through space like a great shadow, misty and wavering of outline, followed by a sound like wings in the darkness; but, when he stopped, fear clutching at his heart, the other resumed his former proportions, and Jones could plainly see his normal outline against the green field behind.

Then the secretary saw him fumbling at his neck, and at the same moment the black beard came away from the face in his hand.

'Then you *are* Thorpe!' he gasped, yet somehow without overwhelming surprise.

They stood facing one another in the lonely lane, trees meeting overhead and hiding the stars, and a sound of mournful sighing among the branches.

'I am Thorpe,' was the answer in a voice that almost seemed part of the wind. 'And I have come out of our far past to help you, for my debt to you is large, and in this life I had but small opportunity to repay.'

Jones thought quickly of the man's kindness to him in the office, and a great wave of feeling surged through him as he began to remember dimly the friend by whose side he had already climbed, perhaps through vast ages of his soul's evolution.

'To help me now?' he whispered.

'You will understand me when you enter into your real memory and recall how great a debt I have to pay for old faithful kindnesses of long ago,' sighed the other in a voice like falling wind.

'Between us, though, there can be no question of *debt*,' Jones heard himself saying, and remembered the reply that floated to him on the air and the smile that lightened for a moment the stern eyes facing him.

'Not of debt, indeed, but of privilege.'

Jones felt his heart leap out towards this man, this old friend, tried by centuries and still faithful. He made a movement to seize his hand. But the other shifted like a thing of mist, and for a moment the clerk's head swam and his eyes seemed to fail.

'Then you are *dead*?' he said under his breath with a slight shiver.

'Five years ago I left the body you knew,' replied Thorpe. 'I tried to help you then instinctively, not fully recognising you. But now I can accomplish far more.'

With an awful sense of foreboding and dread in his heart, the secretary was beginning to understand.

'It has to do with – with – ?'

'Your past dealings with the Manager,' came the answer, as the wind rose louder among the branches overhead and carried off the remainder of the sentence into the air.

Jones's memory, which was just beginning to stir among the deepest layers of all, shut down suddenly with a snap, and he followed his companion over fields and down sweet-smelling lanes where the air was fragrant and cool, till they came to a large house, standing gaunt and lonely in the shadows at the edge of a wood. It was wrapped in utter stillness, with windows heavily draped in black, and the clerk, as he looked, felt such an overpowering wave of sadness invade him that his eyes began to burn and smart, and he was conscious of a desire to shed tears.

The key made a harsh noise as it turned in the lock, and when the door swung open into a lofty hall they heard a confused sound of rustling and whispering, as of a great throng of people pressing forward to meet them. The air seemed full of swaying movement, and Jones was certain he saw hands held aloft and dim faces claiming recognition, while in his heart, already oppressed by the approaching burden of vast accumulated memories, he was aware of the *uncoiling of something* that had been asleep for ages.

As they advanced he heard the doors close with a muffled thunder behind them, and saw that the shadows seemed to retreat and shrink away towards the interior of the house, carrying the hands and faces with them. He heard the wind singing round the walls and over the roof, and its wailing voice mingled with the sound of deep, collective breathing that filled the house like the murmur of a sea; and as they walked up the broad staircase and through the vaulted rooms, where pillars rose like the stems of trees, he knew that the building was crowded, row upon row, with the thronging memories of his own long past.

'This is the *House of the Past*,' whispered Thorpe beside him, as they moved silently from room to room; 'the house of *your* past. It is full from cellar to roof with the memories of what you have done, thought, and felt from the earliest stages of your evolution until now.

'The house climbs up almost to the clouds, and stretches back into the heart of the wood you saw outside, but the remoter halls are filled with the ghosts of ages ago too many to count, and even if we were able to waken them you could not remember them now. Some day, though, they will come and claim you, and you must know them, and answer their questions, for they can never rest till they have exhausted themselves again through you, and justice has been perfectly worked out.

'But now follow me closely, and you shall see the particular memory for which I am permitted to be your guide, so that you may know and understand a great force in your present life, and may use the sword of justice, or rise to the level of a great forgiveness, according to your degree of power.'

Icy thrills ran through the trembling clerk, and as he walked slowly beside his companion he heard from the vaults below, as well as from more distant regions of the vast building, the stirring and sighing of the serried ranks of sleepers, sounding in the still air like a chord swept from unseen strings stretched somewhere among the very foundations of the house.

Stealthily, picking their way among the great pillars, they moved up the sweeping staircase and through several dark corridors and halls, and presently stopped outside a small door in an archway where the shadows were very deep.

'Remain close by my side, and remember to utter no cry,' whispered the voice of his guide, and as the clerk turned to reply he saw his face was stern to whiteness and even shone a little in the darkness.

The room they entered seemed at first to be pitchy black, but gradually the secretary perceived a faint reddish glow against the farther end, and thought he saw figures moving silently to and fro.

'Now watch!' whispered Thorpe, as they pressed close to the wall near the door and waited. 'But remember to keep absolute silence. It is a torture scene.'

Jones felt utterly afraid, and would have turned to fly if he dared, for an indescribable terror seized him and his knees shook; but some power that made escape impossible held him remorselessly there, and with eyes glued on the spots of light he crouched against the wall and waited.

The figures began to move more swiftly, each in its own dim light that shed no radiance beyond itself, and he heard a soft clanking of chains and the voice of a man groaning in pain. Then came the sound of a door closing, and thereafter Jones saw but one figure, the figure of an old man, naked entirely, and fastened with chains to an iron framework on the floor. His memory gave a sudden leap of fear as he looked, for the features and white beard were familiar, and he recalled them as though of yesterday.

The other figures had disappeared, and the old man became the centre of the terrible picture. Slowly, with ghastly groans; as the heat below him increased into a steady glow, the aged body rose in a curve of agony, resting on the iron frame only where the chains held wrists and ankles fast. Cries and gasps filled the air, and Jones felt exactly as though they came from his own throat, and as if the chains were burning into his own wrists and ankles, and the heat scorching the skin and flesh upon his own back. He began to writhe and twist himself.

'Spain!' whispered the voice at his side, 'and four hundred years ago.'

'And the purpose?' gasped the perspiring clerk, though he knew quite well what the answer must be.

'To extort the name of a friend, to his death and betrayal,' came the reply through the darkness.

A sliding panel opened with a little rattle in the wall immediately above the rack, and a face, framed in the same red glow, appeared and looked down upon the dying victim. Jones was only just able to choke a scream, for he recognised the tall dark man of his dreams. With horrible, gloating eyes he gazed down upon the writhing form of the old man, and his lips moved as in speaking, though no words were actually audible.

'He asks again for the name,' explained the other, as the clerk struggled with the intense hatred and loathing that threatened every moment to result in screams and action. His ankles and wrists pained him so that he could scarcely keep still, but a merciless power held him to the scene.

He saw the old man, with a fierce cry, raise his tortured head and spit up into the face at the panel, and then the shutter slid back again, and a moment later the increased glow beneath the body, accompanied by awful writhing, told of the application of further heat. There came the odour of burning flesh; the white beard curled and burned to a crisp; the body fell back limp upon the red-hot iron, and then shot up again in fresh agony; cry after cry, the most awful in the world, rang out with deadened sound between the four walls; and again the panel slid back creaking, and revealed the dreadful face of the torturer.

Again the name was asked for, and again it was refused; and this time, after the closing of the panel, a door opened, and the tall thin man with the evil face came slowly into the chamber. His features were savage with rage and disappointment, and in the dull red glow that fell upon them he looked like a very prince of devils. In his hand he held a pointed iron at white heat.

'Now the murder!' came from Thorpe in a whisper that sounded as if it was outside the building and far away.

Jones knew quite well what was coming, but was unable even to close his eyes. He felt all the fearful pains himself just as though he were actually the sufferer; but now, as he stared, he felt something more besides; and when the tall man deliberately approached the rack and plunged the heated iron first into one eye and then into the other, he heard the faint fizzing of it, and felt his own eyes burst in frightful pain from his head. At the same moment, unable longer to control himself, he uttered a wild shriek and dashed forward to seize the torturer and tear him to a thousand pieces. Instantly, in a flash, the entire scene vanished; darkness rushed in to fill the room, and he felt himself lifted off his feet by some force like a great wind and borne swiftly away into space.

When he recovered his senses he was standing just outside the house and the figure of Thorpe was beside him in the gloom. The great doors were in the act of closing behind him, but before they shut he fancied he caught a glimpse of an immense veiled figure standing upon the threshold, with flaming eyes, and in his hand a bright weapon like a shining sword of fire.

'Come quickly now – all is over!' Thorpe whispered.

'And the dark man – ?' gasped the clerk, as he moved swiftly by the other's side.

'In this present life is the Manager of the company.'

'And the victim?'

'Was yourself!'

'And the friend he – *I* refused to betray?'

'I was that friend,' answered Thorpe, his voice with every moment sounding more and more like the cry of the wind. 'You gave your life in agony to save mine.'

'And again, in this life, we have all three been together?'

'Yes. Such forces are not soon or easily exhausted, and justice is not satisfied till all have reaped what they sowed.'

Jones had an odd feeling that he was slipping away into some other state of consciousness. Thorpe began to seem unreal. Presently he would be unable to ask more questions. He felt utterly sick and faint with it all, and his strength was ebbing.

'Oh, quick!' he cried, 'now tell me more. Why did I see this? What must I do?'

The wind swept across the field on their right and entered the wood beyond with a great roar, and the air round him seemed filled with voices and the rushing of hurried movement.

'To the ends of justice,' answered the other, as though speaking out of the centre of the wind and from a distance, 'which sometimes is entrusted to the hands of those who suffered and were strong. One wrong cannot be put right by another wrong, but your life has been so worthy that the opportunity is given to –'

The voice grew fainter and fainter, already it was far overhead with the rushing wind.

'You may punish or –.' Here Jones lost sight of Thorpe's figure altogether, for he seemed to have vanished and melted away into the wood behind him. His voice sounded far across the trees, very weak, and ever rising.

'Or if you can rise to the level of a great forgiveness –'

The voice became inaudible. . . . The wind came crying out of the wood again.

Jones shivered and stared about him. He shook himself violently and rubbed his eyes. The room was dark, the fire was out; he felt cold and stiff. He got up out of his armchair, still trembling, and lit the gas. Outside the wind was howling, and when he looked at his watch he saw that it was very late and he must go to bed.

He had not even changed his office coat; he must have fallen asleep in the chair as soon as he came in, and he had slept for several hours. Certainly he had eaten no dinner, for he felt ravenous.

III

N ext day, and for several weeks thereafter, the business of the office went on as usual, and Jones did his work well and behaved outwardly with perfect propriety. No more visions troubled him, and his relations with the Manager became, if anything, somewhat smoother and easier.

True, the man *looked* a little different, because the clerk kept seeing him with his inner and outer eye promiscuously, so that one moment he was broad and red-faced, and the next he was tall, thin, and dark, enveloped, as it were, in a sort of black atmosphere tinged with red. While at times a confusion of the two sights took place, and Jones saw the two faces mingled in a composite countenance that was very horrible indeed to contemplate. But, beyond this occasional change in the outward appearance of the Manager, there was nothing that the secretary noticed as the result of his vision, and business went on more or less as before, and perhaps even with a little less friction.

But in the rooms under the roof in Bloomsbury it was different, for there it was perfectly clear to Jones that Thorpe had come to take up his abode with him. He never saw him, but he knew all the time he was there. Every night on returning from his work he was greeted by the well-known whisper, 'Be ready when I give the sign!' and often in the night he woke up suddenly out of deep sleep and was aware that Thorpe had that minute moved away from his bed and was standing waiting and watching somewhere in the darkness of the room. Often he followed him down the stairs, though the dim gas jet on the landings never revealed his outline; and sometimes he did not come into the room at all, but hovered outside the window, peering through the dirty panes, or sending his whisper into the chamber in the whistling of the wind.

For Thorpe had come to stay, and Jones knew that he would not get rid of him until he had fulfilled the ends of justice and accomplished the purpose for which he was waiting.

Meanwhile, as the days passed, he went through a tremendous struggle with himself, and came to the perfectly honest decision that the 'level of a great forgiveness' was impossible for him, and that he must therefore accept the alternative and use the secret knowledge placed in his hands – and execute justice. And once this decision was arrived at, he noticed that Thorpe no longer left him alone during the day as before, but now accompanied him to the office and stayed more or less at his side all through business hours as well. His whisper made itself heard in the streets and in the train, and even in the Manager's room where he worked; sometimes warning, sometimes urging, but never for a moment suggesting the abandonment of the main purpose, and more than once so plainly audible that the clerk felt certain others must have heard it as well as himself.

The obsession was complete. He felt he was always under Thorpe's eye day and night, and he knew he must acquit himself like a man when the moment came, or prove a failure in his own sight as well as in the sight of the other.

And now that his mind was made up, nothing could prevent the carrying out of the sentence. He bought a pistol, and spent his Saturday afternoons practising at a target in lonely places along the Essex shore, marking out in the sand the exact measurements of the Manager's room. Sundays he occupied in like fashion, putting up at an inn overnight for the purpose, spending the money that usually went into the savings bank on travelling expenses and cartridges. Everything was done very thoroughly, for there must be no possibility of failure; and at the end of several weeks he had become so expert with his six-shooter that at a distance of 25 feet, which was the greatest length of the Manager's room, he could pick the inside out of a halfpenny nine times out of a dozen, and leave a clean, unbroken rim.

There was not the slightest desire to delay. He had thought the matter over from every point of view his mind could reach, and his purpose was inflexible. Indeed, he felt proud to think that he had been chosen as the instrument of justice in the infliction of so well-deserved and so terrible a punishment. Vengeance may have had some part in his decision, but he could not help that, for he still felt at times the hot chains burning his wrists and ankles with fierce agony through to the bone. He remembered the hideous pain of his slowly roasting back, and the point when he thought death *must* intervene to end his suffering, but instead new powers of endurance had surged up in him, and awful further stretches of pain had opened up, and unconsciousness seemed farther off than ever. Then at last the hot irons in his eyes. . . . It all came back to him, and caused him to break out in icy perspiration at the mere thought of it . . . the vile face at the panel . . . the expression of the dark face. . . . His fingers worked. His blood boiled. It was utterly impossible to keep the idea of vengeance altogether out of his mind.

Several times he was temporarily baulked of his prey. Odd things happened to stop him when he was on the point of action. The first day, for instance, the Manager fainted from the heat. Another time when he had decided to do the deed, the Manager did not come down to the office at all. And a third time, when his hand was actually in his hip pocket, he suddenly heard Thorpe's horrid whisper telling him to wait, and turning, he saw that the head cashier had entered the room noiselessly without his noticing it. Thorpe evidently knew what he was about, and did not intend to let the clerk bungle the matter.

He fancied, moreover, that the head cashier was watching him. He was always meeting him in unexpected corners and places, and the cashier never seemed to have an adequate excuse for being there. His movements seemed suddenly of particular interest to others in the office as well, for clerks were always being sent to ask him unnecessary questions, and there was apparently a general design to keep him under a sort of surveillance, so that he was never much alone with the Manager in the private room where they worked. And once the cashier had even gone so far as to suggest that he could take his holiday earlier than usual if he liked, as the work had been very arduous of late and the heat exceedingly trying.

He noticed, too, that he was sometimes followed by a certain individual in the streets, a careless-looking sort of man, who never came face to face with him, or actually ran into him, but who was always in his train or omnibus, and whose eye he often caught observing him over the top of his newspaper, and who on one occasion was even waiting at the door of his lodgings when he came out to dine.

There were other indications too, of various sorts, that led him to think something was at work to defeat his purpose, and that he must act at once before these hostile forces could prevent.

And so the end came very swiftly, and was thoroughly approved by Thorpe.

It was towards the close of July, and one of the hottest days London had ever known, for the City was like an oven, and the particles of dust seemed to burn the throats of the unfortunate toilers in street and office. The portly Manager, who suffered cruelly owing to his size, came down perspiring and gasping with the heat. He carried a light-coloured umbrella to protect his head.

'He'll want something more than that, though!' Jones laughed quietly to himself when he saw him enter.

The pistol was safely in his hip pocket, every one of its six chambers loaded.

The Manager saw the smile on his face, and gave him a long steady look as he sat down to his desk in the corner. A few minutes later he touched the bell for the head cashier – a single ring – and then asked Jones to fetch some papers from another safe in the room upstairs.

A deep inner trembling seized the secretary as he noticed these precautions, for he saw that the hostile forces were at work against him, and yet he felt he could delay no longer and must act that very morning, interference or no interference. However, he went obediently up in the lift to the next floor, and while fumbling with the combination of the safe, known only to himself, the cashier, and the Manager, he again heard Thorpe's horrid whisper just behind him:

'You must do it today! You must do it today!'

He came down again with the papers, and found the Manager alone. The room was like a furnace, and a wave of dead heated air met him in the face as he went in. The moment he passed the doorway he realised that he had been the subject of conversation between the head cashier and his enemy. They had been discussing him. Perhaps an inkling of his secret had somehow got into their minds. They had been watching him for days past. They had become suspicious.

Clearly, he must act now, or let the opportunity slip by perhaps for ever. He heard Thorpe's voice in his ear, but this time it was no mere whisper, but a plain human voice, speaking out loud.

'Now!' it said. 'Do it now!'

The room was empty. Only the Manager and himself were in it.

Jones turned from his desk where he had been standing, and locked the door leading into the main office. He saw the army of clerks scribbling in their shirt-sleeves, for the upper half of the door was of glass. He had perfect control of himself, and his heart was beating steadily.

The Manager, hearing the key turn in the lock, looked up sharply.

'What's that you're doing?' he asked quickly.

'Only locking the door, sir,' replied the secretary in a quite even voice.

'Why? Who told you to – ?'

'The voice of Justice, sir,' replied Jones, looking steadily into the hated face.

The Manager looked black for a moment, and stared angrily across the room at him. Then suddenly his expression changed as he stared, and he tried to smile. It was meant to be a kind smile evidently, but it only succeeded in being frightened.

'That *is* a good idea in this weather,' he said lightly, 'but it would be much better to lock it on the *outside*, wouldn't it, Mr. Jones?'

'I think not, sir. You might escape me then. Now you can't.'

Jones took his pistol out and pointed it at the other's face. Down the barrel he saw the features of the tall dark man, evil and sinister. Then the outline trembled a little and the face of the Manager slipped back into its place. It was white as death, and shining with perspiration.

'You tortured me to death four hundred years ago,' said the clerk in the same steady voice, 'and now the dispensers of justice have chosen me to punish you.'

The Manager's face turned to flame, and then back to chalk again. He made a quick movement towards the telephone bell, stretching out a hand to reach it, but at the same moment Jones pulled the trigger and the wrist was shattered, splashing the wall behind with blood.

'That's *one* place where the chains burnt,' he said quietly to himself. His hand was absolutely steady, and he felt that he was a hero.

The Manager was on his feet, with a scream of pain, supporting himself with his right hand on the desk in front of him, but Jones pressed the trigger again, and a bullet flew into the other wrist, so that the big man, deprived of support, fell forward with a crash on to the desk.

'You damned madman!' shrieked the Manager. 'Drop that pistol!'

'That's *another* place,' was all Jones said, still taking careful aim for another shot.

The big man, screaming and blundering, scrambled beneath the desk, making frantic efforts to hide, but the secretary took a step forward and fired two shots in quick succession into his projecting legs, hitting first one ankle and then the other, and smashing them horribly.

'Two more places where the chains burnt,' he said, going a little nearer.

The Manager, still shrieking, tried desperately to squeeze his bulk behind the shelter of the opening beneath the desk, but he was far too large, and his bald head protruded through on the other side. Jones caught him by the scruff of his great neck and dragged him yelping out on to the carpet. He was covered with blood, and flopped helplessly upon his broken wrists.

'Be quick now!' cried the voice of Thorpe.

There was a tremendous commotion and banging at the door, and Jones gripped his pistol tightly. Something seemed to crash through his brain, clearing it for a second, so that he thought he saw beside him a great veiled figure, with drawn sword and flaming eyes, and sternly approving attitude.

'Remember the eyes! Remember the eyes!' hissed Thorpe in the air above him.

Jones felt like a god, with a god's power. Vengeance disappeared from his mind. He was acting impersonally as an instrument in the hands of the Invisibles who dispense justice and balance accounts. He bent down and put the barrel close into the other's face, smiling a little as he saw the childish efforts of the arms to cover his head. Then he pulled the trigger, and a bullet went straight into the right eye, blackening the skin. Moving the pistol two inches the other way, he sent another bullet crashing into the left eye. Then he stood upright over his victim with a deep sigh of satisfaction.

The Manager wriggled convulsively for the space of a single second, and then lay still in death.

There was not a moment to lose, for the door was already broken in and violent hands were at his neck. Jones put the pistol to his temple and once more pressed the trigger with his finger.

But this time there was no report. Only a little dead click answered the pressure, for the secretary had forgotten that the pistol had only six chambers, and that he had used them all. He threw the useless weapon on to the floor, laughing a little out loud, and turned, without a struggle, to give himself up.

'I *had* to do it,' he said quietly, while they tied him. 'It was simply my duty! And now I am ready to face the consequences, and Thorpe will be proud of me. For justice has been done and the gods are satisfied.'

He made not the slightest resistance, and when the two policemen marched him off through the crowd of shuddering little clerks in the office, he again saw the veiled figure moving majestically in front of him, making slow sweeping circles with the flaming sword, to keep back the host of faces that were thronging in upon him from the Other Region.

The Land of Green Ginger

In his luxurious service flat the elderly Mr. Adam sat before the fire with a frown upon his face, a frown not of anger or annoyance but of perplexity. It was the cosy time between tea and dinner; about his armchair lay scattered a number of opened and unopened letters; he was scanning a brief typewritten note, wondering how he should deal with it, and this wonder was the cause of his frown.

'These newspaper symposiums,' he grumbled to himself, 'are a nuisance!' His secretary had gone home, taking away with her the dictated chapters of his book, his twentieth novel – his twentieth *successful* novel, he remembered with a smile that momentarily displaced the frown. 'How I started,' he read the typed sentence before him. 'What made me first begin to write?' The frown came back. Thought ran off into the mists of years ago. . . . He remembered quite well what made him first begin to write. 'But no one would believe me.'. . .

His face grew quite puckered. . . . He finally decided he would dictate in the morning a few commonplace paragraphs, giving facts, of course, yet not this queer incident that had first discovered his gift to himself. It had been due to a shock, this discovery; and a shock, some say, can bring out latent possibilities in the mind hitherto ignored. Circumstances, that is, are necessary for their appearance; unless life produces them, the possibilities remain unknown, inactive.

He remembered the shock in his own case, the queer experience it produced, and the first hint of his imaginative gift that appeared as a result. 'But they'd think I was romancing!'

His pencil, meanwhile, scribbled a few words on the blank part of the letter. . . .

'It is interesting,' he paused a moment to reflect, 'how every important detail of the experience was due to something in my mind at the time. All the ingredients were in me. Something just used them, dramatised them. That's the imaginative gift, I suppose. . . . It shapes the raw material.'

He could see it all as though it were yesterday . . . instead of thirty years ago. . . .

The shock, in his case, had been the sudden total loss of the comfortable fortune he had been brought up to expect. The trustee, his guardian, had played ducks and drakes with it, and at twenty, an orphan, just down from Oxford with a prospect of £2,000 a year, he found himself instead with £50, perhaps less. Two details only bear importantly upon the story: his intense bitterness against the swindling guardian, whom he knew personally; and the question of what he could do to earn his living. These two, had he written the truth for the symposium, Mr. Adam would have stressed. For it was with these two, this thought and this feeling burning intensely in his mind, that he had gone for a walk to think things over. . . .

To him, at the age of twenty, the situation seemed intensely tragic; no one in the world before had ever been so overwhelmed by fate; his anger against the psalm-singing guardian was of that bitter kind that could have killed. The young man was stirred to an intense anger and hatred. He could have murdered Mr. Holyoake. The swindler deserved it. And Adam, dwelling upon the years of dishonest speculation that had left him penniless, meant this precisely. Not that he actually wanted to commit murder, but that he realised the possibility lay in him. He still remembered – with a smile today – how he finally dismissed the idea from his mind: 'What's the use ?' he had reflected, bitterly. 'Even if I did murder him the State would only murder me in return. I should be hanged. Who murders is murdered in his turn.'

In this way the notion was – as he believed – dismissed from his mind.

The other 'important detail' concerned his immediate future. What could he do to earn his living ? He dwelt upon it with eager concentration. He reviewed a dozen futures: the stage, journalism, the motor trade, then in its infancy; insurance, emigrating – he thought of many fields and callings, but realised he was trained for none. The choice of work, of something that he could do, troubled him obsessingly. There were a hundred, a thousand possible futures open to a fellow, he discovered. It was the choice that he found impossible. At a given moment in anybody's life, he reflected, a number of possible things lie waiting – he can take only one, but the multiple choice is there.

He had been walking for some time, and in a circle apparently, for he now found himself wandering towards the waterfront of the ancient port that was his home town. It was after six o'clock on a summer evening, a Saturday, and few people were about. The sunshine fell slanting down the tangle of deserted alleyways. There was a smell of the sea, of tarred ropes, rigging, fish, and these brought back the idea of emigrating. He thought of a cousin who had just gone to some job or other in China. . . .

One notion chased another; his mind was a seething mass of wild ideas, with bitter, turbulent emotion behind them. Then, glancing up, his eye caught suddenly five little words, whose faded black letters shone in a patch of sunshine on the dull brick wall above his head. They were rather romantic little words, and they snatched at something in his mind. He stood and stared. It was merely the name of the alley, of course, yet thought took a new turn.

A kind of enchantment stole over him, for the words, as the poet puts it, walked up and down in his heart. . . . There rose before him a picture of forgotten days when the old port traded with southern isles, when dark-bearded sailors gabbling foreign tongues thronged these narrow alleyways, and the high romance of gallant sailing ships was in the air. . . . The five little words were almost a line of poetry.

'The Land of Green Ginger' was what he read.

Mr. Adam, the young one of thirty years ago, paused, his eyes fastened on the faded lettering in the yellow sunlight. Then he started down the twisting alley, whose high walls now housed nothing more romantic than offices of shipbrokers, notaries, typists, packers, and commissioners of oaths, until his eye noted suddenly an exception – an old furniture shop, with its queer wares overflowing on to the narrow pavement. They were a heterogeneous collection apparently. A circular mirror standing on a three-legged pedestal nearly six feet high reflected his figure, as he moved idly towards the shop a few yards lower down. He saw himself reflected, not without satisfaction – his smart flannel suit, his eyeglass, his straw hat with its Oxford colours. He also saw a bent, thin little old man with a skull-cap on his head standing among the shadows a few feet inside beyond the dingy doorway.

This figure now moved slowly towards him, scenting perhaps a possible customer.

'A fine piece,' said the wheezy voice. 'A perfect bit of glass, me lord! Cheap, too!' He rubbed his hands, nodding his ancient head in the direction of the article. 'It come from Chiney thirty years ago!'

Adam realised that he had been examining his own reflection for some minutes. He entered the shop, as an escape from troubling thoughts more than anything else, and as he did so the old man, bowing and scraping, moved too, backing away before him. The interior was dark, and much larger than the small entrance promised. A single oil-lamp revealed a series of deep, narrow rooms, cluttered up with stuff, among which the bent figure now set down the mirror carefully, for he had carried it in with him.

In the dimness the young man found his own reflection more attractive than before; it was softened, more effective, he decided. The wheezy voice was mentioning a price, rather a trumpery price, considered Mr. Adam, a few shillings only. He did not want to buy it, but anything was better than being alone with his tormenting thoughts, and he went closer to examine it. He bent down, noticing an inscription cut deeply into the dark wood of the framework. It was in Chinese characters. He ran his fingers over them, then looked up to ask:

'*Who looks in me,*' translated the wheezy voice, '*murders – and is murdered.*' And, carrying the mirror with him, the old man retreated a little farther into the shadow of the room beyond.

The young man was startled. He felt his body give an imperceptible twitch he was unable to suppress. His mind likewise gave a twitch. Was it uneasiness? It was, at any rate, surprise, while at the same time he was aware that something drew him, so that, almost involuntarily, he found himself following the retreating figure, who now, still carrying the mirror with him, was on the threshold of the next long room. It was the third extension of the premises, and it was considerably darker than the first two rooms. A chilliness hung in the fusty atmosphere. The place seemed lonely suddenly.

Aware of a faint tremor in him, though not yet of anything more than that, he spoke in a brusque, almost an aggressive voice:

'And what may such rubbish mean?' he inquired, sharply.

'Precisely what it says, me lord,' came the wheezy voice, much lower than before. There was an unpleasant hush in it. And there came a look into the face that hardly invited merriment, which was, perhaps, the very reason why Mr. Adam chose the moment for an audible guffaw. It betrayed him, he realised when it was too late. He felt nervous – and that guffaw had shown his nervousness. More of a chuckle than an actual laugh, it sounded unnatural among this piled-up paraphernalia from foreign lands that gave back no single echo. It sounded dead.

'Does it hold good? 'Mr. Adam challenged, the tone of his voice again betraying him – to himself at least. For the tremor crept somehow from the body into the sound. 'If I buy the thing, for instance, d'you mean to tell me that *I* – that *you* already before me –'

He could not finish the sentence. A shudder stopped his breath, and the voice died on his lips. While speaking he had been looking, not into the old man's face, but into the mirror, where he still saw his own reflection. But it was not this that stopped his speech, and froze his blood. It was something else he saw. With one wrinkled hand the old shopman still clutched the pedestal; but in the other was an unsheathed knife.

'So far, me lord, it has held good,' came his whisper down the long, dim room, and as he spoke he tilted the mirror to a slightly different angle. The young man saw himself in the glass as before, but he now saw something else behind him, too. It lay stretched upon the floor, motionless, crumpled dreadfully, its position not quite natural. One arm was twisted about the face at an angle not possible to life. In the narrow fairway of the room behind him, the room he had already passed, this pitiful, repulsive body lay. To stand where he now stood, the young man realised, he must actually have stepped over it.

'*You* – did – that?' he gasped, in a voice that emitted hardly any sound.

'He looked in the mirror,' came the whispered answer. 'What do you expect?'

'And before that – *he* in turn –'

'It works that way,' the other gave back with an awful grin. Adam felt his body stiffen; yet the blood began to flow in tumult. He felt his fists clench tightly. With his eyes fixed on the shopman and not leaving him for a single instant, he saw that the old man, letting go of the mirror, had suddenly begun to dodge. Light-footed he was, amazingly agile, quick, his movements convulsive, horribly alert. He dodged sideways, backwards, swift as a shadow round his customer, who watched the hideous dance with arrested muscles and with spellbound eyes. The knife gleamed and flashed.

Adam made an effort that seemed to wrench his heart – and the muscles began to function again. His instinct of self-preservation woke. Instinctively he picked up a heavy iron mace from a teak-wood table close beside him. With a strain he could just lift it.

'It's up to *me* then, now – is it?' he cried, his own feet shifting quickly.

'I can defend meself!' shrieked the shopman, dodging with incredible rapidity. 'If *that's* any good to you, me lord!' he yelled, shooting across the floor as an arrow flies, and brandishing his knife.

Moved by a sudden power that surprised himself, the young man leaped towards the pirouetting horror. He made one bound. He swung his heavy mace. The great weapon crashed down upon the ancient skull, driving the cap deep into the split bone. The figure stopped abruptly, uttered a tiny squeak, crumpled, and lay like a great mutilated insect where it fell. It did not move again.

'Murders and *is* murdered!' the other tried to scream, his voice, as in extreme nightmare agony, making no sound upon the air. 'I've done *you* in, at any rate. Then it's *my* turn next, is it – ?'

He turned swiftly, with the feeling that someone watched him from behind.

A tall figure, sure enough, darkened the distant door into the street, the outline of a stranger who bent a little to examine something that stood upon the pavement just outside.

The young man stared and stared. Though in semi-darkness himself, the outline was clearly defined in the evening light. But was it a stranger? He wore a smart flannel suit, a straw hat with Oxford colours. As he straightened up, an eyeglass became visible.

Mr. Adam shot round and stared at the crumpled heap upon the floor at his feet. It was *not* the shopman. An electric shock flowed over him. What he stared down at was a neat flannel suit, a straw hat with Oxford colours.

He shrieked. He raced headlong down the room. He darted at top speed along the next narrow room as well, straight towards the street door, towards the stranger with the tall outline. And this tall outline now came gliding to meet him, very swiftly gliding, silently too, making no sound upon the boarded floor, just as he had seen his own reflected image gliding towards himself in the mirror before. Closer it came and closer, something oddly, dreadfully familiar about it, something that he almost recognised.

It came remorselessly nearer, he could not have stopped it if he tried, while, curiously, he felt that he did not want to, even *must* not, stop it. Like Fate – his own fate – he must meet it; he could not avoid it – because he somehow welcomed it.

He did not pause himself; he even moved faster, till there was but a foot between them. Terrified he was, yet at the same time his courage rose. They met, they slipped into one another, they emerged, and instantaneously though this came about, he had time to recognise – himself... and that same second to find himself standing on the pavement outside, gazing at a mirror on a high three-legged pedestal, while a little, thin, bent old man faced him, wearing a skull-cap and rubbing his hands. It was the shopman evidently, scenting a possible customer.

'A fine piece,' the old man wheezed. His eyes pierced like gimlets. 'And cheap, too. It come from Chiney thirty year ago.'

A wave of pleasant, even delightful, emotion fluttered through the young man's heart, as he bent to read an inscription carved in Chinese characters upon the wooden frame. He ran his finger over them, then looked up to ask.

'*To each*' the wheezy voice translated, '*ten thousand futures. Yet each must choose his own,*' and went on to explain how a learned gentleman had once kindly deciphered the words for him – only the young man was no longer listening. He was staring intently at the upper part of the frame.

'But – the frame's empty!' he cried aloud. 'There *is* no mirror!' And again that marvellous emotion passed fluttering across his heart.

'It got broke,' he heard the wheezy voice explaining ; 'got broke on the vige over. But it's easy put in again, me lord. A fine old piece.' He mentioned a trumpery price, a few shillings merely.

*****

Young Mr. Adam bought it and took it home with him. . . . In due course he entered his cousin's insurance office as a clerk, and one evening he scribbled an account of his adventure in The Land of Green Ginger. Later, he wrote other, longer adventures, too. He had inside him, it seems, some queer gift of scribbling imaginary, possibly imaginative, adventures. . . . A shock had brought it to the surface.

*****

Next morning the elderly Mr. Adam dictated to his secretary a few commonplace paragraphs about 'How I started to write.' They began: 'At the age of twenty I entered an insurance office as a clerk. . . .' They were extremely dull. 'Send it to the editor,' he told his secretary, 'with a line to say I hope it is what he wants; he need not use it otherwise, of course.'

And as he dictated the paragraphs his eye wandered from a long shelf, holding some twenty adventure books, to a mirror on a high three-legged pedestal which, oddly, had no glass, and which, the elderly Mr. Adam knew, had never had one, nor ever would.

The Willows

I

After leaving Vienna, and long before you come to Budapest, the Danube enters a region of singular loneliness and desolation, where its waters spread away on all sides regardless of a main channel, and the country becomes a swamp for miles upon miles, covered by a vast sea of low willow-bushes. On the big maps this deserted area is painted in a fluffy blue, growing fainter in colour as it leaves the banks, and across it may be seen in large straggling letters the word Sumpfe, meaning marshes.

In high flood this great acreage of sand, shingle-beds, and willow-grown islands is almost topped by the water, but in normal seasons the bushes bend and rustle in the free winds, showing their silver leaves to the sunshine in an ever-moving plain of bewildering beauty. These willows never attain to the dignity of trees; they have no rigid trunks; they remain humble bushes, with rounded tops and soft outline, swaying on slender stems that answer to the least pressure of the wind; supple as grasses, and so continually shifting that they somehow give the impression that the entire plain is moving and alive. For the wind sends waves rising and falling over the whole surface, waves of leaves instead of waves of water, green swells like the sea, too, until the branches turn and lift, and then silvery white as their underside turns to the sun.

Happy to slip beyond the control of the stern banks, the Danube here wanders about at will among the intricate network of channels intersecting the islands everywhere with broad avenues down which the waters pour with a shouting sound; making whirlpools, eddies, and foaming rapids; tearing at the sandy banks; carrying away masses of shore and willow-clumps; and forming new islands innumerably which shift daily in size and shape and possess at best an impermanent life, since the flood-time obliterates their very existence.

Properly speaking, this fascinating part of the river's life begins soon after leaving Pressburg, and we, in our Canadian canoe, with gipsy tent and frying-pan on board, reached it on the crest of a rising flood about mid-July. That very same morning, when the sky was reddening before sunrise, we had slipped swiftly through still-sleeping Vienna, leaving it a couple of hours later a mere patch of smoke against the blue hills of the Wienerwald on the horizon; we had breakfasted below Fischeramend under a grove of birch trees roaring in the wind; and had then swept on the tearing current past Orth, Hainburg, Petronell (the old Roman Carnuntum of Marcus Aurelius), and so under the frowning heights of Thelsen on a spur of the Carpathians, where the March steals in quietly from the left and the frontier is crossed between Austria and Hungary.

Racing along at twelve kilometres an hour soon took us well into Hungary, and the muddy waters – sure sign of flood – sent us aground on many a shingle-bed, and twisted us like a cork in many a sudden belching whirlpool before the towers of Pressburg (Hungarian, Poszony) showed against the sky; and then the canoe, leaping like a spirited horse, flew at top speed under the grey walls, negotiated safely the sunken chain of the Fliegende Brucke ferry, turned the corner sharply to the left, and plunged on yellow foam into the wilderness of islands, sandbanks, and swamp-land beyond – the land of the willows.

The change came suddenly, as when a series of bioscope pictures snaps down on the streets of a town and shifts without warning into the scenery of lake and forest. We entered the land of desolation on wings, and in less than half an hour there was neither boat nor fishing-hut nor red roof, nor any single sign of human habitation and civilisation within sight. The sense of remoteness from the world of humankind, the utter isolation, the fascination of this singular world of willows, winds, and waters, instantly laid its spell upon us both, so that we allowed laughingly to one another that we ought by rights to have held some special kind of passport to admit us, and that we had, somewhat audaciously, come without asking leave into a separate little kingdom of wonder and magic – a kingdom that was reserved for the use of others who had a right to it, with everywhere unwritten warnings to trespassers for those who had the imagination to discover them.

Though still early in the afternoon, the ceaseless buffetings of a most tempestuous wind made us feel weary, and we at once began casting about for a suitable camping-ground for the night. But the bewildering character of the islands made landing difficult; the swirling flood carried us in shore and then swept us out again; the willow branches tore our hands as we seized them to stop the canoe, and we pulled many a yard of sandy bank into the water before at length we shot with a great sideways blow from the wind into a backwater and managed to beach the bows in a cloud of spray. Then we lay panting and laughing after our exertions on the hot yellow sand, sheltered from the wind, and in the full blaze of a scorching sun, a cloudless blue sky above, and an immense army of dancing, shouting willow bushes, closing in from all sides, shining with spray and clapping their thousand little hands as though to applaud the success of our efforts.

'What a river!' I said to my companion, thinking of all the way we had travelled from the source in the Black Forest, and how he had often been obliged to wade and push in the upper shallows at the beginning of June.

'Won't stand much nonsense now, will it?' he said, pulling the canoe a little farther into safety up the sand, and then composing himself for a nap.

I lay by his side, happy and peaceful in the bath of the elements – water, wind, sand, and the great fire of the sun – thinking of the long journey that lay behind us, and of the great stretch before us to the Black Sea, and how lucky I was to have such a delightful and charming travelling companion as my friend, the Swede.

We had made many similar journeys together, but the Danube, more than any other river I knew, impressed us from the very beginning with its aliveness. From its tiny bubbling entry into the world among the pinewood gardens of Donaueschingen, until this moment when it began to play the great river-game of losing itself among the deserted swamps, unobserved, unrestrained, it had seemed to us like following the grown of some living creature. Sleepy at first, but later developing violent desires as it became conscious of its deep soul, it rolled, like some huge fluid being, through all the countries we had passed, holding our little craft on its mighty shoulders, playing roughly with us sometimes, yet always friendly and well-meaning, till at length we had come inevitably to regard it as a Great Personage.

How, indeed, could it be otherwise, since it told us so much of its secret life? At night we heard it singing to the moon as we lay in our tent, uttering that odd sibilant note peculiar to itself and said to be caused by the rapid tearing of the pebbles along its bed, so great is its hurrying speed. We knew, too, the voice of its gurgling whirlpools, suddenly bubbling up on a surface previously quite calm; the roar of its shallows and swift rapids; its constant steady thundering below all mere surface sounds; and that ceaseless tearing of its icy waters at the banks. How it stood up and shouted when the rains fell flat upon its face! And how its laughter roared out when the wind blew up-stream and tried to stop its growing speed! We knew all its sounds and voices, its tumblings and foamings, its unnecessary splashing against the bridges; that self-conscious chatter when there were hills to look on; the affected dignity of its speech when it passed through the little towns, far too important to laugh; and all these faint, sweet whisperings when the sun caught it fairly in some slow curve and poured down upon it till the steam rose.

It was full of tricks, too, in its early life before the great world knew it. There were places in the upper reaches among the Swabian forests, when yet the first whispers of its destiny had not reached it, where it elected to disappear through holes in the ground, to appear again on the other side of the porous limestone hills and start a new river with another name; leaving, too, so little water in its own bed that we had to climb out and wade and push the canoe through miles of shallows.

And a chief pleasure, in those early days of its irresponsible youth, was to lie low, like Brer Fox, just before the little turbulent tributaries came to join it from the Alps, and to refuse to acknowledge them when in, but to run for miles side by side, the dividing line well marked, the very levels different, the Danube utterly declining to recognise the newcomer. Below Passau, however, it gave up this particular trick, for there the Inn comes in with a thundering power impossible to ignore, and so pushes and incommodes the parent river that there is hardly room for them in the long twisting gorge that follows, and the Danube is shoved this way and that against the cliffs, and forced to hurry itself with great waves and much dashing to and fro in order to get through in time. And during the fight our canoe slipped down from its shoulder to its breast, and had the time of its life among the struggling waves. But the Inn taught the old river a lesson, and after Passau it no longer pretended to ignore new arrivals.

This was many days back, of course, and since then we had come to know other aspects of the great creature, and across the Bavarian wheat plain of Straubing she wandered so slowly under the blazing June sun that we could well imagine only the surface inches were water, while below there moved, concealed as by a silken mantle, a whole army of Undines, passing silently and unseen down to the sea, and very leisurely too, lest they be discovered.

Much, too, we forgave her because of her friendliness to the birds and animals that haunted the shores. Cormorants lined the banks in lonely places in rows like short black palings; grey crows crowded the shingle-beds; storks stood fishing in the vistas of shallower water that opened up between the islands, and hawks, swans, and marsh birds of all sorts filled the air with glinting wings and singing, petulant cries. It was impossible to feel annoyed with the river's vagaries after seeing a deer leap with a splash into the water at sunrise and swim past the bows of the canoe; and often we saw fawns peering at us from the underbrush, or looked straight into the brown eyes of a stag as we charged full tilt round a corner and entered another reach of the river. Foxes, too, everywhere haunted the banks, tripping daintily among the driftwood and disappearing so suddenly that it was impossible to see how they managed it.

But now, after leaving Pressburg, everything changed a little, and the Danube became more serious. It ceased trifling. It was half-way to the Black Sea, within seeming distance almost of other, stranger countries where no tricks would be permitted or understood. It became suddenly grown-up, and claimed our respect and even our awe. It broke out into three arms, for one thing, that only met again a hundred kilometres farther down, and for a canoe there were no indications which one was intended to be followed.

'If you take a side channel,' said the Hungarian officer we met in the Pressburg shop while buying provisions, 'you may find yourselves, when the flood subsides, forty miles from anywhere, high and dry, and you may easily starve. There are no people, no farms, no fishermen. I warn you not to continue. The river, too, is still rising, and this wind will increase.'

The rising river did not alarm us in the least, but the matter of being left high and dry by a sudden subsidence of the waters might be serious, and we had consequently laid in an extra stock of provisions. For the rest, the officer's prophecy held true, and the wind, blowing down a perfectly clear sky, increased steadily till it reached the dignity of a westerly gale.

It was earlier than usual when we camped, for the sun was a good hour or two from the horizon, and leaving my friend still asleep on the hot sand, I wandered about in desultory examination of our hotel. The island, I found, was less than an acre in extent, a mere sandy bank standing some two or three feet above the level of the river. The far end, pointing into the sunset, was covered with flying spray which the tremendous wind drove off the crests of the broken waves. It was triangular in shape, with the apex up stream.

I stood there for several minutes, watching the impetuous crimson flood bearing down with a shouting roar, dashing in waves against the bank as though to sweep it bodily away, and then swirling by in two foaming streams on either side. The ground seemed to shake with the shock and rush, while the furious movement of the willow bushes as the wind poured over them increased the curious illusion that the island itself actually moved. Above, for a mile or two, I could see the great river descending upon me; it was like looking up the slope of a sliding hill, white with foam, and leaping up everywhere to show itself to the sun.

The rest of the island was too thickly grown with willows to make walking pleasant, but I made the tour, nevertheless. From the lower end the light, of course, changed, and the river looked dark and angry. Only the backs of the flying waves were visible, streaked with foam, and pushed forcibly by the great puffs of wind that fell upon them from behind. For a short mile it was visible, pouring in and out among the islands, and then disappearing with a huge sweep into the willows, which closed about it like a herd of monstrous antediluvian creatures crowding down to drink. They made me think of gigantic sponge-like growths that sucked the river up into themselves. They caused it to vanish from sight. They herded there together in such overpowering numbers.

Altogether it was an impressive scene, with its utter loneliness, its bizarre suggestion; and as I gazed, long and curiously, a singular emotion began to stir somewhere in the depths of me. Midway in my delight of the wild beauty, there crept, unbidden and unexplained, a curious feeling of disquietude, almost of alarm.

A rising river, perhaps, always suggests something of the ominous; many of the little islands I saw before me would probably have been swept away by the morning; this resistless, thundering flood of water touched the sense of awe. Yet I was aware that my uneasiness lay deeper far than the emotions of awe and wonder. It was not that I felt. Nor had it directly to do with the power of the driving wind – this shouting hurricane that might almost carry up a few acres of willows into the air and scatter them like so much chaff over the landscape. The wind was simply enjoying itself, for nothing rose out of the flat landscape to stop it, and I was conscious of sharing its great game with a kind of pleasurable excitement. Yet this novel emotion had nothing to do with the wind. Indeed, so vague was the sense of distress I experienced, that it was impossible to trace it to its source and deal with it accordingly, though I was aware somehow that it had to do with my realisation of our utter insignificance before this unrestrained power of the elements about me. The huge-grown river had something to do with it too – a vague, unpleasant idea that we had somehow trifled with these great elemental forces in whose power we lay helpless every hour of the day and night. For here, indeed, they were gigantically at play together, and the sight appealed to the imagination.

But my emotion, so far as I could understand it, seemed to attach itself more particularly to the willow bushes, to these acres and acres of willows, crowding, so thickly growing there, swarming everywhere the eye could reach, pressing upon the river as though to suffocate it, standing in dense array mile after mile beneath the sky, watching, waiting, listening. And, apart quite from the elements, the willows connected themselves subtly with my malaise, attacking the mind insidiously somehow by reason of their vast numbers, and contriving in some way or other to represent to the imagination a new and mighty power, a power, moreover, not altogether friendly to us.

Great revelations of nature, of course, never fail to impress in one way or another, and I was no stranger to moods of the kind. Mountains overawe and oceans terrify, while the mystery of great forests exercises a spell peculiarly its own. But all these, at one point or another, somewhere link on intimately with human life and human experience. They stir comprehensible, even if alarming, emotions. They tend on the whole to exalt.

With this multitude of willows, however, it was something far different, I felt. Some essence emanated from them that besieged the heart. A sense of awe awakened, true, but of awe touched somewhere by a vague terror. Their serried ranks, growing everywhere darker about me as the shadows deepened, moving furiously yet softly in the wind, woke in me the curious and unwelcome suggestion that we had trespassed here upon the borders of an alien world, a world where we were intruders, a world where we were not wanted or invited to remain – where we ran grave risks perhaps!

The feeling, however, though it refused to yield its meaning entirely to analysis, did not at the time trouble me by passing into menace. Yet it never left me quite, even during the very practical business of putting up the tent in a hurricane of wind and building a fire for the stew-pot. It remained, just enough to bother and perplex, and to rob a most delightful camping-ground of a good portion of its charm. To my companion, however, I said nothing, for he was a man I considered devoid of imagination. In the first place, I could never have explained to him what I meant, and in the second, he would have laughed stupidly at me if I had.

There was a slight depression in the center of the island, and here we pitched the tent. The surrounding willows broke the wind a bit.

'A poor camp,' observed the imperturbable Swede when at last the tent stood upright, 'no stones and precious little firewood. I'm for moving on early tomorrow – eh? This sand won't hold anything.'

But the experience of a collapsing tent at midnight had taught us many devices, and we made the cozy gipsy house as safe as possible, and then set about collecting a store of wood to last till bed-time. Willow bushes drop no branches, and driftwood was our only source of supply. We hunted the shores pretty thoroughly. Everywhere the banks were crumbling as the rising flood tore at them and carried away great portions with a splash and a gurgle.

'The island's much smaller than when we landed,' said the accurate Swede. 'It won't last long at this rate. We'd better drag the canoe close to the tent, and be ready to start at a moment's notice. I shall sleep in my clothes.'

He was a little distance off, climbing along the bank, and I heard his rather jolly laugh as he spoke.

'By Jove!' I heard him call, a moment later, and turned to see what had caused his exclamation. But for the moment he was hidden by the willows, and I could not find him.

'What in the world's this?' I heard him cry again, and this time his voice had become serious.

I ran up quickly and joined him on the bank. He was looking over the river, pointing at something in the water.

'Good heavens, it's a man's body!' he cried excitedly. 'Look!'

A black thing, turning over and over in the foaming waves, swept rapidly past. It kept disappearing and coming up to the surface again. It was about twenty feet from the shore, and just as it was opposite to where we stood it lurched round and looked straight at us. We saw its eyes reflecting the sunset, and gleaming an odd yellow as the body turned over. Then it gave a swift, gulping plunge, and dived out of sight in a flash.

'An otter, by gad!' we exclaimed in the same breath, laughing.

It was an otter, alive, and out on the hunt; yet it had looked exactly like the body of a drowned man turning helplessly in the current. Far below it came to the surface once again, and we saw its black skin, wet and shining in the sunlight.

Then, too, just as we turned back, our arms full of driftwood, another thing happened to recall us to the river bank. This time it really was a man, and what was more, a man in a boat. Now a small boat on the Danube was an unusual sight at any time, but here in this deserted region, and at flood time, it was so unexpected as to constitute a real event. We stood and stared.

Whether it was due to the slanting sunlight, or the refraction from the wonderfully illumined water, I cannot say, but, whatever the cause, I found it difficult to focus my sight properly upon the flying apparition. It seemed, however, to be a man standing upright in a sort of flat-bottomed boat, steering with a long oar, and being carried down the opposite shore at a tremendous pace. He apparently was looking across in our direction, but the distance was too great and the light too uncertain for us to make out very plainly what he was about. It seemed to me that he was gesticulating and making signs at us. His voice came across the water to us shouting something furiously, but the wind drowned it so that no single word was audible. There was something curious about the whole appearance – man, boat, signs, voice – that made an impression on me out of all proportion to its cause.

'He's crossing himself!' I cried. 'Look, he's making the sign of the Cross!'

'I believe you're right,' the Swede said, shading his eyes with his hand and watching the man out of sight. He seemed to be gone in a moment, melting away down there into the sea of willows where the sun caught them in the bend of the river and turned them into a great crimson wall of beauty. Mist, too, had begun to rise, so that the air was hazy.

'But what in the world is he doing at nightfall on this flooded river?' I said, half to myself. 'Where is he going at such a time, and what did he mean by his signs and shouting? D'you think he wished to warn us about something?'

'He saw our smoke, and thought we were spirits probably,' laughed my companion. 'These Hungarians believe in all sorts of rubbish; you remember the shopwoman at Pressburg warning us that no one ever landed here because it belonged to some sort of beings outside man's world! I suppose they believe in fairies and elementals, possibly demons, too. That peasant in the boat saw people on the islands for the first time in his life,' he added, after a slight pause, 'and it scared him, that's all.'

The Swede's tone of voice was not convincing, and his manner lacked something that was usually there. I noted the change instantly while he talked, though without being able to label it precisely.

'If they had enough imagination,' I laughed loudly – I remember trying to make as much noise as I could – 'they might well people a place like this with the old gods of antiquity. The Romans must have haunted all this region more or less with their shrines and sacred groves and elemental deities.'

The subject dropped and we returned to our stew-pot, for my friend was not given to imaginative conversation as a rule. Moreover, just then I remember feeling distinctly glad that he was not imaginative; his stolid, practical nature suddenly seemed to me welcome and comforting. It was an admirable temperament, I felt; he could steer down rapids like a red Indian, shoot dangerous bridges and whirlpools better than any white man I ever saw in a canoe. He was a grand fellow for an adventurous trip, a tower of strength when untoward things happened. I looked at his strong face and light curly hair as he staggered along under his pile of driftwood (twice the size of mine!), and I experienced a feeling of relief. Yes, I was distinctly glad just then that the Swede was – what he was, and that he never made remarks that suggested more than they said.

'The river's still rising, though,' he added, as if following out some thoughts of his own, and dropping his load with a gasp. 'This island will be under water in two days if it goes on.'

'I wish the wind would go down,' I said. 'I don't care a fig for the river.'

The flood, indeed, had no terrors for us; we could get off at ten minutes' notice, and the more water the better we liked it. It meant an increasing current and the obliteration of the treacherous shingle-beds that so often threatened to tear the bottom out of our canoe.

Contrary to our expectations, the wind did not go down with the sun. It seemed to increase with the darkness, howling overhead and shaking the willows round us like straws. Curious sounds accompanied it sometimes, like the explosion of heavy guns, and it fell upon the water and the island in great flat blows of immense power. It made me think of the sounds a planet must make, could we only hear it, driving along through space.

But the sky kept wholly clear of clouds, and soon after supper the full moon rose up in the east and covered the river and the plain of shouting willows with a light like the day.

We lay on the sandy patch beside the fire, smoking, listening to the noises of the night round us, and talking happily of the journey we had already made, and of our plans ahead. The map lay spread in the door of the tent, but the high wind made it hard to study, and presently we lowered the curtain and extinguished the lantern. The firelight was enough to smoke and see each other's faces by, and the sparks flew about overhead like fireworks. A few yards beyond, the river gurgled and hissed, and from time to time a heavy splash announced the falling away of further portions of the bank.

Our talk, I noticed, had to do with the faraway scenes and incidents of our first camps in the Black Forest, or of other subjects altogether remote from the present setting, for neither of us spoke of the actual moment more than was necessary – almost as though we had agreed tacitly to avoid discussion of the camp and its incidents. Neither the otter nor the boatman, for instance, received the honour of a single mention, though ordinarily these would have furnished discussion for the greater part of the evening. They were, of course, distinct events in such a place.

The scarcity of wood made it a business to keep the fire going, for the wind, that drove the smoke in our faces wherever we sat, helped at the same time to make a forced draught. We took it in turn to make some foraging expeditions into the darkness, and the quantity the Swede brought back always made me feel that he took an absurdly long time finding it; for the fact was I did not care much about being left alone, and yet it always seemed to be my turn to grub about among the bushes or scramble along the slippery banks in the moonlight. The long day's battle with wind and water – such wind and such water! – had tired us both, and an early bed was the obvious programme. Yet neither of us made the move for the tent. We lay there, tending the fire, talking in desultory fashion, peering about us into the dense willow bushes, and listening to the thunder of wind and river. The loneliness of the place had entered our very bones, and silence seemed natural, for after a bit the sound of our voices became a trifle unreal and forced; whispering would have been the fitting mode of communication, I felt, and the human voice, always rather absurd amid the roar of the elements, now carried with it something almost illegitimate. It was like talking out loud in church, or in some place where it was not lawful, perhaps not quite safe, to be overheard.

The eeriness of this lonely island, set among a million willows, swept by a hurricane, and surrounded by hurrying deep waters, touched us both, I fancy. Untrodden by man, almost unknown to man, it lay there beneath the moon, remote from human influence, on the frontier of another world, an alien world, a world tenanted by willows only and the souls of willows. And we, in our rashness, had dared to invade it, even to make use of it! Something more than the power of its mystery stirred in me as I lay on the sand, feet to fire, and peered up through the leaves at the stars. For the last time I rose to get firewood.

'When this has burnt up,' I said firmly, 'I shall turn in,' and my companion watched me lazily as I moved off into the surrounding shadows.

For an unimaginative man I thought he seemed unusually receptive that night, unusually open to suggestion of things other than sensory. He too was touched by the beauty and loneliness of the place. I was not altogether pleased, I remember, to recognise this slight change in him, and instead of immediately collecting sticks, I made my way to the far point of the island where the moonlight on plain and river could be seen to better advantage. The desire to be alone had come suddenly upon me; my former dread returned in force; there was a vague feeling in me I wished to face and probe to the bottom.

When I reached the point of sand jutting out among the waves, the spell of the place descended upon me with a positive shock. No mere 'scenery' could have produced such an effect. There was something more here, something to alarm.

I gazed across the waste of wild waters; I watched the whispering willows; I heard the ceaseless beating of the tireless wind; and, one and all, each in its own way, stirred in me this sensation of a strange distress. But the willows especially; for ever they went on chattering and talking among themselves, laughing a little, shrilly crying out, sometimes sighing – but what it was they made so much to-do about belonged to the secret life of the great plain they inhabited. And it was utterly alien to the world I knew, or to that of the wild yet kindly elements. They made me think of a host of beings from another plane of life, another evolution altogether, perhaps, all discussing a mystery known only to themselves. I watched them moving busily together, oddly shaking their big bushy heads, twirling their myriad leaves even when there was no wind. They moved of their own will as though alive, and they touched, by some incalculable method, my own keen sense of the horrible.

There they stood in the moonlight, like a vast army surrounding our camp, shaking their innumerable silver spears defiantly, formed all ready for an attack.

The psychology of places, for some imaginations at least, is very vivid; for the wanderer, especially, camps have their 'note' either of welcome or rejection. At first it may not always be apparent, because the busy preparations of tent and cooking prevent, but with the first pause – after supper usually – it comes and announces itself. And the note of this willow-camp now became unmistakably plain to me; we were interlopers, trespassers; we were not welcomed. The sense of unfamiliarity grew upon me as I stood there watching. We touched the frontier of a region where our presence was resented. For a night's lodging we might perhaps be tolerated; but for a prolonged and inquisitive stay – No! by all the gods of the trees and wilderness. No! We were the first human influences upon this island, and we were not wanted. The willows were against us.

Strange thoughts like these, bizarre fancies, borne I know not whence, found lodgment in my mind as I stood listening. What, I thought, if, after all, these crouching willows proved to be alive; if suddenly they should rise up, like a swarm of living creatures, marshaled by the gods whose territory we had invaded, sweep towards us off the vast swamps, booming overhead in the night – and then settle down! As I looked it was so easy to imagine they actually moved, crept nearer, retreated a little, huddled together in masses, hostile, waiting for the great wind that should finally start them a-running. I could have sworn their aspect changed a little, and their ranks deepened and pressed more closely together.

The melancholy shrill cry of a night-bird sounded overhead, and suddenly I nearly lost my balance as the piece of bank I stood upon fell with a great splash into the river, undermined by the flood. I stepped back just in time, and went on hunting for firewood again, half laughing at the odd fancies that crowded so thickly into my mind and cast their spell upon me. I recalled the Swede's remark about moving on next day, and I was just thinking that I fully agreed with him, when I turned with a start and saw the subject of my thoughts standing immediately in front of me. He was quite close. The roar of the elements had covered his approach.

II

'You've been gone so long,' he shouted above the wind, 'I thought something must have happened to you.'

But there was that in his tone, and a certain look in his face as well, that conveyed to me more than his usual words, and in a flash I understood the real reason for his coming. It was because the spell of the place had entered his soul too, and he did not like being alone.

'River still rising,' he cried, pointing to the flood in the moonlight, 'and the wind's simply awful.'

He always said the same things, but it was the cry for companionship that gave the real importance to his words.

'Lucky,' I cried back, 'our tent's in the hollow. I think it'll hold all right.' I added something about the difficulty of finding wood, in order to explain my absence, but the wind caught my words and flung them across the river, so that he did not hear, but just looked at me through the branches, nodding his head.

'Lucky if we get away without disaster!' he shouted, or words to that effect; and I remember feeling half angry with him for putting the thought into words, for it was exactly what I felt myself. There was disaster impending somewhere, and the sense of presentiment lay unpleasantly upon me.

We went back to the fire and made a final blaze, poking it up with our feet. We took a last look round. But for the wind the heat would have been unpleasant. I put this thought into words, and I remember my friend's reply struck me oddly: that he would rather have the heat, the ordinary July weather, than this 'diabolical wind.'

Everything was snug for the night; the canoe lying turned over beside the tent, with both yellow paddles beneath her; the provision sack hanging from a willow-stem, and the washed-up dishes removed to a safe distance from the fire, all ready for the morning meal.

We smothered the embers of the fire with sand, and then turned in. The flap of the tent door was up, and I saw the branches and the stars and the white moonlight. The shaking willows and the heavy buffetings of the wind against our taut little house were the last things I remembered as sleep came down and covered all with its soft and delicious forgetfulness.

Suddenly I found myself lying awake, peering from my sandy mattress through the door of the tent. I looked at my watch pinned against the canvas, and saw by the bright moonlight that it was past twelve o'clock – the threshold of a new day – and I had therefore slept a couple of hours. The Swede was asleep still beside me; the wind howled as before; something plucked at my heart and made me feel afraid. There was a sense of disturbance in my immediate neighbourhood.

I sat up quickly and looked out. The trees were swaying violently to and fro as the gusts smote them, but our little bit of green canvas lay snugly safe in the hollow, for the wind passed over it without meeting enough resistance to make it vicious. The feeling of disquietude did not pass, however, and I crawled quietly out of the tent to see if our belongings were safe. I moved carefully so as not to waken my companion. A curious excitement was on me.

I was half-way out, kneeling on all fours, when my eye first took in that the tops of the bushes opposite, with their moving tracery of leaves, made shapes against the sky. I sat back on my haunches and stared. It was incredible, surely, but there, opposite and slightly above me, were shapes of some indeterminate sort among the willows, and as the branches swayed in the wind they seemed to group themselves about these shapes, forming a series of monstrous outlines that shifted rapidly beneath the moon. Close, about fifty feet in front of me, I saw these things.

My first instinct was to waken my companion, that he too might see them, but something made me hesitate – the sudden realisation, probably, that I should not welcome corroboration; and meanwhile I crouched there staring in amazement with smarting eyes. I was wide awake. I remember saying to myself that I was not dreaming.

They first became properly visible, these huge figures, just within the tops of the bushes – immense, bronze-coloured, moving, and wholly independent of the swaying of the branches. I saw them plainly and noted, now I came to examine them more calmly, that they were very much larger than human, and indeed that something in their appearance proclaimed them to be not human at all. Certainly they were not merely the moving tracery of the branches against the moonlight. They shifted independently. They rose upwards in a continuous stream from earth to sky, vanishing utterly as soon as they reached the dark of the sky. They were interlaced one with another, making a great column, and I saw their limbs and huge bodies melting in and out of each other, forming this serpentine line that bent and swayed and twisted spirally with the contortions of the wind-tossed trees. They were nude, fluid shapes, passing up the bushes, within the leaves almost – rising up in a living column into the heavens. Their faces I never could see. Unceasingly they poured upwards, swaying in great bending curves, with a hue of dull bronze upon their skins.

I stared, trying to force every atom of vision from my eyes. For a long time I thought they must every moment disappear and resolve themselves into the movements of the branches and prove to be an optical illusion. I searched everywhere for a proof of reality, when all the while I understood quite well that the standard of reality had changed. For the longer I looked the more certain I became that these figures were real and living, though perhaps not according to the standards that the camera and the biologist would insist upon.

Far from feeling fear, I was possessed with a sense of awe and wonder such as I have never known. I seemed to be gazing at the personified elemental forces of this haunted and primeval region. Our intrusion had stirred the powers of the place into activity. It was we who were the cause of the disturbance, and my brain filled to bursting with stories and legends of the spirits and deities of places that have been acknowledged and worshipped by men in all ages of the world's history. But, before I could arrive at any possible explanation, something impelled me to go farther out, and I crept forward on the sand and stood upright. I felt the ground still warm under my bare feet; the wind tore at my hair and face; and the sound of the river burst upon my ears with a sudden roar. These things, I knew, were real, and proved that my senses were acting normally. Yet the figures still rose from earth to heaven, silent, majestically, in a great spiral of grace and strength that overwhelmed me at length with a genuine deep emotion of worship. I felt that I must fall down and worship – absolutely worship.

Perhaps in another minute I might have done so, when a gust of wind swept against me with such force that it blew me sideways, and I nearly stumbled and fell. It seemed to shake the dream violently out of me. At least it gave me another point of view somehow. The figures still remained, still ascended into heaven from the heart of the night, but my reason at last began to assert itself. It must be a subjective experience, I argued – none the less real for that, but still subjective. The moonlight and the branches combined to work out these pictures upon the mirror of my imagination, and for some reason I projected them outwards and made them appear objective. I knew this must be the case, of course. I took courage, and began to move forward across the open patches of sand. By Jove, though, was it all hallucination? Was it merely subjective? Did not my reason argue in the old futile way from the little standard of the known?

I only know that great column of figures ascended darkly into the sky for what seemed a very long period of time, and with a very complete measure of reality as most men are accustomed to gauge reality. Then suddenly they were gone!

And, once they were gone and the immediate wonder of their great presence had passed, fear came down upon me with a cold rush. The esoteric meaning of this lonely and haunted region suddenly flamed up within me, and I began to tremble dreadfully. I took a quick look round – a look of horror that came near to panic – calculating vainly ways of escape; and then, realising how helpless I was to achieve anything really effective, I crept back silently into the tent and lay down again upon my sandy mattress, first lowering the door-curtain to shut out the sight of the willows in the moonlight, and then burying my head as deeply as possible beneath the blankets to deaden the sound of the terrifying wind.

As though further to convince me that I had not been dreaming, I remember that it was a long time before I fell again into a troubled and restless sleep; and even then only the upper crust of me slept, and underneath there was something that never quite lost consciousness, but lay alert and on the watch.

But this second time I jumped up with a genuine start of terror. It was neither the wind nor the river that woke me, but the slow approach of something that caused the sleeping portion of me to grow smaller and smaller till at last it vanished altogether, and I found myself sitting bolt upright – listening.

Outside there was a sound of multitudinous little patterings. They had been coming, I was aware, for a long time, and in my sleep they had first become audible. I sat there nervously wide awake as though I had not slept at all. It seemed to me that my breathing came with difficulty, and that there was a great weight upon the surface of my body. In spite of the hot night, I felt clammy with cold and shivered. Something surely was pressing steadily against the sides of the tent and weighing down upon it from above. Was it the body of the wind? Was this the pattering rain, the dripping of the leaves? The spray blown from the river by the wind and gathering in big drops? I thought quickly of a dozen things.

Then suddenly the explanation leaped into my mind: a bough from the poplar, the only large tree on the island, had fallen with the wind. Still half caught by the other branches, it would fall with the next gust and crush us, and meanwhile its leaves brushed and tapped upon the tight canvas surface of the tent. I raised a loose flap and rushed out, calling to the Swede to follow.

But when I got out and stood upright I saw that the tent was free. There was no hanging bough; there was no rain or spray; nothing approached.

A cold, grey light filtered down through the bushes and lay on the faintly gleaming sand. Stars still crowded the sky directly overhead, and the wind howled magnificently, but the fire no longer gave out any glow, and I saw the east reddening in streaks through the trees. Several hours must have passed since I stood there before watching the ascending figures, and the memory of it now came back to me horribly, like an evil dream. Oh, how tired it made me feel, that ceaseless raging wind! Yet, though the deep lassitude of a sleepless night was on me, my nerves were tingling with the activity of an equally tireless apprehension, and all idea of repose was out of the question. The river I saw had risen further. Its thunder filled the air, and a fine spray made itself felt through my thin sleeping shirt.

Yet nowhere did I discover the slightest evidence of anything to cause alarm. This deep, prolonged disturbance in my heart remained wholly unaccounted for.

My companion had not stirred when I called him, and there was no need to waken him now. I looked about me carefully, noting everything; the turned-over canoe; the yellow paddles –

two of them, I'm certain; the provision sack and the extra lantern hanging together from the tree; and, crowding everywhere about me, enveloping all, the willows, those endless, shaking willows. A bird uttered its morning cry, and a string of duck passed with whirring flight overhead in the twilight. The sand whirled, dry and stinging, about my bare feet in the wind.

I walked round the tent and then went out a little way into the bush, so that I could see across the river to the farther landscape, and the same profound yet indefinable emotion of distress seized upon me again as I saw the interminable sea of bushes stretching to the horizon, looking ghostly and unreal in the wan light of dawn. I walked softly here and there, still puzzling over that odd sound of infinite pattering, and of that pressure upon the tent that had wakened me. It must have been the wind, I reflected – the wind bearing upon the loose, hot sand, driving the dry particles smartly against the taut canvas – the wind dropping heavily upon our fragile roof.

Yet all the time my nervousness and malaise increased appreciably.

I crossed over to the farther shore and noted how the coastline had altered in the night, and what masses of sand the river had torn away. I dipped my hands and feet into the cool current, and bathed my forehead. Already there was a glow of sunrise in the sky and the exquisite freshness of coming day. On my way back I passed purposely beneath the very bushes where I had seen the column of figures rising into the air, and midway among the clumps I suddenly found myself overtaken by a sense of vast terror. From the shadows a large figure went swiftly by. Someone passed me, as sure as ever man did. . . .

It was a great staggering blow from the wind that helped me forward again, and once out in the more open space, the sense of terror diminished strangely. The winds were about and walking, I remember saying to myself, for the winds often move like great presences under the trees. And altogether the fear that hovered about me was such an unknown and immense kind of fear, so unlike anything I had ever felt before, that it woke a sense of awe and wonder in me that did much to counteract its worst effects; and when I reached a high point in the middle of the island from which I could see the wide stretch of river, crimson in the sunrise, the whole magical beauty of it all was so overpowering that a sort of wild yearning woke in me and almost brought a cry up into the throat.

But this cry found no expression, for as my eyes wandered from the plain beyond to the island round me and noted our little tent half hidden among the willows, a dreadful discovery leaped out at me, compared to which my terror of the walking winds seemed as nothing at all.

For a change, I thought, had somehow come about in the arrangement of the landscape. It was not that my point of vantage gave me a different view, but that an alteration had apparently been effected in the relation of the tent to the willows, and of the willows to the tent. Surely the bushes now crowded much closer – unnecessarily, unpleasantly close. They had moved nearer.

Creeping with silent feet over the shifting sands, drawing imperceptibly nearer by soft, unhurried movements, the willows had come closer during the night. But had the wind moved them, or had they moved of themselves? I recalled the sound of infinite small patterings and the pressure upon the tent and upon my own heart that caused me to wake in terror. I swayed for a moment in the wind like a tree, finding it hard to keep my upright position on the sandy hillock. There was a suggestion here of personal agency, of deliberate intention, of aggressive hostility, and it terrified me into a sort of rigidity.

Then the reaction followed quickly. The idea was so bizarre, so absurd, that I felt inclined to laugh. But the laughter came no more readily than the cry, for the knowledge that my mind was so receptive to such dangerous imaginings brought the additional terror that it was through our minds and not through our physical bodies that the attack would come, and was coming.

The wind buffeted me about, and, very quickly it seemed, the sun came up over the horizon, for it was after four o'clock, and I must have stood on that little pinnacle of sand longer than I knew, afraid to come down to close quarters with the willows. I returned quietly, creepily, to the tent, first taking another exhaustive look round and – yes, I confess it – making a few measurements. I paced out on the warm sand the distances between the willows and the tent, making a note of the shortest distance particularly.

I crawled stealthily into my blankets. My companion, to all appearances, still slept soundly, and I was glad that this was so. Provided my experiences were not corroborated, I could find strength somehow to deny them, perhaps. With the daylight I could persuade myself that it was all a subjective hallucination, a fantasy of the night, a projection of the excited imagination.

Nothing further came in to disturb me, and I fell asleep almost at once, utterly exhausted, yet still in dread of hearing again that weird sound of multitudinous pattering, or of feeling the pressure upon my heart that had made it difficult to breathe.

The sun was high in the heavens when my companion woke me from a heavy sleep and announced that the porridge was cooked and there was just time to bathe. The grateful smell of frizzling bacon entered the tent door.

'River still rising,' he said, 'and several islands out in midstream have disappeared altogether. Our own island's much smaller.'

'Any wood left?' I asked sleepily.

'The wood and the island will finish tomorrow in a dead heat,' he laughed, 'but there's enough to last us till then.'

I plunged in from the point of the island, which had indeed altered a lot in size and shape during the night, and was swept down in a moment to the landing-place opposite the tent. The water was icy, and the banks flew by like the country from an express train. Bathing under such conditions was an exhilarating operation, and the terror of the night seemed cleansed out of me by a process of evaporation in the brain. The sun was blazing hot; not a cloud showed itself anywhere; the wind, however, had not abated one little jot.

Quite suddenly then the implied meaning of the Swede's words flashed across me, showing that he no longer wished to leave post-haste, and had changed his mind. 'Enough to last till tomorrow' – he assumed we should stay on the island another night. It struck me as odd. The night before he was so positive the other way. How had the change come about?

Great crumblings of the banks occurred at breakfast, with heavy splashings and clouds of spray which the wind brought into our frying-pan, and my fellow-traveller talked incessantly about the difficulty the Vienna-Pesth steamers must have to find the channel in flood. But the state of his mind interested and impressed me far more than the state of the river or the difficulties of the steamers. He had changed somehow since the evening before. His manner was different – a trifle excited, a trifle shy, with a sort of suspicion about his voice and gestures. I hardly know how to describe it now in cold blood, but at the time I remember being quite certain of one thing – that he had become frightened?

He ate very little breakfast, and for once omitted to smoke his pipe. He had the map spread open beside him, and kept studying its markings.

'We'd better get off sharp in an hour,' I said presently, feeling for an opening that must bring him indirectly to a partial confession at any rate. And his answer puzzled me uncomfortably: 'Rather! If they'll let us.'

'Who'll let us? The elements?' I asked quickly, with affected indifference.

'The powers of this awful place, whoever they are,' he replied, keeping his eyes on the map. 'The gods are here, if they are anywhere at all in the world.'

'The elements are always the true immortals,' I replied, laughing as naturally as I could manage, yet knowing quite well that my face reflected my true feelings when he looked up gravely at me and spoke across the smoke:

'We shall be fortunate if we get away without further disaster.'

This was exactly what I had dreaded, and I screwed myself up to the point of the direct question. It was like agreeing to allow the dentist to extract the tooth; it had to come anyhow in the long run, and the rest was all pretence.

'Further disaster! Why, what's happened?'

'For one thing – the steering paddle's gone,' he said quietly.

'The steering paddle gone!' I repeated, greatly excited, for this was our rudder, and the Danube in flood without a rudder was suicide. 'But what –'

'And there's a tear in the bottom of the canoe,' he added, with a genuine little tremor in his voice.

I continued staring at him, able only to repeat the words in his face somewhat foolishly. There, in the heat of the sun, and on this burning sand, I was aware of a freezing atmosphere descending round us. I got up to follow him, for he merely nodded his head gravely and led the way towards the tent a few yards on the other side of the fireplace. The canoe still lay there as I had last seen her in the night, ribs uppermost, the paddles, or rather, the paddle, on the sand beside her.

'There's only one,' he said, stooping to pick it up. 'And here's the rent in the base-board.'

It was on the tip of my tongue to tell him that I had clearly noticed two paddles a few hours before, but a second impulse made me think better of it, and I said nothing. I approached to see.

There was a long, finely made tear in the bottom of the canoe where a little slither of wood had been neatly taken clean out; it looked as if the tooth of a sharp rock or snag had eaten down her length, and investigation showed that the hole went through. Had we launched out in her without observing it we must inevitably have foundered. At first the water would have made the wood swell so as to close the hole, but once out in mid-stream the water must have poured in, and the canoe, never more than two inches above the surface, would have filled and sunk very rapidly.

'There, you see an attempt to prepare a victim for the sacrifice,' I heard him saying, more to himself than to me, 'two victims rather,' he added as he bent over and ran his fingers along the slit.

I began to whistle – a thing I always do unconsciously when utterly nonplussed – and purposely paid no attention to his words. I was determined to consider them foolish.

'It wasn't there last night,' he said presently, straightening up from his examination and looking anywhere but at me.

'We must have scratched her in landing, of course,' I stopped whistling to say. 'The stones are very sharp.'

I stopped abruptly, for at that moment he turned round and met my eye squarely. I knew just as well as he did how impossible my explanation was. There were no stones, to begin with.

'And then there's this to explain, too,' he added quietly, handing me the paddle and pointing to the blade.

A new and curious emotion spread freezingly over me as I took and examined it. The blade was scraped down all over, beautifully scraped, as though someone had sand-papered it with care, making it so thin that the first vigorous stroke must have snapped it off at the elbow.

'One of us walked in his sleep and did this thing,' I said feebly, 'or – or it has been filed by the constant stream of sand particles blown against it by the wind, perhaps.'

'Ah,' said the Swede, turning away, laughing a little, 'you can explain everything.'

'The same wind that caught the steering paddle and flung it so near the bank that it fell in with the next lump that crumbled,' I called out after him, absolutely determined to find an explanation for everything he showed me.

'I see,' he shouted back, turning his head to look at me before disappearing among the willow bushes.

Once alone with these perplexing evidences of personal agency, I think my first thoughts took the form of 'One of us must have done this thing, and it certainly was not I.' But my second thought decided how impossible it was to suppose, under all the circumstances, that either of us had done it. That my companion, the trusted friend of a dozen similar expeditions, could have knowingly had a hand in it, was a suggestion not to be entertained for a moment. Equally absurd seemed the explanation that this imperturbable and densely practical nature had suddenly become insane and was busied with insane purposes.

Yet the fact remained that what disturbed me most, and kept my fear actively alive even in this blaze of sunshine and wild beauty, was the clear certainty that some curious alteration had come about in his mind – that he was nervous, timid, suspicious, aware of goings on he did not speak about, watching a series of secret and hitherto unmentionable events – waiting, in a word, for a climax that he expected, and, I thought, expected very soon. This grew up in my mind intuitively – I hardly knew how.

I made a hurried examination of the tent and its surroundings, but the measurements of the night remained the same. There were deep hollows formed in the sand I now noticed for the first time, basin-shaped and of various depths and sizes, varying from that of a tea-cup to a large bowl. The wind, no doubt, was responsible for these miniature craters, just as it was for lifting the paddle and tossing it towards the water. The rent in the canoe was the only thing that seemed quite inexplicable; and, after all, it was conceivable that a sharp point had caught it when we landed. The examination I made of the shore did not assist this theory, but all the same I clung to it with that diminishing portion of my intelligence which I called my 'reason.' An explanation of some kind was an absolute necessity, just as some working explanation of the universe is necessary – however absurd – to the happiness of every individual who seeks to do his duty in the world and face the problems of life. The simile seemed to me at the time an exact parallel.

I at once set the pitch melting, and presently the Swede joined me at the work, though under the best conditions in the world the canoe could not be safe for traveling till the following day. I drew his attention casually to the hollows in the sand.

'Yes,' he said, 'I know. They're all over the island. But you can explain them, no doubt!'

'Wind, of course,' I answered without hesitation. 'Have you never watched those little whirlwinds in the street that twist and twirl everything into a circle? This sand's loose enough to yield, that's all.'

He made no reply, and we worked on in silence for a bit. I watched him surreptitiously all the time, and I had an idea he was watching me. He seemed, too, to be always listening attentively to something I could not hear, or perhaps for something that he expected to hear, for he kept turning about and staring into the bushes, and up into the sky, and out across the water where it was visible through the openings among the willows. Sometimes he even put his hand to his ear and held it there for several minutes. He said nothing to me, however, about it, and I asked no questions. And meanwhile, as he mended that torn canoe with the skill and address of a red Indian, I was glad to notice his absorption in the work, for there was a vague dread in my heart that he would speak of the changed aspect of the willows. And, if he had noticed that, my imagination could no longer be held a sufficient explanation of it.

III

At length, after a long pause, he began to talk.

'Queer thing,' he added in a hurried sort of voice, as though he wanted to say something and get it over. 'Queer thing. I mean, about that otter last night.'

I had expected something so totally different that he caught me with surprise, and I looked up sharply.

'Shows how lonely this place is. Otters are awfully shy things –'

'I don't mean that, of course,' he interrupted. 'I mean – do you think – did you think it really was an otter?'

'What else, in the name of Heaven, what else?'

'You know, I saw it before you did, and at first it seemed – so much bigger than an otter.'

'The sunset as you looked upstream magnified it, or something,' I replied.

He looked at me absently a moment, as though his mind were busy with other thoughts.

'It had such extraordinary yellow eyes,' he went on half to himself.

'That was the sun too,' I laughed, a trifle boisterously. 'I suppose you'll wonder next if that fellow in the boat –'

I suddenly decided not to finish the sentence. He was in the act again of listening, turning his head to the wind, and something in the expression of his face made me halt. The subject dropped, and we went on with our caulking. Apparently he had not noticed my unfinished sentence. Five minutes later, however, he looked at me across the canoe, the smoking pitch in his hand, his face exceedingly grave.

'I did rather wonder, if you want to know,' he said slowly, 'what that thing in the boat was. I remember thinking at the time it was not a man. The whole business seemed to rise quite suddenly out of the water.'

I laughed again boisterously in his face, but this time there was impatience, and a strain of anger, too, in my feeling.

'Look here now,' I cried, 'this place is quite queer enough without going out of our way to imagine things! That boat was an ordinary boat, and the man in it was an ordinary man, and they were both going downstream as fast as they could lick. And that otter was an otter, so don't let's play the fool about it!'

He looked steadily at me with the same grave expression. He was not in the least annoyed. I took courage from his silence.

'And, for Heaven's sake,' I went on, 'don't keep pretending you hear things, because it only gives me the jumps, and there's nothing to hear but the river and this cursed old thundering wind.'

'You fool!' he answered in a low, shocked voice, 'You utter fool. That's just the way all victims talk. As if you didn't understand just as well as I do!' he sneered with scorn in his voice, and a sort of resignation. 'The best thing you can do is to keep quiet and try to hold your mind as firm as possible. This feeble attempt at self-deception only makes the truth harder when you're forced to meet it.'

My little effort was over, and I found nothing more to say, for I knew quite well his words were true, and that I was the fool, not he. Up to a certain stage in the adventure he kept ahead of me easily, and I think I felt annoyed to be out of it, to be thus proved less psychic, less sensitive than himself to these extraordinary happenings, and half ignorant all the time of what was going on under my very nose. He knew from the very beginning, apparently. But at the moment I wholly missed the point of his words about the necessity of there being a victim, and that we ourselves were destined to satisfy the want. I dropped all pretence thenceforward, but thenceforward likewise my fear increased steadily to the climax.

'But you're quite right about one thing,' he added, before the subject passed, 'and that is that we're wiser not to talk about it, or even to think about it, because what one thinks finds expression in words, and what one says, happens.'

That afternoon, while the canoe dried and hardened, we spent trying to fish, testing the leak, collecting wood, and watching the enormous flood of rising water. Masses of driftwood swept near our shores sometimes, and we fished for them with long willow branches. The island grew perceptibly smaller as the banks were torn away with great gulps and splashes. The weather kept brilliantly fine till about four o'clock, and then for the first time for three days the wind showed signs of abating. Clouds began to gather in the southwest, spreading thence slowly over the sky.

This lessening of the wind came as a great relief, for the incessant roaring, banging, and thundering had irritated our nerves. Yet the silence that came about five o'clock with its sudden cessation was in a manner quite as oppressive. The booming of the river had everything in its own way then; it filled the air with deep murmurs, more musical than the wind noises, but infinitely more monotonous. The wind held many notes, rising, falling, always beating out some sort of great elemental tune; whereas the river's song lay between three notes at most – dull pedal notes, that held a lugubrious quality foreign to the wind, and somehow seemed to me, in my then nervous state, to sound wonderfully well the music of doom.

It was extraordinary, too, how the withdrawal suddenly of bright sunlight took everything out of the landscape that made for cheerfulness; and since this particular landscape had already managed to convey the suggestion of something sinister, the change of course was all the more unwelcome and noticeable.

For me, I know, the darkening outlook became distinctly more alarming, and I found myself more than once calculating how soon after sunset the full moon would get up in the east, and whether the gathering clouds would greatly interfere with her lighting of the little island.

With this general hush of the wind – though it still indulged in occasional brief gusts – the river seemed to me to grow blacker, the willows to stand more densely together. The latter, too, kept up a sort of independent movement of their own, rustling among themselves when no wind stirred, and shaking oddly from the roots upwards. When common objects in this way become charged with the suggestion of horror, they stimulate the imagination far more than things of unusual appearance; and these bushes, crowding huddled about us, assumed for me in the darkness a bizarre grotesquerie of appearance that lent to them somehow the aspect of purposeful and living creatures. Their very ordinariness, I felt, masked what was malignant and hostile to us. The forces of the region drew nearer with the coming of night. They were focusing upon our island, and more particularly upon ourselves. For thus, somehow, in the terms of the imagination, did my really indescribable sensations in this extraordinary place present themselves.

I had slept a good deal in the early afternoon, and had thus recovered somewhat from the exhaustion of a disturbed night, but this only served apparently to render me more susceptible than before to the obsessing spell of the haunting. I fought against it, laughing at my feelings as absurd and childish, with very obvious physiological explanations, yet, in spite of every effort, they gained in strength upon me so that I dreaded the night as a child lost in a forest must dread the approach of darkness.

The canoe we had carefully covered with a waterproof sheet during the day, and the one remaining paddle had been securely tied by the Swede to the base of a tree, lest the wind should rob us of that too. From five o'clock onwards I busied myself with the stew-pot and preparations for dinner, it being my turn to cook that night. We had potatoes, onions, bits of bacon fat to add flavour, and a general thick residue from former stews at the bottom of the pot; with black bread broken up into it the result was most excellent, and it was followed by a stew of plums with sugar and a brew of strong tea with dried milk. A good pile of wood lay close at hand, and the absence of wind made my duties easy. My companion sat lazily watching me, dividing his attentions between cleaning his pipe and giving useless advice – an admitted privilege of the off-duty man. He had been very quiet all the afternoon, engaged in re-caulking the canoe, strengthening the tent ropes, and fishing for driftwood while I slept. No more talk about undesirable things had passed between us, and I think his only remarks had to do with the gradual destruction of the island, which he declared was not fully a third smaller than when we first landed.

The pot had just begun to bubble when I heard his voice calling to me from the bank, where he had wandered away without my noticing. I ran up.

'Come and listen,' he said, 'and see what you make of it.' He held his hand cupwise to his ear, as so often before.

'Now do you hear anything?' he asked, watching me curiously.

We stood there, listening attentively together. At first I heard only the deep note of the water and the hissings rising from its turbulent surface. The willows, for once, were motionless and silent. Then a sound began to reach my ears faintly, a peculiar sound – something like the humming of a distant gong. It seemed to come across to us in the darkness from the waste of swamps and willows opposite. It was repeated at regular intervals, but it was certainly neither the sound of a bell nor the hooting of a distant steamer. I can liken it to nothing so much as to the sound of an immense gong, suspended far up in the sky, repeating incessantly its muffled metallic note, soft and musical, as it was repeatedly struck. My heart quickened as I listened.

'I've heard it all day,' said my companion. 'While you slept this afternoon it came all round the island. I hunted it down, but could never get near enough to see – to localise it correctly. Sometimes it was overhead, and sometimes it seemed under the water. Once or twice, too, I could have sworn it was not outside at all, but within myself – you know – the way a sound in the fourth dimension is supposed to come.'

I was too much puzzled to pay much attention to his words. I listened carefully, striving to associate it with any known familiar sound I could think of, but without success. It changed in the direction, too, coming nearer, and then sinking utterly away into remote distance. I cannot say that it was ominous in quality, because to me it seemed distinctly musical, yet I must admit it set going a distressing feeling that made me wish I had never heard it.

'The wind blowing in those sand-funnels,' I said determined to find an explanation, 'or the bushes rubbing together after the storm perhaps.'

'It comes off the whole swamp,' my friend answered.

'It comes from everywhere at once.' He ignored my explanations. 'It comes from the willow bushes somehow –'

'But now the wind has dropped,' I objected. 'The willows can hardly make a noise by themselves, can they?'

His answer frightened me, first because I had dreaded it, and secondly, because I knew intuitively it was true.

'It is because the wind has dropped we now hear it. It was drowned before. It is the cry, I believe, of the –'

I dashed back to my fire, warned by the sound of bubbling that the stew was in danger, but determined at the same time to escape further conversation. I was resolute, if possible, to avoid the exchanging of views. I dreaded, too, that he would begin about the gods, or the elemental forces, or something else disquieting, and I wanted to keep myself well in hand for what might happen later. There was another night to be faced before we escaped from this distressing place, and there was no knowing yet what it might bring forth.

'Come and cut up bread for the pot,' I called to him, vigorously stirring the appetizing mixture. That stew-pot held sanity for us both, and the thought made me laugh.

He came over slowly and took the provision sack from the tree, fumbling in its mysterious depths, and then emptying the entire contents upon the ground-sheet at his feet.

'Hurry up!' I cried; 'it's boiling.'

The Swede burst out into a roar of laughter that startled me. It was forced laughter, not artificial exactly, but mirthless.

'There's nothing here!' he shouted, holding his sides.

'Bread, I mean.'

'It's gone. There is no bread. They've taken it!'

I dropped the long spoon and ran up. Everything the sack had contained lay upon the ground-sheet, but there was no loaf.

The whole dead weight of my growing fear fell upon me and shook me. Then I burst out laughing too. It was the only thing to do: and the sound of my laughter also made me understand his. The stain of psychical pressure caused it – this explosion of unnatural laughter in both of us; it was an effort of repressed forces to seek relief; it was a temporary safety-valve. And with both of us it ceased quite suddenly.

'How criminally stupid of me!' I cried, still determined to be consistent and find an explanation. 'I clean forgot to buy a loaf at Pressburg. That chattering woman put everything out of my head, and I must have left it lying on the counter or –'

'The oatmeal, too, is much less than it was this morning,' the Swede interrupted.

Why in the world need he draw attention to it? I thought angrily.

'There's enough for tomorrow,' I said, stirring vigorously, 'and we can get lots more at Komorn or Gran. In twenty-four hours we shall be miles from here.'

'I hope so – to God,' he muttered, putting the things back into the sack, 'unless we're claimed first as victims for the sacrifice,' he added with a foolish laugh. He dragged the sack into the tent, for safety's sake, I suppose, and I heard him mumbling to himself, but so indistinctly that it seemed quite natural for me to ignore his words.

Our meal was beyond question a gloomy one, and we ate it almost in silence, avoiding one another's eyes, and keeping the fire bright. Then we washed up and prepared for the night, and, once smoking, our minds unoccupied with any definite duties, the apprehension I had felt all day long became more and more acute. It was not then active fear, I think, but the very vagueness of its origin distressed me far more thatn if I had been able to ticket and face it squarely. The curious sound I have likened to the note of a gong became now almost incessant, and filled the stillness of the night with a faint, continuous ringing rather than a series of distinct notes. At one time it was behind and at another time in front of us. Sometimes I fancied it came from the bushes on our left, and then again from the clumps on our right. More often it hovered directly overhead like the whirring of wings. It was really everywhere at once, behind, in front, at our sides and over our heads, completely surrounding us. The sound really defies description. But nothing within my knowledge is like that ceaseless muffled humming rising off the deserted world of swamps and willows.

We sat smoking in comparative silence, the strain growing every minute greater. The worst feature of the situation seemed to me that we did not know what to expect, and could therefore make no sort of preparation by way of defence. We could anticipate nothing. My explanations made in the sunshine, moreover, now came to haunt me with their foolish and wholly unsatisfactory nature, and it was more and more clear to us that some kind of plain talk with my companion was inevitable, whether I liked it or not. After all, we had to spend the night together, and to sleep in the same tent side by side. I saw that I could not get along much longer without the support of his mind, and for that, of course, plain talk was imperative. As long as possible, however, I postponed this little climax, and tried to ignore or laugh at the occasional sentences he flung into the emptiness.

Some of these sentences, moreover, were confoundedly disquieting to me, coming as they did to corroborate much that I felt myself; corroboration, too – which made it so much more convincing – from a totally different point of view. He composed such curious sentences, and hurled them at me in such an inconsequential sort of way, as though his main line of thought was secret to himself, and these fragments were mere bits he found it impossible to digest. He got rid of them by uttering them. Speech relieved him. It was like being sick.

'There are things about us, I'm sure, that make for disorder, disintegration, destruction, our destruction,' he said once, while the fire blazed between us. 'We've strayed out of a safe line somewhere.'

And, another time, when the gong sounds had come nearer, ringing much louder than before, and directly over our heads, he said as though talking to himself:

'I don't think a gramophone would show any record of that. The sound doesn't come to me by the ears at all. The vibrations reach me in another manner altogether, and seem to be within me, which is precisely how a fourth dimensional sound might be supposed to make itself heard.'

I purposely made no reply to this, but I sat up a little closer to the fire and peered about me into the darkness. The clouds were massed all over the sky, and no trace of moonlight came through. Very still, too, everything was, so that the river and the frogs had things all their own way.

'It has that about it,' he went on, 'which is utterly out of common experience. It is unknown. Only one thing describes it really; it is a non-human sound; I mean a sound outside humanity.'

Having rid himself of this indigestible morsel, he lay quiet for a time, but he had so admirably expressed my own feeling that it was a relief to have the thought out, and to have confined it by the limitation of words from dangerous wandering to and fro in the mind.

The solitude of that Danube camping-place, can I ever forget it? The feeling of being utterly alone on an empty planet! My thoughts ran incessantly upon cities and the haunts of men. I would have given my soul, as the saying is, for the 'feel' of those Bavarian villages we had passed through by the score; for the normal, human commonplaces; peasants drinking beer, tables beneath the trees, hot sunshine, and a ruined castle on the rocks behind the red-roofed church. Even the tourists would have been welcome.

Yet what I felt of dread was no ordinary ghostly fear. It was infinitely greater, stranger, and seemed to arise from some dim ancestral sense of terror more profoundly disturbing than anything I had known or dreamed of. We had 'strayed,' as the Swede put it, into some region or some set of conditions where the risks were great, yet unintelligible to us; where the frontiers of some unknown world lay close about us. It was a spot held by the dwellers in some outer space, a sort of peep-hole whence they could spy upon the earth, themselves unseen, a point where the veil between had worn a little thin. As the final result of too long a sojourn here, we should be carried over the border and deprived of what we called 'our lives,' yet by mental, not physical, processes. In that sense, as he said, we should be the victims of our adventure – a sacrifice.

It took us in different fashion, each according to the measure of his sensitiveness and powers of resistance. I translated it vaguely into a personification of the mightily disturbed elements, investing them with the horror of a deliberate and malefic purpose, resentful of our audacious intrusion into their breeding-place; whereas my friend threw it into the unoriginal form at first of a trespass on some ancient shrine, some place where the old gods still held sway, where the emotional forces of former worshippers still clung, and the ancestral portion of him yielded to the old pagan spell.

At any rate, here was a place unpolluted by men, kept clean by the winds from coarsening human influences, a place where spiritual agencies were within reach and aggressive. Never, before or since, have I been so attacked by indescribable suggestions of a 'beyond region,' of another scheme of life, another revolution not parallel to the human. And in the end our minds would succumb under the weight of the awful spell, and we should be drawn across the frontier into their world.

Small things testified to the amazing influence of the place, and now in the silence round the fire they allowed themselves to be noted by the mind. The very atmosphere had proved itself a magnifying medium to distort every indication: the otter rolling in the current, the hurrying boatman making signs, the shifting willows, one and all had been robbed of its natural character, and revealed in something of its other aspect – as it existed across the border to that other region. And this changed aspect I felt was now not merely to me, but to the race. The whole experience whose verge we touched was unknown to humanity at all. It was a new order of experience, and in the true sense of the word unearthly.

'It's the deliberate, calculating purpose that reduces one's courage to zero,' the Swede said suddenly, as if he had been actually following my thoughts. 'Otherwise imagination might count for much. But the paddle, the canoe, the lessening food –'

'Haven't I explained all that once?' I interrupted viciously.

'You have,' he answered dryly; 'you have indeed.'

He made other remarks too, as usual, about what he called the 'plain determination to provide a victim'; but, having now arranged my thoughts better, I recognised that this was simply the cry of his frightened soul against the knowledge that he was being attacked in a vital part, and that he would be somehow taken or destroyed. The situation called for a courage and calmness of reasoning that neither of us could compass, and I have never before been so clearly conscious of two persons in me – the one that explained everything, and the other that laughed at such foolish explanations, yet was horribly afraid.

Meanwhile, in the pitchy night the fire died down and the wood pile grew small. Neither of us moved to replenish the stock, and the darkness consequently came up very close to our faces. A few feet beyond the circle of firelight it was inky black. Occasionally a stray puff of wind set the willows shivering about us, but apart from this not very welcome sound a deep and depressing silence reigned, broken only by the gurgling of the river and the humming in the air overhead.

We both missed, I think, the shouting company of the winds.

At length, at a moment when a stray puff prolonged itself as though the wind were about to rise again, I reached the point for me of saturation, the point where it was absolutely necessary to find relief in plain speech, or else to betray myself by some hysterical extravagance that must have been far worse in its effect upon both of us. I kicked the fire into a blaze, and turned to my companion abruptly. He looked up with a start.

'I can't disguise it any longer,' I said; 'I don't like this place, and the darkness, and the noises, and the awful feelings I get. There's something here that beats me utterly. I'm in a blue funk, and that's the plain truth. If the other shore was – different, I swear I'd be inclined to swim for it!'

The Swede's face turned very white beneath the deep tan of sun and wind. He stared straight at me and answered quietly, but his voice betrayed his huge excitement by its unnatural calmness. For the moment, at any rate, he was the strong man of the two. He was more phlegmatic, for one thing.

'It's not a physical condition we can escape from by running away,' he replied, in the tone of a doctor diagnosing some grave disease; 'we must sit tight and wait. There are forces close here that could kill a herd of elephants in a second as easily as you or I could squash a fly. Our only chance is to keep perfectly still. Our insignificance perhaps may save us.'

I put a dozen questions into my expression of face, but found no words. It was precisely like listening to an accurate description of a disease whose symptoms had puzzled me.

'I mean that so far, although aware of our disturbing presence, they have not found us – not 'located' us, as the Americans say,' he went on. 'They're blundering about like men hunting for a leak of gas. The paddle and canoe and provisions prove that. I think they feel us, but cannot actually see us. We must keep our minds quiet – it's our minds they feel. We must control our thoughts, or it's all up with us.'

'Death, you mean?' I stammered, icy with the horror of his suggestion.

'Worse – by far,' he said. 'Death, according to one's belief, means either annihilation or release from the limitations of the senses, but it involves no change of character. You don't suddenly alter just because the body's gone. But this means a radical alteration, a complete change, a horrible loss of oneself by substitution – far worse than death, and not even annihilation. We happen to have camped in a spot where their region touches ours, where the veil between has worn thin' – horrors! he was using my very own phrase, my actual words – 'so that they are aware of our being in their neighbourhood.'

'But who are aware?' I asked.

I forgot the shaking of the willows in the windless calm, the humming overhead, everything except that I was waiting for an answer that I dreaded more than I can possibly explain.

He lowered his voice at once to reply, leaning forward a little over the fire, an indefinable change in his face that made me avoid his eyes and look down upon the ground.

'All my life,' he said, 'I have been strangely, vividly conscious of another region – not far removed from our own world in one sense, yet wholly different in kind – where great things go on unceasingly, where immense and terrible personalities hurry by, intent on vast purposes compared to which earthly affairs, the rise and fall of nations, the destinies of empires, the fate of armies and continents, are all as dust in the balance; vast purposes, I mean, that deal directly with the soul, and not indirectly with mere expressions of the soul –'

'I suggest just now –' I began, seeking to stop him, feeling as though I was face to face with a madman. But he instantly overbore me with his torrent that had to come.

'You think,' he said, 'it is the spirit of the elements, and I thought perhaps it was the old gods. But I tell you now it is – neither. These would be comprehensible entities, for they have relations with men, depending upon them for worship or sacrifice, whereas these beings who are now about us have absolutely nothing to do with mankind, and it is mere chance that their space happens just at this spot to touch our own.'

The mere conception, which his words somehow made so convincing, as I listened to them there in the dark stillness of that lonely island, set me shaking a little all over. I found it impossible to control my movements.

'And what do you propose?' I began again.

'A sacrifice, a victim, might save us by distracting them until we could get away,' he went on, 'just as the wolves stop to devour the dogs and give the sleigh another start. But – I see no chance of any other victim now.'

I stared blankly at him. The gleam in his eye was dreadful. Presently he continued.

IV

'It's the willows, of course. The willows mask the others, but the others are feeling about for us. If we let our minds betray our fear, we're lost, lost utterly.' He looked at me with an expression so calm, so determined, so sincere, that I no longer had any doubts as to his sanity. He was as sane as any man ever was. 'If we can hold out through the night,' he added, 'we may get off in the daylight unnoticed, or rather, undiscovered.'

'But you really think a sacrifice would –'

That gong-like humming came down very close over our heads as I spoke, but it was my friend's scared face that really stopped my mouth.

'Hush!' he whispered, holding up his hand. 'Do not mention them more than you can help. Do not refer to them by name. To name is to reveal; it is the inevitable clue, and our only hope lies in ignoring them, in order that they may ignore us.'

'Even in thought?' He was extraordinarily agitated.

'Especially in thought. Our thoughts make spirals in their world. We must keep them out of our minds at all costs if possible.'

I raked the fire together to prevent the darkness having everything its own way. I never longed for the sun as I longed for it then in the awful blackness of that summer night.

'Were you awake all last night?' he went on suddenly.

'I slept badly a little after dawn,' I replied evasively, trying to follow his instructions, which I knew instinctively were true, 'but the wind, of course –'

'I know. But the wind won't account for all the noises.'

'Then you heard it too?'

'The multiplying countless little footsteps I heard,' he said, adding, after a moment's hesitation, 'and that other sound –'

'You mean above the tent, and the pressing down upon us of something tremendous, gigantic?'

He nodded significantly.

'It was like the beginning of a sort of inner suffocation?' I said.

'Partly, yes. It seemed to me that the weight of the atmosphere had been altered – had increased enormously, so that we should have been crushed.'

'And that,' I went on, determined to have it all out, pointing upwards where the gong-like note hummed ceaselessly, rising and falling like wind. 'What do you make of that?'

'It's their sound,' he whispered gravely. 'It's the sound of their world, the humming in their region. The division here is so thin that it leaks through somehow. But, if you listen carefully, you'll find it's not above so much as around us. It's in the willows. It's the willows themselves humming, because here the willows have been made symbols of the forces that are against us.'

I could not follow exactly what he meant by this, yet the thought and idea in my mind were beyond question the thought and idea in his. I realised what he realised, only with less power of analysis than his. It was on the tip of my tongue to tell him at last about my hallucination of the ascending figures and the moving bushes, when he suddenly thrust his face again close into mine across the firelight and began to speak in a very earnest whisper. He amazed me by his calmness and pluck, his apparent control of the situation. This man I had for years deemed unimaginative, stolid!

'Now listen,' he said. 'The only thing for us to do is to go on as though nothing had happened, follow our usual habits, go to bed, and so forth; pretend we feel nothing and notice nothing.

It is a question wholly of the mind, and the less we think about them the better our chance of escape. Above all, don't think, for what you think happens!'

'All right,' I managed to reply, simply breathless with his words and the strangeness of it all; 'all right, I'll try, but tell me one more thing first. Tell me what you make of those hollows in the ground all about us, those sand-funnels?'

'No!' he cried, forgetting to whisper in his excitement. 'I dare not, simply dare not, put the thought into words. If you have not guessed I am glad. Don't try to. They have put it into my mind; try your hardest to prevent their putting it into yours.'

He sank his voice again to a whisper before he finished, and I did not press him to explain. There was already just about as much horror in me as I could hold. The conversation came to an end, and we smoked our pipes busily in silence.

Then something happened, something unimportant apparently, as the way is when the nerves are in a very great state of tension, and this small thing for a brief space gave me an entirely different point of view. I chanced to look down at my sand-shoe – the sort we used for the canoe – and something to do with the hole at the toe suddenly recalled to me the London shop where I had bought them, the difficulty the man had in fitting me, and other details of the uninteresting but practical operation. At once, in its train, followed a wholesome view of the modern sceptical world I was accustomed to move in at home. I thought of roast beef, and ale, motor-cars, policemen, brass bands, and a dozen other things that proclaimed the soul of ordinariness or utility. The effect was immediate and astonishing even to myself. Psychologically, I suppose, it was simply a sudden and violent reaction after the strain of living in an atmosphere of things that to the normal consciousness must seem impossible and incredible. But, whatever the cause, it momentarily lifted the spell from my heart, and left me for the short space of a minute feeling free and utterly unafraid. I looked up at my friend opposite.

'You damned old pagan!' I cried, laughing aloud in his face.

'You imaginative idiot! You superstitious idolater! You –'

I stopped in the middle, seized anew by the old horror. I tried to smother the sound of my voice as something sacrilegious. The Swede, of course, heard it too – the strange cry overhead in the darkness – and that sudden drop in the air as though something had come nearer.

He had turned ashen white under the tan. He stood bolt upright in front of the fire, stiff as a rod, staring at me.

'After that,' he said in a sort of helpless, frantic way, 'we must go! We can't stay now; we must strike camp this very instant and go on – down the river.'

He was talking, I saw, quite wildly, his words dictated by abject terror – the terror he had resisted so long, but which had caught him at last.

'In the dark?' I exclaimed, shaking with fear after my hysterical outburst, but still realising our position better than he did. 'Sheer madness! The river's in flood, and we've only got a single paddle. Besides, we only go deeper into their country! There's nothing ahead for fifty miles but willows, willows, willows!'

He sat down again in a state of semi-collapse. The positions, by one of those kaleidoscopic changes nature loves, were suddenly reversed, and the control of our forces passed over into my hands. His mind at last had reached the point where it was beginning to weaken.

'What on earth possessed you to do such a thing?' he whispered with the awe of genuine terror in his voice and face.

I crossed round to his side of the fire. I took both his hands in mine, kneeling down beside him and looking straight into his frightened eyes.

'We'll make one more blaze,' I said firmly, 'and then turn in for the night. At sunrise we'll be off full speed for Komorn. Now, pull yourself together a bit, and remember your own advice about not thinking fear!'

He said no more, and I saw that he would agree and obey. In some measure, too, it was a sort of relief to get up and make an excursion into the darkness for more wood. We kept close together, almost touching, groping among the bushes and along the bank. The humming overhead never ceased, but seemed to me to grow louder as we increased our distance from the fire. It was shivery work!

We were grubbing away in the middle of a thickish clump of willows where some driftwood from a former flood had caught high among the branches, when my body was seized in a grip that made me half drop upon the sand. It was the Swede. He had fallen against me, and was clutching me for support. I heard his breath coming and going in short gasps.

'Look! By my soul!' he whispered, and for the first time in my experience I knew what it was to hear tears of terror in a human voice. He was pointing to the fire, some fifty feet away. I followed the direction of his finger, and I swear my heart missed a beat.

There, in front of the dim glow, something was moving.

I saw it through a veil that hung before my eyes like the gauze drop-curtain used at the back of a theater – hazily a little. It was neither a human figure nor an animal. To me it gave the strange impression of being as large as several animals grouped together, like horses, two or three, moving slowly. The Swede, too, got a similar result, though expressing it differently, for he thought it was shaped and sized like a clump of willow bushes, rounded at the top, and moving all over upon its surface – 'coiling upon itself like smoke,' he said afterwards.

'I watched it settle downwards through the bushes,' he sobbed at me. 'Look, by God! It's coming this way! Oh, oh!' – he gave a kind of whistling cry. 'They've found us.'

I gave one terrified glance, which just enabled me to see that the shadowy form was swinging towards us through the bushes, and then I collapsed backwards with a crash into the branches.

These failed, of course, to support my weight, so that with the Swede on top of me we fell in a struggling heap upon the sand. I really hardly knew what was happening. I was conscious only of a sort of enveloping sensation of icy fear that plucked the nerves out of their fleshly covering, twisted them this way and that, and replaced them quivering. My eyes were tightly shut; something in my throat choked me; a feeling that my consciousness was expanding, extending out into space, swiftly gave way to another feeling that I was losing it altogether, and about to die.

An acute spasm of pain passed through me, and I was aware that the Swede had hold of me in such a way that he hurt me abominably. It was the way he caught at me in falling.

But it was the pain, he declared afterwards, that saved me; it caused me to forget them and think of something else at the very instant when they were about to find me. It concealed my mind from them at the moment of discovery, yet just in time to evade their terrible seizing of me. He himself, he says, actually swooned at the same moment, and that was what saved him.

I only know that at a later date, how long or short is impossible to say, I found myself scrambling up out of the slippery network of willow branches, and saw my companion standing in front of me holding out a hand to assist me. I stared at him in a dazed way, rubbing the arm he had twisted for me. Nothing came to me to say, somehow.

'I lost consciousness for a moment or two,' I heard him say. 'That's what saved me. It made me stop thinking about them.'

'You nearly broke my arm in two,' I said, uttering my only connected thought at the moment. A numbness came over me.

'That's what saved you!' he replied. 'Between us, we've managed to set them off on a false tack somewhere. The humming has ceased. It's gone – for the moment at any rate!'

A wave of hysterical laughter seized me again, and this time spread to my friend too – great healing gusts of shaking laughter that brought a tremendous sense of relief in their train. We made our way back to the fire and put the wood on so that it blazed at once. Then we saw that the tent had fallen over and lay in a tangled heap upon the ground.

We picked it up, and during the process tripped more than once and caught our feet in sand.

'It's those sand-funnels,' exclaimed the Swede, when the tent was up again and the firelight lit up the ground for several yards about us. 'And look at the size of them!'

All round the tent and about the fireplace where we had seen the moving shadows there were deep funnel-shaped hollows in the sand, exactly similar to the ones we had already found over the island, only far bigger and deeper, beautifully formed, and wide enough in some instances to admit the whole of my foot and leg.

Neither of us said a word. We both knew that sleep was the safest thing we could do, and to bed we went accordingly without further delay, having first thrown sand on the fire and taken the provision sack and the paddle inside the tent with us. The canoe, too, we propped in such a way at the end of the tent that our feet touched it, and the least motion would disturb and wake us.

In case of emergency, too, we again went to bed in our clothes, ready for a sudden start.

It was my firm intention to lie awake all night and watch, but the exhaustion of nerves and body decreed otherwise, and sleep after a while came over me with a welcome blanket of oblivion. The fact that my companion also slept quickened its approach. At first he fidgeted and constantly sat up, asking me if I 'heard this' or 'heard that.' He tossed about on his cork mattress, and said the tent was moving and the river had risen over the point of the island, but each time I went out to look I returned with the report that all was well, and finally he grew calmer and lay still. Then at length his breathing became regular and I heard unmistakable sounds of snoring – the first and only time in my life when snoring has been a welcome and calming influence.

This, I remember, was the last thought in my mind before dozing off.

A difficulty in breathing woke me, and I found the blanket over my face. But something else besides the blanket was pressing upon me, and my first thought was that my companion had rolled off his mattress on to my own in his sleep. I called to him and sat up, and at the same moment it came to me that the tent was surrounded. That sound of multitudinous soft pattering was again audible outside, filling the night with horror.

I called again to him, louder than before. He did not answer, but I missed the sound of his snoring, and also noticed that the flap of the tent was down. This was the unpardonable sin. I crawled out in the darkness to hook it back securely, and it was then for the first time I realised positively that the Swede was not here. He had gone.

I dashed out in a mad run, seized by a dreadful agitation, and the moment I was out I plunged into a sort of torrent of humming that surrounded me completely and came out of every quarter of the heavens at once. It was that same familiar humming – gone mad! A swarm of great invisible bees might have been about me in the air. The sound seemed to thicken the very atmosphere, and I felt that my lungs worked with difficulty.

But my friend was in danger, and I could not hesitate.

The dawn was just about to break, and a faint whitish light spread upwards over the clouds from a thin strip of clear horizon. No wind stirred. I could just make out the bushes and river beyond, and the pale sandy patches. In my excitement I ran frantically to and fro about the island, calling him by name, shouting at the top of my voice the first words that came into my head. But the willows smothered my voice, and the humming muffled it, so that the sound only travelled a few feet round me. I plunged among the bushes, tripping headlong, tumbling over roots, and scraping my face as I tore this way and that among the preventing branches.

Then, quite unexpectedly, I came out upon the island's point and saw a dark figure outlined between the water and the sky. It was the Swede. And already he had one foot in the river! A moment more and he would have taken the plunge.

I threw myself upon him, flinging my arms about his waist and dragging him shorewards with all my strength. Of course he struggled furiously, making a noise all the time just like that cursed humming, and using the most outlandish phrases in his anger about 'going inside to Them,' and 'taking the way of the water and the wind,' and God only knows what more besides, that I tried in vain to recall afterwards, but which turned me sick with horror and amazement as I listened. But in the end I managed to get him into the comparative safety of the tent, and flung him breathless and cursing upon the mattress where I held him until the fit had passed.

I think the suddenness with which it all went and he grew calm, coinciding as it did with the equally abrupt cessation of the humming and pattering outside – I think this was almost the strangest part of the whole business perhaps. For he had just opened his eyes and turned his tired face up to me so that the dawn threw a pale light upon it through the doorway, and said, for all the world just like a frightened child:

'My life, old man – it's my life I owe you. But it's all over now anyhow. They've found a victim in our place!'

Then he dropped back upon his blankets and went to sleep literally under my eyes. He simply collapsed, and began to snore again as healthily as though nothing had happened and he had never tried to offer his own life as a sacrifice by drowning. And when the sunlight woke him three hours later – hours of ceaseless vigil for me – it became so clear to me that he remembered absolutely nothing of what he had attempted to do, that I deemed it wise to hold my peace and ask no dangerous questions.

He woke naturally and easily, as I have said, when the sun was already high in a windless hot sky, and he at once got up and set about the preparation of the fire for breakfast. I followed him anxiously at bathing, but he did not attempt to plunge in, merely dipping his head and making some remark about the extra coldness of the water.

'River's falling at last,' he said, 'and I'm glad of it.'

'The humming has stopped too,' I said.

He looked up at me quietly with his normal expression. Evidently he remembered everything except his own attempt at suicide.

'Everything has stopped,' he said, 'because –'

He hesitated. But I knew some reference to that remark he had made just before he fainted was in his mind, and I was determined to know it.

'Because 'They've found another victim'?' I said, forcing a little laugh.

'Exactly,' he answered, 'exactly! I feel as positive of it as though – as though – I feel quite safe again, I mean,' he finished.

He began to look curiously about him. The sunlight lay in hot patches on the sand. There was no wind. The willows were motionless. He slowly rose to feet.

'Come,' he said; 'I think if we look, we shall find it.'

He started off on a run, and I followed him. He kept to the banks, poking with a stick among the sandy bays and caves and little backwaters, myself always close on his heels.

'Ah!' he exclaimed presently, 'Ah!'

The tone of his voice somehow brought back to me a vivid sense of the horror of the last twenty-four hours, and I hurried up to join him. He was pointing with his stick at a large black object that lay half in the water and half on the sand. It appeared to be caught by some twisted willow roots so that the river could not sweep it away. A few hours before the spot must have been under water.

'See,' he said quietly, 'the victim that made our escape possible!'

And when I peered across his shoulder I saw that his stick rested on the body of a man. He turned it over. It was the corpse of a peasant, and the face was hidden in the sand. Clearly the man had been drowned, but a few hours before, and his body must have been swept down upon our island somewhere about the hour of the dawn – at the very time the fit had passed.

'We must give it a decent burial, you know.'

'I suppose so,' I replied. I shuddered a little in spite of myself, for there was something about the appearance of that poor drowned man that turned me cold.

The Swede glanced up sharply at me, an undecipherable expression on his face, and began clambering down the bank. I followed him more leisurely. The current, I noticed, had torn away much of the clothing from the body, so that the neck and part of the chest lay bare.

Halfway down the bank my companion suddenly stopped and held up his hand in warning; but either my foot slipped, or I had gained too much momentum to bring myself quickly to a halt, for I bumped into him and sent him forward with a sort of leap to save himself. We tumbled together on to the hard sand so that our feet splashed into the water. And, before anything could be done, we had collided a little heavily against the corpse.

The Swede uttered a sharp cry. And I sprang back as if I had been shot.

At the moment we touched the body there rose from its surface the loud sound of humming – the sound of several hummings – which passed with a vast commotion as of winged things in the air about us and disappeared upwards into the sky, growing fainter and fainter till they finally ceased in the distance. It was exactly as though we had disturbed some living yet invisible creatures at work.

My companion clutched me, and I think I clutched him, but before either of us had time properly to recover from the unexpected shock, we saw that a movement of the current was turning the corpse round so that it became released from the grip of the willow roots. A moment later it had turned completely over, the dead face uppermost, staring at the sky. It lay on the edge of the main stream. In another moment it would be swept away.

The Swede started to save it, shouting again something I did not catch about a 'proper burial' – and then abruptly dropped upon his knees on the sand and covered his eyes with his hands. I was beside him in an instant.

I saw what he had seen.

For just as the body swung round to the current the face and the exposed chest turned full towards us, and showed plainly how the skin and flesh were indented with small hollows, beautifully formed, and exactly similar in shape and kind to the sand-funnels that we had found all over the island.

'Their mark!' I heard my companion mutter under his breath. 'Their awful mark!'

And when I turned my eyes again from his ghastly face to the river, the current had done its work, and the body had been swept away into mid-stream and was already beyond our reach and almost out of sight, turning over and over on the waves like an otter.

The Man Who Lived Backwards

I f it is true that most people have one secret they never share, it is also true that many have an experience they never tell, not so much from fear of ridicule or being disbelieved as from utter inability to describe it intelligibly. Language has grown gradually: it describes the experience of the race; anything beyond human experience exposes the poverty of language at once. No words exist.

Professor Zeitt had something of the sort, it seems. He was an ardent physicist, astrophysics his speciality; he knew all about waves, he was one of the few who really understood Relativity; he was a wireless expert, too. If Jeans, Whitehead and Eddington were in his pocket, the mystery of space-time was in his mind. He chatted as easily about other dimensions in time as most people do about shares and commodities. Conceptions of time beyond our one-dimensional kind were always in his thoughts.

He was also an experimenter; he made, it appears, audacious experiments, some of them psychological. That he ever suffered from overwork, from cerebral excitement of a rather dangerous sort, is open to question. To myself, who enjoyed the privilege, or suffered the affliction, of hearing his experience, there seemed no sign of delusion, hallucination, or mental disturbance. I remain convinced that he told me something that had actually happened – to an able, clear-headed, if unusual man.

It happened to him on a winter's night as he sat alone in his flat – a Sunday evening, the servants out, and his wife away in Paris. His married life was unhappy, childless, ill-assorted. He had made a mistake. There was another girl he should have chosen.

Now, at forty, he realised this, though without undue bitterness, for he blamed himself. Her money had made his career possible. This particular day had been passed in strenuous exercise. His body, he admits, was over-tired, perhaps, but his mind, at any rate, was resting delightfully – he was reading a story of crime over the fire – delicious relaxation, he called it. The room was dim, only the reading-lamp turned on. Facing him in the wall was a long pier glass.

The book, *It Doesn't Pay*, was the life of a burglar told by himself – Black, if memory serves me, the author – and he was near the end. In his mind, as he read the last chapter, stretched a picture of the man's whole life, not actually realised, perhaps, but lying there in perspective. Like a map, it existed serially and all at once, though he now focused attention on its close. As a cinema screen, it could have turned back, of course, and repeated any particular section. The whole of the burglar's life lay between the book covers; it was present, any portion of it accessible by turning back the pages. Its end was vivid at the moment merely because he, Zeitt, focused attention upon that part, that moment. And so, as was usual with him, he realised that his own life, similarly, existed serially, complete, the whole map there, while he was conscious of himself at the moment called forty, merely because he focused attention on that moment. Only, in his own case, Time made turning back impossible. If time had another dimension, he could have turned back to earlier sections.

He admits his general awareness of this idea in the background of his mind. For it was habitual. Such ideas lay always in his thought. But at the moment, thought and interest were centred on Black's adventures, these other ideas not consciously to the fore – when something in the semi-darkened room suddenly drew his attention. The room, he felt positive, had altered; and this alteration was in his immediate surroundings. Very close to him this abrupt change had come about. And he looked up from his page, startled a little, 'as though an unexpected sound had disturbed me,' were his words, 'something, anyhow, that *drew* my attention actively.'

The winter's night was still, the Sunday traffic negligible, the flat empty, yet he was positive that someone stood in the room in close proximity to him. As he raised his eyes, he looked automatically at the reflection of himself in the pier glass opposite. He saw himself deep in the easy chair, the open book on his knee, the shaded lamp behind his head, and at the same instant saw also the reflection of a tall, straight figure that passed swiftly behind his chair from right to left. Simultaneously with this, and before thought had time to spread, he felt something that, he declares, he had never felt before, something entirely new. Accustomed mentally to contemplate ultimate zero and the colds of outer space, he was instantly conscious now that all about him, in brain and nerves as well, was a sudden cold of another kind altogether, a kind hitherto unexperienced. This cold brought horror with it. He felt as if hanging in interstellar space, adrift from all known moorings, on the brink of something that horrified because it was utterly unknown. By 'unknown' he meant he had never experienced it himself. There was no 'up' or 'down', because there was nothing to which 'up' or 'down' could be referred; similarly, 'backwards' or 'forwards' held no meaning. Nor could he know whether he was in motion or stationary. He was merely 'relative'. With a tremendous effort, however, he managed to cling tenaciously with his ordinary mind to ordinary, familiar standards. In the first second all this came to him.

At the same time, he knew that the figure, now passing behind his chair, would appear in a fractional moment beside or in front of him, and even as he realised this, it happened. The figure moved beside him, then in front, then stopped and looked at him. Expecting his muscles somehow to be paralysed by the shock of unusual fear, and that he would be unable to move, he now found that this was not the case. As he saw the tall, straight figure come to a dead stop in front of him, not two feet away, he rose quickly to his feet and faced it. The book fell to the carpet with a thud. It was a young man he looked at straight in the eyes. He was able, even at this moment, to note his sensations. The habit of years worked truly. The intense, strange, different cold, he thus asserts, persisted. It numbed something in him that must have otherwise reasoned, reflected, criticised. These faculties, at any rate, did not function. All that happened seemed not natural, supernatural. The sensation of unbelievable fear that had turned him dizzy was gone. Having terrorised him, it disappeared. His breath became oddly, immensely accelerated. An idea of death slipped his thought. But all these, passing, left an exhilaration beyond all words.

It was under this intensification of consciousness that he then at once began to speak. The figure spoke, too. They spoke together. He emphasised this simultaneous utterance, though the spoken words were not always quite identical:

'Of course, I know you. I know who you are,' he said. 'You are myself.'

The figure, a young man in a light, summery suit smiled eagerly.

'I was twenty-five then,' said Zeitt. 'I *am* twenty-five,' said the other. And, as they uttered together, came all the emotions of troubled love, of doubt, of being drawn in two different directions by worldly considerations and by personal inclination, with all the fever of a young man's indecision.

'If only I could see ahead,' Zeitt heard himself saying, while simultaneously sounded: *'If only I could go back.'*

They looked into each other's eyes while uttering the next words, identical words this time :

'I exist at that point where my attention is fixed at a given moment. But there's really no need to. I can choose my moment, alter my attention – forwards or backwards. Can't I?'

The young figure smiled, a curiously passionate expression in the eyes. In Zeitt rose the tumultuous passion for a girl, as against the affection and respect for another girl whose worldly possessions would enable him to follow his dream.

'I can go backwards or forwards,' both spoke together, 'by changing my type of consciousness. It's open. It's here, it's now, both accessible, as between the covers of a book – if only I could escape from being fixed on a point so stupidly. If only I knew how.'

'*I do*,' grinned the other, while Zeitt laughed audibly, a laugh of audacious triumph, using the same words exactly. 'I do.'

'I can change my consciousness, make it different,' cried Zeitt. 'I see the way. My life is serial, all at once, whole. I am not fixed at any point. I am in time of two dimensions.'

'*I always am*,' said the other, bending his head down to read a letter, whose wet ink still glistened.

'I will destroy it. I won't send it,' exclaimed Zeitt, despising himself for proposing to a girl he did not really love.

The young figure tore the letter he held into tiny pieces and turned to throw them into the fire. But there was no fire, only a gas stove burning, and the room was a shabby lodging-house room. Zeitt gazed about him. The picture of the girl he really loved possessed his mind. 'I'll go to her – go back to her. I'll go tomorrow.' His speech fumbled slightly.

'*I'll go to her now*,' said the figure decisively, his young face alight, as he moved across the faded carpet to a waste-paper basket beside the draughty window.

'I'll change it – change the past,' and Zeitt realised he was shouting now aloud, amazing joy and wonder in him, as he watched the shower of small, torn bits of paper flutter down.

The figure came suddenly very close, so close that there seemed hardly room to stand without touching, as though space could not possibly contain both of them on that one spot, then closer still, all over one another.

'*That would be too dislocating – for others – and until all can do it,*' sounded the voice very faintly. Professor Zeitt declares it sounded inside himself. '*I'll make the effort, anyhow. A result of sorts may come.*' The voice died out. The figure was no longer there.

Zeitt, the physicist, found himself alone. He stooped down and picked up the fallen book. The heat of the blazing coal fire scorched his face, but did not affect the curious internal cold that lay, like a touch from interstellar space, over his entire being. He turned on all the lights, and before sitting down to finish Black's book, he wrote down the dialogue and description as given above. It was bald, but as accurate as he could make it.

Long afterwards, as I listened to his account, watching his face, I saw a light in his eyes I have never seen before in any human eyes.

'The major part of the experience,' he added, 'the *important* part,' he emphasised, 'is beyond any power or words at my command.'

The distinguished man, now famous and happily remarried, smiled as he said this. He shivered a little. They'd say I dreamed it,' he remarked, shrugging his shoulders. Yet within a few short weeks of the experience, his wife had run off with another man, and Professor Zeitt, finding the girl he loved a widow, had married her.

Ancient Sorceries

I

There are, it would appear, certain wholly unremarkable persons, with none of the characteristics that invite adventure, who yet once or twice in the course of their smooth lives undergo an experience so strange that the world catches its breath – and looks the other way! And it was cases of this kind, perhaps, more than any other, that fell into the widespread net of John Silence, the psychic doctor, and, appealing to his deep humanity, to his patience, and to his great qualities of spiritual sympathy, led often to the revelation of problems of the strangest complexity, and of the profoundest possible human interest.

Matters that seemed almost too curious and fantastic for belief he loved to trace to their hidden sources. To unravel a tangle in the very soul of things – and to release a suffering human soul in the process – was with him a veritable passion. And the knots he untied were, indeed, often passing strange.

The world, of course, asks for some plausible basis to which it can attach credence – something it can, at least, pretend to explain. The adventurous type it can understand: such people carry about with them an adequate explanation of their exciting lives, and their characters obviously drive them into the circumstances which produce the adventures. It expects nothing else from them, and is satisfied. But dull, ordinary folk have no right to out-of-the-way experiences, and the world having been led to expect otherwise, is disappointed with them, not to say shocked. Its complacent judgement has been rudely disturbed.

'Such a thing happen to *that* man!' it cries '– a commonplace person like that! It is too absurd! There must be something wrong!'

Yet there could be no question that something did actually happen to little Arthur Vezin, something of the curious nature he described to Dr Silence. Outwardly, or inwardly, it happened beyond a doubt, and in spite of the jeers of his few friends who heard the tale, and observed wisely that 'such a thing might perhaps have come to Iszard, that crack-brained Iszard, or to that odd fish Minski, but it could never have happened to commonplace little Vezin, who was fore-ordained to live and die according to scale.'

But, whatever his method of death was, Vezin certainly did not 'live according to scale' so far as this particular event in his otherwise uneventful life was concerned; and to hear him recount it, and watch his pale delicate features change, and hear his voice grow softer and more hushed as he proceeded, was to know the conviction that his halting words perhaps failed sometimes to convey. He lived the thing over again each time he told it. His whole personality became muffled in the recital. It subdued him more than ever, so that the tale became a lengthy apology for an experience that he deprecated. He appeared to excuse himself and ask your pardon for having dared to take part in so fantastic an episode. For little Vezin was a timid, gentle, sensitive soul, rarely able to assert himself, tender to man and beast, and almost constitutionally unable to say No, or to claim many things that should rightly have been his. His whole scheme of life seemed utterly remote from anything more exciting than missing a train or losing an umbrella on an omnibus. And when this curious event came upon him he was already more years beyond forty than his friends suspected or he cared to admit.

John Silence, who heard him speak of his experience more than once, said that he sometimes left out certain details and put in others; yet they were all obviously true. The whole scene was unforgettably cinematographed on to his mind. None of the details were imagined or invented. And when he told the story with them all complete, the effect was undeniable. His appealing brown eyes shone, and much of the charming personality, usually so carefully repressed, came forward and revealed itself. His modesty was always there, of course, but in the telling he forgot the present and allowed himself to appear almost vividly as he lived again in the past of his adventure.

He was on the way home when it happened, crossing northern France from some mountain trip or other where he buried himself solitary-wise every summer. He had nothing but an unregistered bag in the rack, and the train was jammed to suffocation, most of the passengers being unredeemed holiday English. He disliked them, not because they were his fellow-countrymen, but because they were noisy and obtrusive, obliterating with their big limbs and tweed clothing all the quieter tints of the day that brought him satisfaction and enabled him to melt into insignificance and forget that he was anybody. These English clashed about him like a brass band, making him feel vaguely that he ought to be more self-assertive and obstreperous, and that he did not claim insistently enough all kinds of things that he didn't want and that were really valueless, such as corner seats, windows up or down, and so forth.

So that he felt uncomfortable in the train, and wished the journey were over and he was back again living with his unmarried sister in Surbiton.

And when the train stopped for ten panting minutes at the little station in northern France, and he got out to stretch his legs on the platform, and saw to his dismay a further batch of the British Isles debouching from another train, it suddenly seemed impossible to him to continue the journey. Even *his* flabby soul revolted, and the idea of staying a night in the little town and going on next day by a slower, emptier train, flashed into his mind. The guard was already shouting *'envoiture'* and the corridor of his compartment was already packed when the thought came to him. And, for once, he acted with decision and rushed to snatch his bag.

Finding the corridor and steps impassable, he tapped at the window (for he had a corner seat) and begged the Frenchman who sat opposite to hand his luggage out to him, explaining in his wretched French that he intended to break the journey there. And this elderly Frenchman, he declared, gave him a look, half of warning, half of reproach, that to his dying day he could never forget; handed the bag through the window of the moving train; and at the same time poured into his ears a long sentence, spoken rapidly and low, of which he was able to comprehend only the last few words: *à cause du sommeil et à cause des chats.'*

In reply to Dr Silence, whose singular psychic acuteness at once seized upon this Frenchman as a vital point in the adventure, Vezin admitted that the man had impressed him favourably from the beginning, though without being able to explain why. They had sat facing one another during the four hours of the journey, and though no conversation had passed between them – Vezin was timid about his stuttering French – he confessed that his eyes were being continually drawn to his face, almost, he felt, to rudeness, and that each, by a dozen nameless little politenesses and attentions, had evinced the desire to be kind. The men liked each other and their personalities did not clash, or would not have clashed had they chanced to come to terms of acquaintance. The Frenchman, indeed, seemed to have exercised a silent protective influence over the insignificant little Englishman, and without words or gestures betrayed that he wished him well and would gladly have been of service to him.

'And this sentence that he hurled at you after the bag?' asked John Silence, smiling that peculiarly sympathetic smile that always melted the prejudices of his patient, 'were you unable to follow it exactly?'

'It was so quick and low and vehement,' explained Vezin, in his small voice, 'that I missed practically the whole of it. I only caught the few words at the very end, because he spoke them so clearly, and his face was bent down out of the carriage window so near to mine.'

'*À cause du sommeil et à cause des chats,*' repeated Dr Silence, as though half speaking to himself.

'That's it exactly,' said Vezin; 'which, I take it, means something like 'because of sleep and because of the cats', doesn't it?'

'Certainly, that's how I should translate it,' the doctor observed shortly, evidently not wishing to interrupt more than necessary.

'And the rest of the sentence – all the first part I couldn't understand, I mean – was a warning not to do something – not to stop in the town, or at some particular place in the town, perhaps. That was the impression it made on me.'

Then, of course, the train rushed off, and left Vezin standing on the platform alone and rather forlorn.

The little town climbed in straggling fashion up a sharp hill rising out of the plain at the back of the station, and was crowned by the twin towers of the ruined cathedral peeping over the summit. From the station itself it looked uninteresting and modern, but the fact was that the medieval position lay out of sight just beyond the crest. And once he reached the top and entered the old streets, he stepped clean out of modern life into a bygone century. The noise and bustle of the crowded train seemed days away. The spirit of this silent hill-town, remote from tourists and motor-cars, dreaming its own quiet life under the autumn sun, rose up and cast its spell upon him. Long before he recognised this spell he acted under it. He walked softly, almost on tiptoe down the winding narrow streets where the gables all but met over his head, and he entered the doorway of the solitary inn with a deprecating and modest demeanour that was in itself an apology for intruding upon the place and disturbing its dream.

At first, however, Vezin said, he noticed very little of all this. The attempt at analysis came much later. What struck him then was only the delightful contrast of the silence and peace after the dust and noisy rattle of the train. He felt soothed and stroked like a cat.

'Like a cat, you said?' interrupted John Silence, quickly catching him up.

'Yes. At the very start I felt that.' He laughed apologetically. 'I felt as though the warmth and the stillness and the comfort made me purr. It seemed to be the general mood of the whole place – then.'

The inn, a rambling ancient house, the atmosphere of the old coaching days still about it, apparently did not welcome him too warmly. He felt he was only tolerated, he said. But it was cheap and comfortable, and the delicious cup of afternoon tea he ordered at once made him feel really very pleased with himself for leaving the train in this bold, original way. For to him it had seemed bold and original. He felt something of a dog. His room, too, soothed him with its dark panelling and low irregular ceiling, and the long sloping passage that led to it seemed the natural pathway to a real Chamber of Sleep – a little dim cubby hole out of the world where noise could not enter. It looked upon the courtyard at the back. It was all very charming, and made him think of himself as dressed in very soft velvet somehow, and the floors seemed padded, the walls provided with cushions. The sounds of the streets could not penetrate there. It was an atmosphere of absolute rest that surrounded him.

On engaging the two-franc room he had interviewed the only person who seemed to be about that sleepy afternoon, an elderly waiter with Dundreary whiskers and a drowsy courtesy, who had ambled lazily towards him across the stone yard; but on coming downstairs again for a little promenade in the town before dinner he encountered the proprietress herself. She was a large woman whose hands, feet, and features seemed to swim towards him out of a sea of person. They emerged, so to speak. But she had great dark, vivacious eyes that counteracted the bulk of her body, and betrayed the fact that in reality she was both vigorous and alert. When he first caught sight of her she was knitting in a low chair against the sunlight of the wall, and something at once made him see her as a great tabby cat, dozing, yet awake, heavily sleepy, and yet at the same time prepared for instantaneous action. A great mouser on the watch occurred to him.

She took him in with a single comprehensive glance that was polite without being cordial. Her neck, he noticed, was extraordinarily supple in spite of its proportions, for it turned so easily to follow him, and the head it carried bowed so very flexibly.

'But when she looked at me, you know,' said Vezin, with that little apologetic smile in his brown eyes, and that faintly deprecating gesture of the shoulders that was characteristic of him, 'the odd notion came to me that really she had intended to make quite a different movement, and that with a single bound she could have leaped at me across the width of that stone yard and pounced upon me like some huge cat upon a mouse.'

He laughed a little soft laugh, and Dr Silence made a note in his book without interrupting, while Vezin proceeded in a tone as though he feared he had already told too much and more than we could believe.

'Very soft, yet very active she was, for all her size and mass, and I felt she knew what I was doing even after I had passed and was behind her back. She spoke to me, and her voice was smooth and running. She asked if I had my luggage, and was comfortable in my room, and then added that dinner was at seven o'clock, and that they were very early people in this little country town. Clearly, she intended to convey that late hours were not encouraged.'

Evidently, she contrived by voice and manner to give him the impression that here he would be 'managed', that everything would be arranged and planned for him, and that he had nothing to do but fall into the groove and obey. No decided action or sharp personal effort would be looked for from him. It was the very reverse of the train. He walked quietly out into the street feeling soothed and peaceful. He realised that he was in a *milieu* that suited him and stroked him the right way. It was so much easier to be obedient. He began to purr again, and to feel that all the town purred with him.

About the streets of that little town he meandered gently, falling deeper and deeper into the spirit of repose that characterised it. With no special aim he wandered up and down, and to and fro. The September sunshine fell slantingly over the roofs. Down winding alleyways, fringed with tumbling gables and open casements, he caught fairylike glimpses of the great plain below, and of the meadows and yellow copses lying like a dream-map in the haze. The spell of the past held very potently here, he felt.

The streets were full of picturesquely garbed men and women, all busy enough, going their respective ways; but no one took any notice of him or turned to stare at his obviously English appearance. He was even able to forget that with his tourist appearance he was a false note in a charming picture, and he melted more and more into the scene, feeling delightfully insignificant and unimportant and unselfconscious. It was like becoming part of a softly-coloured dream which he did not even realise to be a dream.

On the eastern side the hill fell away more sharply, and the plain below ran off rather suddenly into a sea of gathering shadows in which the little patches of woodland looked like islands and the stubble fields like deep water. Here he strolled along the old ramparts of ancient fortifications that once had been formidable, but now were only vision-like with their charming mingling of broken grey walls and wayward vine and ivy. From the broad coping on which he sat for a moment, level with the rounded tops of clipped plane trees, he saw the esplanade far below lying in shadow. Here and there a yellow sunbeam crept in and lay upon the fallen yellow leaves, and from the height he looked down and saw that the townsfolk were walking to and fro in the cool of the evening. He could just hear the sound of their slow footfalls, and the murmur of their voices floated up to him through the gaps between the trees. The figures looked like shadows as he caught glimpses of their quiet movements far below.

He sat there for some time pondering, bathed in the waves of murmurs and half-lost echoes that rose to his ears, muffled by the leaves of the plane trees. The whole town, and the little hill out of which it grew as naturally as an ancient wood, seemed to him like a being lying there half asleep on the plain and crooning to itself as it dozed.

And, presently, as he sat lazily melting into its dream, a sound of horns and strings and wood instruments rose to his ears, and the town band began to play at the far end of the crowded terrace below to the accompaniment of a very soft, deep-throated drum. Vezin was very sensitive to music, knew about it intelligently, and had even ventured, unknown to his friends, upon the composition of quiet melodies with low-running chords which he played to himself with the soft pedal when no one was about. And this music floating up through the trees from an invisible and doubtless very picturesque band of the townspeople wholly charmed him. He recognised nothing that they played, and it sounded as though they were simply improvising without a conductor. No definitely marked time ran through the pieces, which ended and began oddly after the fashion of wind through an Aeolian harp. It was part of the place and scene, just as the dying sun light and faintly-breathing wind were part of the scene and hour, and the mellow notes of old-fashioned plaintive horns, pierced here and there by the sharper strings, all half smothered by the continuous booming of the deep drum, touched his soul with a curiously potent spell that was almost too engrossing to be quite pleasant.

There was a certain queer sense of bewitchment in it all. The music seemed to him oddly unartificial. It made him think of trees swept by the wind, of night breezes singing among wires and chimney-stacks, or in the rigging of invisible ships; or – and the simile leaped up in his thoughts with a sudden sharpness of suggestion – a chorus of animals, of wild creatures, somewhere in desolate places of the world, crying and singing as animals will, to the moon. He could fancy he heard the wailing, half-human cries of cats upon the tiles at night, rising and falling with weird intervals of sound, and this music, muffled by distance and the trees, made him think of a queer company of these creatures on some roof far away in the sky, uttering their solemn music to one another and the moon in chorus.

It was, he felt at the time, a singular image to occur to him, yet it expressed his sensation pictorially better than anything else. The instruments played such impossibly odd intervals, and the crescendos and diminuendos were so very suggestive of cat-land on the tiles at night, rising swiftly, dropping without warning to deep notes again, and all in such strange confusion of discords and accords. But, at the same time a plaintive sweetness resulted on the whole, and the discords of these half-broken instruments were so singular that they did not distress his musical soul like fiddles out of tune.

He listened a long time, wholly surrendering himself as his character was, and then strolled homewards in the dusk as the air grew chilly.

'There was nothing to alarm?' put in Dr Silence briefly.

'Absolutely nothing,' said Vezin; 'but you know it was all so fantastical and charming that my imagination was profoundly impressed. Perhaps, too,' he continued, gently explanatory, 'it was this stirring of my imagination that caused other impressions; for, as I walked back, the spell of the place began to steal over me in a dozen ways, though all intelligible ways. But there were other things I could not account for in the least, even then.'

'Incidents, you mean?'

'Hardly incidents, I think. A lot of vivid sensations crowded themselves upon my mind and I could trace them to no causes. It was just after sunset and the tumbled old buildings traced magical outlines against an opalescent sky of gold and red. The dusk was running down the twisted streets. All round the hill the plain pressed in like a dim sea, its level rising with the darkness. The spell of this kind of scene, you know, can be very moving, and it was so that night. Yet I felt that what came to me had nothing directly to do with the mystery and wonder of the scene.'

'Not merely the subtle transformations of the spirit that come with beauty,' put in the doctor, noticing his hesitation.

'Exactly,' Vezin went on, duly encouraged and no longer so fearful of our smiles at his expense. 'The impressions came from somewhere else. For instance, down the busy main street where men and women were bustling home from work, shopping at stalls and barrows, idly gossiping in groups, and all the rest of it, I saw that I aroused no interest and that no one turned to stare at me as a foreigner and stranger. I was utterly ignored, and my presence among them excited no special interest or attention.

'And then, quite suddenly, it dawned upon me with conviction that all the time this indifference and inattention were merely feigned. Everybody as a matter of fact was watching me closely. Every movement I made was known and observed. Ignoring me was all a pretence – an elaborate pretence.'

He paused a moment and looked at us to see if we were smiling, and then continued, reassured –

'It is useless to ask me how I noticed this, because I simply cannot explain it. But the discovery gave me something of a shock. Before I got back to the inn, however, another curious thing rose up strongly in my mind and forced my recognition of it as true. And this, too, I may as well say at once, was equally inexplicable to me. I mean I can only give you the fact, as fact it was to me.'

The little man left his chair and stood on the mat before the fire. His diffidence lessened from now onwards, and he lost himself again in the magic of the old adventure. His eyes shone a little already as he talked.

'Well,' he went on, his soft voice rising somewhat with his excitement, 'I was in a shop when it came to me first – though the idea must have been at work for a long time subconsciously to appear in so complete a form all at once. I was buying socks, I think,' he laughed, 'and struggling with my dreadful French, when it struck me that the woman in the shop did not care two pins whether I bought anything or not. She was indifferent whether she made a sale or did not make a sale. She was only pretending to sell.

'This sounds a very small and fanciful incident to build upon what follows. But really it was not small. I mean it was the spark that lit the line of powder and ran along to the big blaze in my mind.

'For the whole town, I suddenly realised, was something other than I so far saw it. The real activities and interests of the people were elsewhere and otherwise than appeared. Their true lives lay somewhere out of sight behind the scenes. Their busyness was but the outward semblance that masked their actual purposes. They bought and sold, and ate and drank, and walked about the streets, yet all the while the main stream of their existence lay somewhere beyond my ken, underground, in secret places. In the shops and at the stalls they did not care whether I purchased their articles or not; at the inn, they were indifferent to my staying or going; their life lay remote from my own, springing from hidden, mysterious sources, coursing out of sight, unknown. It was all a great elaborate pretence, assumed possibly for my benefit, or possibly for purposes of their own. But the main current of their energies ran elsewhere. I almost felt as an unwelcome foreign substance might be expected to feel when it has found its way into the human system and the whole body organises itself to eject it or to absorb it. The town was doing this very thing to me.

'This bizarre notion presented itself forcibly to my mind as I walked home to the inn, and I began busily to wonder wherein the true life of this town could lie and what were the actual interests and activities of its hidden life.

'And, now that my eyes were partly opened, I noticed other things too that puzzled me, first of which, I think, was the extraordinary silence of the whole place. Positively, the town was muffled. Although the streets were paved with cobbles the people moved about silently, softly, with padded feet, like cats. Nothing made noise. All was hushed, subdued, muted. The very voices were quiet, low-pitched like purring. Nothing clamourous, vehement or emphatic seemed able to live in the drowsy atmosphere of soft dreaming that soothed this little hill-town into its sleep. It was like the woman at the inn – an outward repose screening intense inner activity and purpose.

'Yet there was no sign of lethargy or sluggishness anywhere about it. The people were active and alert. Only a magical and uncanny softness lay over them all like a spell.'

Vezin passed his hand across his eyes for a moment as though the memory had become very vivid. His voice had run off into a whisper so that we heard the last part with difficulty. He was telling a true thing obviously, yet something that he both liked and hated telling.

'I went back to the inn,' he continued presently in a louder voice, 'and dined. I felt a new strange world about me. My old world of reality receded. Here, whether I liked it or not, was something new and incomprehensible. I regretted having left the train so impulsively. An adventure was upon me, and I loathed adventures as foreign to my nature. Moreover, this was the beginning apparently of an adventure somewhere deep within me, in a region I could not check or measure, and a feeling of alarm mingled itself with my wonder – alarm for the stability of what I had for forty years recognised as my 'personality'.

'I went upstairs to bed, my mind teeming with thoughts that were unusual to me, and of rather a haunting description. By way of relief I kept thinking of that nice, prosaic noisy train and all those wholesome, blustering passengers. I almost wished I were with them again. But my dreams took me elsewhere. I dreamed of cats, and soft-moving creatures, and the silence of life in a dim muffled world beyond the senses.'

II

Vezin stayed on from day to day, indefinitely, much longer than he had intended. He felt in a kind of dazed, somnolent condition. He did nothing in particular, but the place fascinated him and he could not decide to leave. Decisions were always very difficult for him and he sometimes wondered how he had ever brought himself to the point of leaving the train. It seemed as though someone else must have arranged it for him, and once or twice his thoughts ran to the swarthy Frenchman who had sat opposite. If only he could have understood that long sentence ending so strangely with '*à cause du sommeil et à cause des chats.*' He wondered what it all meant.

Meanwhile the hushed softness of the town held him prisoner and he sought in his muddling, gentle way to find out where the mystery lay, and what it was all about. But his limited French and his constitutional hatred of active investigation made it hard for him to buttonhole anybody and ask questions. He was content to observe, and watch, and remain negative.

The weather held on calm and hazy, and this just suited him. He wandered about the town till he knew every street and alley. The people suffered him to come and go without let or hindrance, though it became clearer to him every day that he was never free himself from observation. The town watched him as a cat watches a mouse. And he got no nearer to finding out what they were all so busy with or where the main stream of their activities lay. This remained hidden. The people were as soft and mysterious as cats.

But that he was continually under observation became more evident from day to day.

For instance, when he strolled to the end of the town and entered a little green public garden beneath the ramparts and seated himself upon one of the empty benches in the sun, he was quite alone – at first. Not another seat was occupied; the little park was empty, the paths deserted. Yet, within ten minutes of his coming, there must have been fully twenty persons scattered about him, some strolling aimlessly along the gravel walks, staring at the flowers, and others seated on the wooden benches enjoying the sun like himself. None of them appeared to take any notice of him; yet he understood quite well they had all come there to watch. They kept him under close observation. In the street they had seemed busy enough, hurrying upon various errands; yet these were suddenly all forgotten and they had nothing to do but loll and laze in the sun, their duties unremembered. Five minutes after he left, the garden was again deserted, the seats vacant. But in the crowded street it was the same thing again; he was never alone. He was ever in their thoughts.

By degrees, too, he began to see how it was he was so cleverly watched, yet without the appearance of it. The people did nothing *directly*. They behaved *obliquely*. He laughed in his mind as the thought thus clothed itself in words, but the phrase exactly described it. They looked at him from angles which naturally should have led their sight in another direction altogether. Their movements were oblique, too, so far as these concerned himself. The straight, direct thing was not their way evidently. They did nothing obviously. If he entered a shop to buy, the woman walked instantly away and busied herself with something at the farther end of the counter, though answering at once when he spoke, showing that she knew he was there and that this was only her way of attending to him. It was the fashion of the cat she followed. Even in the dining-room of the inn, the be-whiskered and courteous waiter, lithe and silent in all his movements, never seemed able to come straight to his table for an order or a dish. He came by zigzags, indirectly, vaguely, so that he appeared to be going to another table altogether, and only turned suddenly at the last moment, and was there beside him.

Vezin smiled curiously to himself as he described how he began to realise these things. Other tourists there were none in the hostel, but he recalled the figures of one or two old men, inhabitants, who took their *déjeuner* and dinner there, and remembered how fantastically they entered the room in similar fashion. First, they paused in the doorway, peering about the room, and then, after a temporary inspection, they came in, as it were, sideways, keeping close to the walls so that he wondered which table they were making for, and at the last minute making almost a little quick run to their particular seats. And again he thought of the ways and methods of cats.

Other small incidents, too, impressed him as all part of this queer, soft town with its muffled, indirect life, for the way some of the people appeared and disappeared with extraordinary swiftness puzzled him exceedingly. It may have been all perfectly natural, he knew, yet he could not make it out how the alleys swallowed them up and shot them forth in a second of time when there were no visible doorways or openings near enough to explain the phenomenon. Once he followed two elderly women who, he felt, had been particularly examining him from across the street – quite near the inn this was – and saw them turn the corner a few feet only in front of him. Yet when he sharply followed on their heels he saw nothing but an utterly deserted alley stretching in front of him with no sign of a living thing. And the only opening through which they could have escaped was a porch some fifty yards away, which not the swiftest human runner could have reached in time.

And in just such sudden fashion people appeared when he never expected them. Once when he heard a great noise of fighting going on behind a low wall, and hurried up to see what was going on, what should he see but a group of girls and women engaged in vociferous conversation which instantly hushed itself to the normal whispering note of the town when his head appeared over the wall. And even then none of them turned to look at him directly, but slunk off with the most unaccountable rapidity into doors and sheds across the yard. And their voices, he thought, had sounded so like, so strangely like, the angry snarling of fighting animals, almost of cats.

The whole spirit of the town, however, continued to evade him as something elusive, protean, screened from the outer world, and at the same time intensely, genuinely vital; and, since he now formed part of its life, this concealment puzzled and irritated him; more – it began rather to frighten him.

Out of the mists that slowly gathered about his ordinary surface thoughts, there rose again the idea that the inhabitants were waiting for him to declare himself, to take an attitude, to do this, or to do that; and that when he had done so they in their turn would at length make some direct response, accepting or rejecting him. Yet the vital matter concerning when his decision was awaited came no nearer to him.

Once or twice he purposely followed little processions or groups of the citizens in order to find out, if possible, on what purpose they were bent; but they always discovered him in time and dwindled away, each individual going his or her own way. It was always the same: he never could learn what their main interest was. The cathedral was ever empty, the old church of St Martin, at the other end of the town, deserted. They shopped because they had to, and not because they wished to. The booths stood neglected, the stalls unvisited, the little cafés desolate. Yet the streets were always full, the townsfolk ever on the bustle.

'Can it be,' he thought to himself, yet with a deprecating laugh that he should have dared to think anything so odd, 'can it be that these people are people of the twilight, that they live only at night their real life, and come out honestly only with the dusk? That during the day they make a sham though brave pretence, and after the sun is down their true life begins? Have they the souls of night-things, and is the whole blessed town in the hands of the cats?'

The fancy somehow electrified him with little shocks of shrinking and dismay. Yet, though he affected to laugh, he knew that he was beginning to feel more than uneasy, and that strange forces were tugging with a thousand invisible cords at the very centre of his being. Something utterly remote from his ordinary life, something that had not waked for years, began faintly to stir in his soul, sending feelers abroad into his brain and heart, shaping queer thoughts and penetrating even into certain of his minor actions. Something exceedingly vital to himself, to his soul, hung in the balance.

And, always when he returned to the inn about the hour of sunset, he saw the figures of the townsfolk stealing through the dusk from their shop doors, moving sentry-wise to and fro at the corners of the streets, yet always vanishing silently like shadows at his near approach. And as the inn invariably closed its doors at ten o'clock he had never yet found the opportunity he rather half-heartedly sought to see for himself what account the town could give of itself at night.

'– *à cause du sommeil et à cause des chats*' – the words now rang in his ears more and more often, though still as yet without any definite meaning.

Moreover, something made him sleep like the dead.

III

I t was, I think, on the fifth day – though in this detail his
story sometimes varied – that he made a definite discovery
which increased his alarm and brought him up to a rather sharp
climax. Before that he had already noticed that a change was
going forward and certain subtle transformations being brought
about in his character which modified several of his minor
habits. And he had affected to ignore them. Here, however, was
something he could no longer ignore; and it startled him.

At the best of times he was never very positive, always negative
rather, compliant and acquiescent; yet, when necessity arose
he was capable of reasonably vigorous action and could take a
strongish decision. The discovery he now made that brought
him up with such a sharp turn was that this power had positively
dwindled to nothing. He found it impossible to make up his
mind. For, on this fifth day, he realised that he had stayed long
enough in the town and that for reasons he could only vaguely
define to himself it was wiser *and safer* that he should leave.

And he found that he could not leave!

This is difficult to describe in words, and it was more by
gesture and the expression of his face that he conveyed to Dr
Silence the state of impotence he had reached. All this spying
and watching, he said, had as it were spun a net about his feet
so that he was trapped and powerless to escape; he felt like a fly
that had blundered into the intricacies of a great web; he was
caught, imprisoned, and could not get away. It was a distressing
sensation. A numbness had crept over his will till it had become
almost incapable of decision. The mere thought of vigorous

action – action towards escape – began to terrify him. All the currents of his life had turned inwards upon himself, striving to bring to the surface something that lay buried almost beyond reach, determined to force his recognition of something he had long forgotten – forgotten years upon years, centuries almost ago. It seemed as though a window deep within his being would presently open and reveal an entirely new world, yet somehow a world that was not unfamiliar. Beyond that, again, he fancied a great curtain hung; and when that too rolled up he would see still farther into this region and at last understand something of the secret life of these extraordinary people.

'Is this why they wait and watch?' he asked himself with rather a shaking heart, 'for the time when I shall join them – or refuse to join them? Does the decision rest with me after all, and not with them?'

And it was at this point that the sinister character of the adventure first really declared itself, and he became genuinely alarmed. The stability of his rather fluid personality was at stake, he felt, and something in his heart turned coward.

Why otherwise should he have suddenly taken to walking stealthily, silently, making as little sound as possible, forever looking behind him? Why else should he have moved almost on tiptoe about the passages of the practically deserted inn, and when he was abroad have found himself deliberately taking advantage of what cover presented itself? And why, if he was not afraid, should the wisdom of staying indoors after sun down have suddenly occurred to him as eminently desirable? Why, indeed?

And, when John Silence gently pressed him for an explanation of these things, he admitted apologetically that he had none to give.

'It was simply that I feared something might happen to me unless I kept a sharp look-out. I felt afraid. It was instinctive,' was all he could say. 'I got the impression that the whole town was after me – wanted me for something; and that if it got me I should lose myself, or at least the Self I knew, in some unfamiliar state of consciousness. But I am not a psychologist, you know,' he added meekly, 'and I cannot define it better than that.'

It was while lounging in the courtyard half an hour before the evening meal that Vezin made this discovery, and he at once went upstairs to his quiet room at the end of the winding passage to think it over alone. In the yard it was empty enough, true, but there was always the possibility that the big woman whom he dreaded would come out of some door, with her pretence of knitting, to sit and watch him. This had happened several times, and he could not endure the sight of her. He still remembered his original fancy, bizarre though it was, that she would spring upon him the moment his back was turned and land with one single crushing leap upon his neck. Of course it was nonsense, but then it haunted him, and once an idea begins to do that it ceases to be nonsense. It has clothed itself in reality.

He went upstairs accordingly. It was dusk, and the oil lamps had not yet been lit in the passages. He stumbled over the uneven surface of the ancient flooring, passing the dim outlines of doors along the corridor – doors that he had never once seen opened – rooms that seemed never occupied. He moved, as his habit now was, stealthily and on tiptoe.

Half-way down the last passage to his own chamber there was a sharp turn, and it was just here, while groping round the walls with outstretched hands, that his fingers touched something that was not wall – something that moved. It was soft and warm in texture, indescribably fragrant, and about the height of his shoulder; and he immediately thought of a furry, sweet-smelling kitten. The next minute he knew it was something quite different.

Instead of investigating, however, – his nerves must have been too overwrought for that, he said, – he shrank back as closely as possible against the wall on the other side. The thing, whatever it was, slipped past him with a sound of rustling, and retreating with light footsteps down the passage behind him, was gone. A breath of warm, scented air was wafted to his nostrils.

Vezin caught his breath for an instant and paused, stock-still, half leaning against the wall – and then almost ran down the remaining distance and entered his room with a rush, locking the door hurriedly behind him. Yet it was not fear that made him run: it was excitement, pleasurable excitement. His nerves were tingling, and a delicious glow made itself felt all over his body. In a flash it came to him that this was just what he had felt twenty-five years ago as a boy when he was in love for the first time. Warm currents of life ran all over him and mounted to his brain in a whirl of soft delight. His mood was suddenly become tender, melting, loving.

The room was quite dark, and he collapsed upon the sofa by the window, wondering what had happened to him and what it all meant. But the only thing he understood clearly in that instant was that something in him had swiftly, magically changed: he no longer wished to leave, or to argue with himself about leaving. The encounter in the passageway had changed all that. The strange perfume of it still hung about him, bemusing his heart and mind. For he knew that it was a girl who had passed him, a girl's face that his fingers had brushed in the darkness, and he felt in some extraordinary way as though he had been actually kissed by her, kissed full upon the lips.

Trembling, he sat upon the sofa by the window and struggled to collect his thoughts. He was utterly unable to understand how the mere passing of a girl in the darkness of a narrow passageway could communicate so electric a thrill to his whole being that he still shook with the sweetness of it. Yet, there it was! And he found it as useless to deny as to attempt analysis.

Some ancient fire had entered his veins, and now ran coursing through his blood; and that he was forty-five instead of twenty did not matter one little jot. Out of all the inner turmoil and confusion emerged the one salient fact that the mere atmosphere, the merest casual touch, of this girl, unseen, unknown in the darkness, had been sufficient to stir dormant fires in the centre of his heart, and rouse his whole being from a state of feeble sluggishness to one of tearing and tumultuous excitement.

After a time, however, the number of Vezin's years began to assert their cumulative power; he grew calmer; and when a knock came at length upon his door and he heard the waiter's voice suggesting that dinner was nearly over, he pulled himself together and slowly made his way downstairs into the dining-room.

Everyone looked up as he entered, for he was very late, but he took his customary seat in the far corner and began to eat. The trepidation was still in his nerves, but the fact that he had passed through the courtyard and hall without catching sight of a petticoat served to calm him a little. He ate so fast that he had almost caught up with the current stage of the table d' hôte, when a slight commotion in the room drew his attention.

His chair was so placed that the door and the greater portion of the long *sale à manger* were behind him, yet it was not necessary to turn round to know that the same person he had passed in the dark passage had now come into the room. He felt the presence long before he heard or saw any one. Then he became aware that the old men, the only other guests, were rising one by one in their places, and exchanging greetings with someone who passed among them from table to table. And when at length he turned with his heart beating furiously to ascertain for himself, he saw the form of a young girl, lithe and slim, moving down the centre of the room and making straight for his own table in the corner. She moved wonderfully, with sinuous grace, like a young panther, and her approach filled him with such delicious bewilderment that he was utterly unable to tell at first what her face was like, or discover what it was about the whole presentment of the creature that filled him anew with trepidation and delight.

'Ah, Ma'mselle est de retour!' he heard the old waiter murmur at his side, and he was just able to take in that she was the daughter of the proprietress, when she was upon him, and he heard her voice. She was addressing him. Something of red lips he saw and laughing white teeth, and stray wisps of fine dark hair about the temples; but all the rest was a dream in which his own emotions rose like a thick cloud before his eyes and prevented his seeing accurately, or knowing exactly what he did. He was aware that she greeted him with a charming little bow; that her beautiful large eyes looked searchingly into his own; that the perfume he had noticed in the dark passage again assailed his nostrils, and that she was bending a little towards him and leaning with one hand on the table at his side. She was quite close to him – that was the chief thing he knew – explaining that she had been asking after the comfort of her mother's guests, and was now introducing herself to the latest arrival – himself.

'M'sieur has already been here a few days,' he heard the waiter say; and then her own voice, sweet as singing, replied –

'Ah, but M'sieur is not going to leave us just yet, I hope. My mother is too old to look after the comfort of our guests properly, but now I am here I will remedy all that.' She laughed deliciously. 'M'sieur shall be well looked after.'

Vezin, struggling with his emotion and desire to be polite, half rose to acknowledge the pretty speech, and to stammer some sort of reply, but as he did so his hand by chance touched her own that was resting upon the table, and a shock that was for all the world like a shock of electricity, passed from her skin into his body. His soul wavered and shook deep within him.

He caught her eyes fixed upon his own with a look of most curious intentness, and the next moment he knew that he had sat down wordless again on his chair, that the girl was already half-way across the room, and that he was trying to eat his salad with a dessert-spoon and a knife.

Longing for her return, and yet dreading it, he gulped down the remainder of his dinner, and then went at once to his bedroom to be alone with his thoughts. This time the passages were lighted, and he suffered no exciting contretemps; yet the winding corridor was dim with shadows, and the last portion, from the bend of the walls onwards, seemed longer than he had ever known it. It ran downhill like the pathway on a mountain-side, and as he tiptoed softly down it he felt that by rights it ought to have led him clean out of the house into the heart of a great forest. The world was singing with him. Strange fancies filled his brain, and once in the room, with the door securely locked, he did not light the candles, but sat by the open window thinking long, long thoughts that came unbidden in troops to his mind.

IV

This part of the story he told to Dr Silence, without special coaxing, it is true, yet with much stammering embarrassment. He could not in the least understand, he said, how the girl had managed to affect him so profoundly, and even before he had set eyes upon her. For her mere proximity in the darkness had been sufficient to set him on fire. He knew nothing of enchantments, and for years had been a stranger to anything approaching tender relations with any member of the opposite sex, for he was encased in shyness, and realised his overwhelming defects only too well. Yet this bewitching young creature came to him deliberately. Her manner was unmistakable, and she sought him out on every possible occasion. Chaste and sweet she was undoubtedly, yet frankly inviting; and she won him utterly with the first glance of her shining eyes, even if she had not already done so in the dark merely by the magic of her invisible presence.

'You felt she was altogether wholesome and good?' queried the doctor. 'You had no reaction of any sort – for instance, of alarm?'

Vezin looked up sharply with one of his inimitable little apologetic smiles. It was some time before he replied. The mere memory of the adventure had suffused his shy face with blushes, and his brown eyes sought the floor again before he answered.

I don't think I can quite say that,' he explained presently.

I acknowledged certain qualms, sitting up in my room afterwards. A conviction grew upon me that there was something about her – how shall I express it? – well, something unholy. It is not impurity in any sense, physical or mental, that I mean, but something quite indefinable that gave me a vague sensation of the creeps. She drew me, and at the same time repelled me, more than – than –'

He hesitated, blushing furiously, and unable to finish the sentence.

'Nothing like it has ever come to me before or since,' he concluded, with lame confusion. I suppose it was, as you suggested just now, something of an enchantment. At any rate, it was strong enough to make me feel that I would stay in that awful little haunted town for years if only I could see her every day, hear her voice, watch her wonderful movements, and sometimes, perhaps, touch her hand.'

'Can you explain to me what you felt was the source of her power?' John Silence asked, looking purposely anywhere but at the narrator.

'I am surprised that *you* should ask me such a question,' answered Vezin, with the nearest approach to dignity he could manage. I think no man can describe to another convincingly wherein lies the magic of the woman who ensnares him. I certainly cannot. I can only say this slip of a girl bewitched me, and the mere knowledge that she was living and sleeping in the same house filled me with an extraordinary sense of delight.

'But there's one thing I can tell you,' he went on earnestly, his eyes aglow, 'namely, that she seemed to sum up and synthesise in herself all the strange hidden forces that operated so mysteriously in the town and its inhabitants. She had the silken movements of the panther, going smoothly, silently to and fro, and the same indirect, oblique methods as the townsfolk, screening, like them, secret purposes of her own – purposes that I was sure had *me* for their objective. She kept me, to my terror and delight, ceaselessly under observation, yet so carelessly, so consummately, that another man less sensitive, if I may say so' – he made a deprecating gesture – 'or less prepared by what had gone before, would never have noticed it at all. She was always still, always reposeful, yet she seemed to be everywhere at once, so that I never could escape from her. I was continually meeting the stare and laughter of her great eyes, in the corners of the rooms, in the passages, calmly looking at me through the windows, or in the busiest parts of the public streets.'

Their intimacy, it seems, grew very rapidly after this first encounter which had so violently disturbed the little man's equilibrium. He was naturally very prim, and prim folk live mostly in so small a world that anything violently unusual may shake them clean out of it, and they therefore instinctively distrust originality. But Vezin began to forget his primness after a while. The girl was always modestly behaved, and as her mother's representative she naturally had to do with the guests in the hotel. It was not out of the way that a spirit of camaraderie should spring up. Besides, she was young, she was charmingly pretty, she was French, and – she obviously liked him.

At the same time, there was something indescribable – a certain indefinable atmosphere of other places, other times – that made him try hard to remain on his guard, and sometimes made him catch his breath with a sudden start. It was all rather like à delirious dream, half delight, half dread, he confided in a whisper to Dr Silence; and more than once he hardly knew quite what he was doing or saying, as though he were driven forward by impulses he scarcely recognised as his own.

And though the thought of leaving presented itself again and again to his mind, it was each time with less insistence, so that he stayed on from day to day, becoming more and more a part of the sleepy life of this dreamy medieval town, losing more and more of his recognisable personality. Soon, he felt, the Curtain within would roll up with an awful rush, and he would find himself suddenly admitted into the secret purposes of the hidden life that lay behind it all. Only, by that time, he would have become transformed into an entirely different being.

And, meanwhile, he noticed various little signs of the intention to make his stay attractive to him: flowers in his bedroom, a more comfortable armchair in the corner, and even special little extra dishes on his private table in the dining-room. Conversations, too, with 'Mademoiselle Ilsé' became more and more frequent and pleasant, and although they seldom travelled beyond the weather, or the details of the town, the girl, he noticed, was never in a hurry to bring them to an end, and often contrived to interject little odd sentences that he never properly understood, yet felt to be significant.

And it was these stray remarks, full of a meaning that evaded him, that pointed to some hidden purpose of her own and made him feel uneasy. They all had to do, he felt sure, with reasons for his staying on in the town indefinitely.

'And has M'sieur not even yet come to a decision?' she said softly in his ear, sitting beside him in the sunny yard before *déjeuner*, the acquaintance having progressed with significant rapidity. 'Because, if it's so difficult, we must all try together to help him!'

The question startled him, following upon his own thoughts. It was spoken with a pretty laugh, and a stray bit of hair across one eye, as she turned and peered at him half roguishly. Possibly he did not quite understand the French of it, for her near presence always confused his small knowledge of the language distressingly. Yet the words, and her manner, and something else that lay behind it all in her mind, frightened him. It gave such point to his feeling that the town was waiting for him to make his mind up on some important matter.

At the same time, her voice, and the fact that she was there so close beside him in her soft dark dress, thrilled him inexpressibly.

'It is true I find it difficult to leave,' he stammered, losing his way deliciously in the depths of her eyes, 'and especially now that Mademoiselle Ilsé has come.'

He was surprised at the success of his sentence, and quite delighted with the little gallantry of it. But at the same time he could have bitten his tongue off for having said it.

'Then after all you like our little town, or you would not be pleased to stay on,' she said, ignoring the compliment.

'I am enchanted with it, and enchanted with you,' he cried, feeling that his tongue was somehow slipping beyond the control of his brain. And he was on the verge of saying all manner of other things of the wildest description, when the girl sprang lightly up from her chair beside him, and made to go.

'It is *soupe à l'oignon* today!' she cried, laughing back at him through the sunlight, 'and I must go and see about it. Otherwise, you know, M'sieur will not enjoy his dinner, and then, perhaps, he will leave us!'

He watched her cross the courtyard, moving with all the grace and lightness of the feline race, and her simple black dress clothed her, he thought, exactly like the fur of the same supple species. She turned once to laugh at him from the porch with the glass door, and then stopped a moment to speak to her mother, who sat knitting as usual in her corner seat just inside the hallway.

But how was it, then, that the moment his eye fell upon this ungainly woman, the pair of them appeared suddenly as other than they were? Whence came that transforming dignity and sense of power that enveloped them both as by magic? What was it about that massive woman that made her appear instantly regal, and set her on a throne in some dark and dreadful scenery, wielding asceptre over the red glare of some tempestuous orgy? And why did this slender stripling of a girl graceful as a willow, lithe as a young leopard, assume suddenly an air of sinister majesty, and move with flame and smoke about her head, and the darkness of night beneath her feet?

Vezin caught his breath and sat there transfixed. Then, almost simultaneously with its appearance, the queer notion vanished again, and the sunlight of day caught them both, and he heard her laughing to her mother about the *soupe à l'oignon,* and saw her glancing back at him over her dear little shoulder with a smile that made him think of a dew-kissed rose bending lightly before summer airs.

And, indeed, the onion soup was particularly excellent that day, because he saw another cover laid at his small table and, with fluttering heart, heard the waiter murmur by way of explanation that 'Ma'mselle Ilsé would honour M'sieur today at *déjeuner,* as her custom sometimes is with her mother's guests.'

So actually she sat by him all through that delirious meal, talking quietly to him in easy French, seeing that he was well looked after, mixing the salad dressing, and even helping him with her own hand. And, later in the afternoon, while he was smoking in the courtyard, longing for a sight of her as soon as her duties were done, she came again to his side, and when he rose to meet her, she stood facing him a moment, full of a perplexing sweet shyness before she spoke –

'My mother thinks you ought to know more of the beauties of our little town, and *I* think so too! Would M'sieur like me to be his guide, perhaps? I can show him everything, for our family has lived here for many generations.'

She had him by the hand, indeed, before he could find a single word to express his pleasure, and led him, all unresisting, out into the street, yet in such a way that it seemed perfectly natural she should do so, and without the faintest suggestion of boldness or immodesty. Her face glowed with the pleasure and interest of it, and with her short dress and tumbled hair she looked every bit the charming child of seventeen that she was, innocent and playful, proud of her native town, and alive beyond her years to the sense of its ancient beauty.

So they went over the town together, and she showed him what she considered its chief interest: the tumble-down old house where her forebears had lived; the sombre, aristocratic looking mansion where her mother's family dwelt for centuries, and the ancient market-place where several hundred years before the witches had been burnt by the score. She kept up a lively running stream of talk about it all, of which he understood not a fiftieth part as he trudged along by her side, cursing his forty-five years and feeling all the yearnings of his early manhood revive and jeer at him. And, as she talked, England and Surbiton seemed very far away indeed, almost in another age of the world's history. Her voice touched something immeasurably old in him, something that slept deep. It lulled the surface parts of his consciousness to sleep, allowing what was far more ancient to awaken. Like the town, with its elaborate pretence of modern active life, the upper layers of his being became dulled, soothed, muffled, and what lay underneath began to stir in its sleep. That big Curtain swayed a little to and fro. Presently it might lift altogether. . . .

He began to understand a little better at last. The mood of the town was reproducing itself in him. In proportion as his ordinary external self became muffled, that inner secret life, that was far more real and vital, asserted itself. And this girl was surely the high-priestess of it all, the chief instrument of its accomplishment. New thoughts, with new interpretations, flooded his mind as she walked beside him through the winding streets, while the picturesque old gabled town, softly coloured in the sunset, had never appeared to him so wholly wonderful and seductive.

And only one curious incident came to disturb and puzzle him, slight in itself, but utterly inexplicable, bringing white terror into the child's face and a scream to her laughing lips. He had merely pointed to a column of blue smoke that rose from the burning autumn leaves and made a picture against the red roofs, and had then run to the wall and called her to his side to watch the flames shooting here and there through the heap of rubbish. Yet, at the sight of it, as though taken by surprise, her face had altered dreadfully, and she had turned and run like the wind, calling out wild sentences to him as she ran, of which he had not understood a single word, except that the fire apparently frightened her, and she wanted to get quickly away from it, and to get him away too.

Yet five minutes later she was as calm and happy again as though nothing had happened to alarm or waken troubled thoughts in her, and they had both forgotten the incident.

They were leaning over the ruined ramparts together listening to the weird music of the band as he had heard it the first day of his arrival. It moved him again profoundly as it had done before, and somehow he managed to find his tongue and his best French. The girl leaned across the stones close beside him. No one was about. Driven by some remorseless engine within he began to stammer something – he hardly knew what – of his strange admiration for her. Almost at the first word she sprang lightly off the wall and came up smiling in front of him, just touching his knees as he sat there. She was hatless as usual, and the sun caught her hair and one side of her cheek and throat.

'Oh, I'm *so* glad!' she cried, clapping her little hands softly in his face, 'so very glad, because that means that if you like me you must also like what I do, and what I belong to.'

Already he regretted bitterly having lost control of himself. Something in the phrasing of her sentence chilled him. He knew the fear of embarking upon an unknown and dangerous sea.

'You will take part in our real life, I mean,' she added softly, with an indescribable coaxing of manner, as though she noticed his shrinking. 'You will come back to us.'

Already this slip of a child seemed to dominate him; he felt the power coming over him more and more; something emanated from her that stole over his senses and made him aware that her personality, for all its simple grace, held forces that were stately, imposing, august. He saw her again moving through smoke and flame amid broken and tempestuous scenery, alarmingly strong, her terrible mother by her side. Dimly this shone through her smile and appearance of charming innocence.

'You will, I know,' she repeated, holding him with her eyes.

They were quite alone up there on the ramparts, and the sensation that she was overmastering him stirred a wild sensuousness in his blood. The mingled abandon and reserve in her attracted him furiously, and all of him that was man rose up and resisted the creeping influence, at the same time acclaiming it with the full delight of his forgotten youth. An irresistible desire came to him to question her, to summon what still remained to him of his own little personality in an effort to retain the right to his normal self.

The girl had grown quiet again, and was now leaning on the broad wall close beside him, gazing out across the darkening plain, her elbows on the coping, motionless as a figure carved in stone. He took his courage in both hands.

'Tell me, Ilsé,' he said, unconsciously imitating her own purring softness of voice, yet aware that he was utterly in earnest, 'what is the meaning of this town, and what is this real life you speak of? And why is it that the people watch me from morning to night? Tell me what it all means? And, tell me,' he added more quickly with passion in his voice, 'what you really are – yourself?'

She turned her head and looked at him through half-closed eyelids, her growing inner excitement betraying itself by the faint colour that ran like a shadow across her face.

'It seems to me,' – he faltered oddly under her gaze – 'that I have some right to know –'

Suddenly she opened her eyes to the full. 'You love me, then?' she asked softly.

'I swear,' he cried impetuously, moved as by the force of a rising tide, 'I never felt before – I have never known any other girl who –'

'Then you *have* the right to know,' she calmly interrupted his confused confession; 'for love shares all secrets.'

She paused, and a thrill like fire ran swiftly through him. Her words lifted him off the earth, and he felt a radiant happiness, followed almost the same instant in horrible contrast by the thought of death. He became aware that she had turned her eyes upon his own and was speaking again.

'The real life I speak of,' she whispered, 'is the old, old life within, the life of long ago, the life to which you, too, once belonged, and to which you still belong.'

A faint wave of memory troubled the deeps of his soul as her low voice sank into him. What she was saying he knew instinctively to be true, even though he could not as yet understand its full purport. His present life seemed slipping from him as he listened, merging his personality in one that was far older and greater. It was this loss of his present self that brought to him the thought of death.

'You came here,' she went on, 'with the purpose of seeking it, and the people felt your presence and are waiting to know what you decide, whether you will leave them without having found it, or whether –'

Her eyes remained fixed upon his own, but her face began to change, growing larger and darker with an expression of age.

'It is their thoughts constantly playing about your soul that makes you feel they watch you. They do not watch you with their eyes. The purposes of their inner life are calling to you, seeking to claim you. You were all part of the same life long, long ago, and now they want you back again among them.'

Vezin's timid heart sank with dread as he listened; but the girl's eyes held him with a net of joy so that he had no wish to escape. She fascinated him, as it were, clean out of his normal self.

'Alone, however, the people could never have caught and held you,' she resumed. 'The motive force was not strong enough; it has faded through all these years. But I' – she paused a moment and looked at him with complete confidence in her splendid eyes – 'I possess the spell to conquer you and hold you: the spell

ANCIENT SORCERIES

of old love. I can win you back again and make you live the
old life with me, for the force of the ancient tie between us, if I
choose to use it, is irresistible. And I *do* choose to use it. I still
want you. And you, dear soul of my dim past' – she pressed
closer to him so that her breath passed across his eyes, and her
voice positively sang – 'I mean to have you, for you love me and
are utterly at my mercy.'

Vezin heard, and yet did not hear; understood, yet did not
understand. He had passed into a condition of exaltation. The
world was beneath his feet, made of music and flowers, and he
was flying somewhere far above it through the sunshine of pure
delight. He was breathless and giddy with the wonder of her
words. They intoxicated him. And, still, the terror of it all, the
dreadful thought of death, pressed ever behind her sentences.
For flames shot through her voice out of black smoke and licked
at his soul.

And they communicated with one another, it seemed to him,
by a process of swift telepathy, for his French could never have
compassed all he said to her. Yet she understood perfectly, and
what she said to him was like the recital of verses long since
known. And the mingled pain and sweetness of it as he listened
were almost more than his little soul could hold.

'Yet I came here wholly by chance –' he heard himself saying.

'No,' she cried with passion, 'you came here because I called
you. I have called to you for years, and you came with the whole
force of the past behind you. You had to come, for I own you,
and I claim you.'

She rose again and moved closer, looking at him with a certain
insolence in the face – the insolence of power.

The sun had set behind the towers of the old cathedral and
the darkness rose up from the plain and enveloped them. The
music of the band had ceased. The leaves of the plane trees hung
motionless, but the chill of the autumn evening rose about them
and made Vezin shiver. There was no sound but the sound of

their voices and the occasional soft rustle of the girl's dress. He could hear the blood rushing in his ears. He scarcely realised where he was or what he was doing. Some terrible magic of the imagination drew him deeply down into the tombs of his own being, telling him in no unfaltering voice that her words shadowed forth the truth. And this simple little French maid, speaking beside him with so strange authority, he saw curiously alter into quite another being. As he stared into her eyes, the picture in his mind grew and lived, dressing itself vividly to his inner vision with a degree of reality he was compelled to acknowledge. As once before, he saw her tall and stately, moving through wild and broken scenery of forests and mountain caverns, the glare of flames behind her head and clouds of shifting smoke about her feet. Dark leaves encircled her hair, flying loosely in the wind, and her limbs shone through the merest rags of clothing. Others were about her too, and ardent eyes on all sides cast delirious glances upon her, but her own eyes were always for one only, one whom she held by the hand. For she was leading the dance in some tempestuous orgy to the music of chanting voices, and the dance she led circled about a great and awful Figure on a throne, brooding over the scene through lurid vapours, while innumerable other wild faces and forms crowded furiously about her in the dance. But the one she held by the hand he knew to be himself, and the monstrous shape upon the throne he knew to be her mother.

The vision rose within him, rushing to him down the long years of buried time, crying aloud to him with the voice of memory reawakened. . . . And then the scene faded away and he saw the clear circle of the girl's eyes gazing steadfastly into his own, and she became once more the pretty little daughter of the innkeeper, and he found his voice again.

'And you,' he whispered tremblingly – 'you child of visions and enchantment, how is it that you so bewitch me that I loved you even before I saw?'

She drew herself up beside him with an air of rare dignity.

'The call of the Past,' she said; 'and besides,' she added proudly, 'in the real life I am a princess –'

'A princess!' he cried.

' – and my mother is a queen!'

At this, little Vezin utterly lost his head. Delight tore at his heart and swept him into sheer ecstasy. To hear that sweet singing voice, and to see those adorable little lips utter such things, upset his balance beyond all hope of control. He took her in his arms and covered her unresisting face with kisses.

But even while he did so, and while the hot passion swept him, he felt that she was soft and loathsome, and that her answering kisses stained his very soul. . . . And when, presently, she had freed herself and vanished into the darkness, he stood there, leaning against the wall in a state of collapse, creeping with horror from the touch of her yielding body, and inwardly raging at the weakness that he already dimly realised must prove his undoing.

And from the shadows of the old buildings into which she disappeared there rose in the stillness of the night a singular, long-drawn cry, which at first he took for laughter, but which later he was sure he recognised as the almost human wailing of a cat.

V

For a long time Vezin leant there against the wall, alone with his surging thoughts and emotions. He understood at length that he had done the one thing necessary to call down upon him the whole force of this ancient Past. For in those passionate kisses he had acknowledged the tie of olden days, and had revived it. And the memory of that soft impalpable caress in the darkness of the inn corridor came back to him with a shudder. The girl had first mastered him, and then led him to the one act that was necessary for her purpose. He had been waylaid, after the lapse of centuries – caught, and conquered.

Dimly he realised this, and sought to make plans for his escape. But, for the moment at any rate, he was powerless to manage his thoughts or will, for the sweet, fantastic madness of the whole adventure mounted to his brain like a spell, and he gloried in the feeling that he was utterly enchanted and moving in a world so much larger and wilder than the one he had ever been accustomed to.

The moon, pale and enormous, was just rising over the sea-like plain, when at last he rose to go. Her slanting rays drew all the houses into new perspective, so that their roofs, already glistening with dew, seemed to stretch much higher into the sky than usual, and their gables and quaint old towers lay far away in its purple reaches.

The cathedral appeared unreal in a silver mist. He moved softly, keeping to the shadows; but the streets were all deserted and very silent; the doors were closed, the shutters fastened. Not a soul was astir. The hush of night lay over everything; it was like a town of the dead, a churchyard with gigantic and grotesque tombstones.

Wondering where all the busy life of the day had so utterly disappeared to, he made his way to a back door that entered the inn by means of the stables, thinking thus to reach his room unobserved. He reached the courtyard safely and crossed it by keeping close to the shadow of the wall. He sidled down it, mincing along on tiptoe, just as the old men did when they entered the *salle à manger.* He was horrified to find himself doing this instinctively. A strange impulse came to him, catching him somehow in the centre of his body – an impulse to drop upon all fours and run swiftly and silently. He glanced upwards and the idea came to him to leap up upon the window-sill overhead instead of going round by the stairs. This occurred to him as the easiest, and most natural way. It was like the beginning of some horrible transformation of himself into something else. He was fearfully strung up.

The moon was higher now, and the shadows very dark along the side of the street where he moved. He kept among the deepest of them, and reached the porch with the glass doors.

But here there was light; the inmates, unfortunately, were still about. Hoping to slip across the hall unobserved and reach the stairs, he opened the door carefully and stole in. Then he saw that the hall was not empty. A large dark thing lay against the wall on his left. At first he thought it must be household articles. Then it moved, and he thought it was an immense cat, distorted in some way by the play of light and shadow. Then it rose straight up before him and he saw that it was the proprietress.

What she had been doing in this position he could only venture a dreadful guess, but the moment she stood up and faced him he was aware of some terrible dignity clothing her about that instantly recalled the girl's strange saying that she was a queen. Huge and sinister she stood there under the little oil lamp; alone with him in the empty hall. Awe stirred in his heart, and the roots of some ancient fear. He felt that he must bow to her and make some kind of obeisance. The impulse was fierce and irresistible, as of long habit. He glanced quickly about him. There was no one there. Then he deliberately inclined his head towards her. He bowed.

'Enfin! M'sieur s'est donc décidé. C'est bien alors. J'en suis contente.'

Her words came to him sonorously as through a great open space.

Then the great figure came suddenly across the flagged hall at him and seized his trembling hands. Some overpowering force moved with her and caught him.

'On pourrait faire un p'tit tour ensemble, n'est-ce pas? Nous y allons cette nuit et il faut s'exercer un peu d'avance pour cela. Ilsé, Ilsé, viens donc ici. Viens vite!'

And she whirled him round in the opening steps of some dance that seemed oddly and horribly familiar. They made no sound on the stones, this strangely assorted couple. It was all soft and stealthy. And presently, when the air seemed to thicken like smoke, and a red glare as of flame shot through it, he was aware that someone else had joined them and that his hand the mother had released was now tightly held by the daughter. Ilsé had come in answer to the call, and he saw her with leaves of vervain twined in her dark hair, clothed in tattered vestiges of some curious garment, beautiful as the night, and horribly, odiously, loathsomely seductive.

'To the Sabbath! To the Sabbath!' they cried. 'On to the! Witches' Sabbath!'

Up and down that narrow hall they danced, the women on each side of him, to the wildest measure he had ever imagined, yet which he dimly, dreadfully remembered, till the lamp on the wall flickered and went out, and they were left in total darkness. And the devil woke in his heart with a thousand vile suggestions and made him afraid.

Suddenly they released his hands and he heard the voice of the mother cry that it was time, and they must go. Which way they went he did not pause to see. He only realised that he was free, and he blundered through the darkness till he found the stairs and then tore up them to his room as though all hell was at his heels.

He flung himself on the sofa, with his face in his hands, and groaned. Swiftly, reviewing a dozen ways of immediate escape, all equally impossible, he finally decided that the only thing to do for the moment was to sit quiet and wait. He must see what was going to happen. At least in the privacy of his own bedroom he would be fairly safe. The door was locked. He crossed over and softly opened the window which gave upon the courtyard and also permitted a partial view of the hall through the glass doors.

As he did so the hum and murmur of a great activity reached his ears from the streets beyond – the sound of footsteps and voices muffled by distance. He leaned out cautiously and listened. The moonlight was clear and strong now, but his own window was in shadow, the silver disc being still behind the house. It came to him irresistibly that the inhabitants of the town, who a little while before had all been invisible behind closed doors, were now issuing forth, busy upon some secret and unholy errand. He listened intently.

At first everything about him was silent, but soon he became aware of movements going on in the house itself. Rustlings and cheepings came to him across that still, moonlit yard. A concourse of living beings sent the hum of their activity into the night. Things were on the move everywhere. A biting, pungent odour rose through the air, coming he knew not whence. Presently his eyes became glued to the windows of the opposite wall where the moonshine fell in a soft blaze.

The roof overhead, and behind him, was reflected clearly in the panes of glass, and he saw the outlines of dark bodies moving with long footsteps over the tiles and along the coping.

They passed swiftly and silently, shaped like immense cats, in an endless procession across the pictured glass, and then appeared to leap down to a lower level where he lost sight of them. He just caught the soft thudding of their leaps. Sometimes their shadows fell upon the white wall opposite, and then he could not make out whether they were the shadows of human beings or of cats. They seemed to change swiftly from one to the other. The transformation looked horribly real, for they leaped like human beings, yet changed swiftly in the air immediately afterwards, and dropped like animals.

The yard, too, beneath him, was now alive with the creeping movements of dark forms all stealthily drawing towards the porch with the glass doors. They kept so closely to the wall that he could not determine their actual shape, but when he saw that they passed on to the great congregation that was gathering in the hall, he understood that these were the creatures whose leaping shadows he had first seen reflected in the window-panes opposite. They were coming from all parts of the town, reaching the appointed meeting-place across the roofs and tiles, and springing from level to level till they came to the yard.

Then a new sound caught his ear, and he saw that the windows all about him were being softly opened, and that to each window came a face. A moment later figures began dropping hurriedly down into the yard. And these figures, as they lowered themselves down from the windows, were human, he saw; but once safely in the yard they fell upon all fours and changed in the swiftest possible second into – cats – huge, silent cats. They ran in streams to join the main body in the hall beyond.

So, after all, the rooms in the house had not been empty and unoccupied.

Moreover, what he saw no longer filled him with amazement. For he remembered it all. It was familiar. It had all happened before just so, hundreds of times, and he himself had taken part in it and known the wild madness of it all. The outline of the old building changed, the yard grew larger, and he seemed to be staring down upon it from a much greater height through smoky vapours. And, as he looked, half remembering, the old pains of long ago, fierce and sweet, furiously assailed him, and the blood stirred horribly as he heard the Call of the Dance again in his heart and tasted the ancient magic of Ilsé whirling by his side.

Suddenly he started back. A great lithe cat had leaped softly up from the shadows below on to the sill close to his face, and was staring fixedly at him with the eyes of a human. 'Come,' it seemed to say, 'come with us to the Dance! Change as of old! Transform yourself swiftly and come!' Only too well he understood the creature's soundless call.

It was gone again in a flash with scarcely a sound of its padded feet on the stones, and then others dropped by the score down the side of the house, past his very eyes, all changing as they fell and darting away rapidly, softly, towards the gathering point. And again he felt the dreadful desire to do likewise; to murmur the old incantation, and then drop upon hands and knees and run swiftly for the great flying leap into the air. Oh, how the passion of it rose within him like a flood, twisting his very entrails, sending his heart's desire flaming forth into the night for the old, old Dance of the Sorcerers at the Witches' Sabbath! The whirl of the stars was about him; once more he met the magic of the moon. The power of the wind, rushing from precipice and forest, leaping from cliff to cliff across the valleys, tore him away. . . . He heard the cries of the dancers and their wild laughter, and with this savage girl in his embrace he danced furiously about the dim Throne where sate the Figure with the sceptre of majesty. . . .

Then, suddenly, all became hushed and still, and the fever died down a little in his heart. The calm moonlight flooded a courtyard empty and deserted. They had started. The procession was off into the sky. And he was left behind – alone.

Vezin tiptoed softly across the room and unlocked the door.

The murmur from the streets, growing momentarily as he

advanced, met his ears. He made his way with the utmost caution down the corridor. At the head of the stairs he paused and listened. Below him, the hall where they had gathered was dark and still, but through opened doors and windows on the far side of the building came the sound of a great throng moving farther and farther into the distance.

He made his way down the creaking wooden stairs, dreading yet longing to meet some straggler who should point the way, but finding no one; across the dark hall, so lately thronged with living, moving things, and out through the opened front doors into the street. He could not believe that he was really left behind, really forgotten, that he had been purposely permitted to escape. It perplexed him.

Nervously he peered about him, and up and down the street; then, seeing nothing, advanced slowly down the pavement.

The whole town, as he went, showed itself empty and deserted, as though a great wind had blown everything alive out of it. The doors and windows of the houses stood open to the night; nothing stirred; moonlight and silence lay over all. The night lay about him like a cloak. The air, soft and cool, caressed his cheek like the touch of a great furry paw. He gained confidence and began to walk quickly, though still keeping to the shadowed side. Nowhere could he discover the faintest sign of the great unholy exodus he knew had just taken place. The moon sailed high over all in a sky cloudless and serene.

Hardly realising where he was going, he crossed the open market-place and so came to the ramparts, whence he knew a pathway descended to the high road and along which he could make good his escape to one of the other little towns that lay to the northward, and so to the railway.

But first he paused and gazed out over the scene at his feet where the great plain lay like a silver map of some dream country. The still beauty of it entered his heart, increasing his sense of bewilderment and unreality. No air stirred, the leaves of the plane trees stood motionless, the near details were defined with the sharpness of day against dark shadows, and in the distance the fields and woods melted away into haze and shimmering mistiness.

But the breath caught in his throat and he stood stockstill as though transfixed when his gaze passed from the horizon and fell upon the near prospect in the depth of the valley at his feet. The whole lower slopes of the hill, that lay hid from the brightness of the moon, were aglow, and through the glare he saw countless moving forms, shifting thick and fast between the openings of the trees; while overhead, like leaves driven by the wind, he discerned flying shapes that hovered darkly one moment against the sky and then settled down with cries and weird singing through the branches into the region that was aflame.

Spellbound, he stood and stared for a time that he could not measure. And then, moved by one of the terrible impulses that seemed to control the whole adventure, he climbed swiftly upon the top of the broad coping, and balanced a moment where the valley gaped at his feet. But in that very instant, as he stood hovering, a sudden movement among the shadows of the houses caught his eye, and he turned to see the outline of a large animal dart swiftly across the open space behind him, and land with a flying leap upon the top of the wall a little lower down. It ran like the wind to his feet and then rose up beside him upon the ramparts. A shiver seemed to run through the moonlight, and his sight trembled for a second. His heart pulsed fearfully. Ilsé stood beside him, peering into his face.

Some dark substance, he saw, stained the girl's face and skin, shining in the moonlight as she stretched her hands towards him; she was dressed in wretched tattered garments that yet became her mightily; rue and vervain twined about her temples; her eyes glittered with unholy light. He only just controlled the wild impulse to take her in his arms and leap with her from their giddy perch into the valley below.

'See!' she cried, pointing with an arm on which the rags fluttered in the rising wind towards the forest aglow in the distance. 'See where they await us! The woods are alive! Already the Great Ones are there, and the dance will soon begin! The slave is here! Anoint yourself and come!'

Though a moment before the sky was clear and cloudless, yet even while she spoke the face of the moon grew dark and the wind began to toss in the crests of the plane trees at his feet. Stray gusts brought the sounds of hoarse singing and crying from the lower slopes of the hill, and the pungent odour he had already noticed about the courtyard of the inn rose about him in the air.

'Transform, transform!' she cried again, her voice rising like a song. 'Rub well your skin before you fly. Come! Come with me to the Sabbath, to the madness of its furious delight, to the sweet abandonment of its evil worship! See! The Great Ones are there, and the terrible Sacraments prepared. The Throne is occupied. Anoint and come! Anoint and come!

She grew to the height of a tree beside him, leaping upon the wall with flaming eyes and hair strewn upon the night. He too began to change swiftly. Her hands touched the skin of his face and neck, streaking him with the burning salve that sent the old magic into his blood with the power before which fades all that is good.

A wild roar came up to his ears from the heart of the wood, and the girl, when she heard it, leaped upon the wall in the frenzy of her wicked joy.

'Satan is there!' she screamed, rushing upon him and striving to draw him with her to the edge of the wall. 'Satan has come! The Sacraments call us! Come, with your dear apostate soul, and we will worship and dance till the moon dies and the world is forgotten!'

Just saving himself from the dreadful plunge, Vezin struggled to release himself from her grasp, while the passion tore at his reins and all but mastered him. He shrieked aloud, not knowing what he said, and then he shrieked again. It was the old impulses, the old awful habits instinctively finding voice; for though it seemed to him that he merely shrieked nonsense, the words he uttered really had meaning in them, and were intelligible. It was the ancient call. And it was heard below. It was answered.

The wind whistled at the skirts of his coat as the air round him darkened with many flying forms crowding upwards out of the valley. The crying of hoarse voices smote upon his ears, coming closer. Strokes of wind buffeted him, tearing him this way and that along the crumbling top of the stone wall; and Ilsé clung to him with her long shining arms, smooth and bare, holding him fast about the neck. But not Ilsé alone, for a dozen of them surrounded him, dropping out of the air. The pungent odour of the anointed bodies stifled him, exciting him to the old madness of the Sabbath, the dance of the witches and sorcerers doing honour to the personified Evil of the world.

'Anoint and away! Anoint and away!' they cried in wild chorus about him. 'To the Dance that never dies! To the sweet and fearful fantasy of evil!'

Another moment and he would have yielded and gone, for his will turned soft and the flood of passionate memory all but overwhelmed him, when – so can a small thing alter the whole course of an adventure – he caught his foot upon a loose stone in the edge of the wall, and then fell with a sudden crash on to the ground below. But he fell towards the houses, in the open space of dust and cobble stones, and fortunately not into the gaping depth of the valley on the farther side.

And they, too, came in a tumbling heap about him, like flies upon a piece of food, but as they fell he was released for a moment from the power of their touch, and in that brief instant of freedom there flashed into his mind the sudden intuition that saved him. Before he could regain his feet he saw them scrabbling awkwardly back upon the wall, as though batlike they could only fly by dropping from a height, and had no hold upon him in the open. Then, seeing them perched there in a row like cats upon a roof, all dark and singularly shapeless, their eyes like lamps, the sudden memory came back to him of Ilsé's terror at the sight of fire.

Quick as a flash he found his matches and lit the dry leaves that lay under the wall.

Dry and withered, they caught fire at once, and the wind carried the flame in a long line down the length of the wall, licking upwards as it ran; and with shrieks and wailings, the crowded row of forms upon the top melted away into the air on the other side, and were gone with a great rush and whirring of their bodies down into the heart of the haunted valley, leaving Vezin breathless and shaken in the middle of the deserted ground.

'Ilsé!' he called feebly; 'Ilsé!' for his heart ached to think that she was really gone to the great Dance without him, and that he had lost the opportunity of its fearful joy. Yet at the same time his relief was so great, and he was so dazed and troubled in mind with the whole thing, that he hardly knew what he was saying, and only cried aloud in the fierce storm of his emotion. . . .

The fire under the wall ran its course, and the moonlight came out again, soft and clear, from its temporary eclipse. With one last shuddering look at the ruined ramparts, and a feeling of horrid wonder for the haunted valley beyond, where the shapes still crowded and flew, he turned his face towards the town and slowly made his way in the direction of the hotel.

And as he went, a great wailing of cries, and a sound of howling, followed him from the gleaming forest below, growing fainter and fainter with the bursts of wind as he disappeared between the houses.

VI

'It may seem rather abrupt to you, this sudden tame ending,' said Arthur Vezin, glancing with flushed face and timid eyes at Dr Silence sitting there with his notebook,' but the fact is – er – from that moment my memory seems to have failed rather. I have no distinct recollection of how I got home or what precisely I did.

'It appears I never went back to the inn at all. I only dimly recollect racing down a long white road in the moonlight, past woods and villages, still and deserted, and then the dawn came up, and I saw the towers of a biggish town and so came to a station.

'But, long before that, I remember pausing somewhere on the road and looking back to where the hill-town of my adventure stood up in the moonlight, and thinking how exactly like a great monstrous cat it lay there upon the plain, its huge front paws lying down the two main streets, and the twin and broken towers of the cathedral marking its torn ears against the sky. That picture stays in my mind with the utmost vividness to this day.

'Another thing remains in my mind from that escape – namely, the sudden sharp reminder that I had not paid my bill, and the decision I made, standing there on the dusty highroad, that the small baggage I had left behind would more than settle for my indebtedness.

'For the rest, I can only tell you that I got coffee and bread at a café on the outskirts of this town I had come to, and soon after found my way to the station and caught a train later in the day. That same evening I reached London.'

'And how long altogether,' asked John Silence quietly, 'do you think you stayed in the town of the adventure?'

Vezin looked up sheepishly.

'I was coming to that,' he resumed, with apologetic wrigglings of his body. 'In London I found that I was a whole week out in my reckoning of time. I had stayed over a week in the town, and it ought to have been September 15th – instead of which it was only September 10th!'

'So that, in reality, you had only stayed a night or two in the inn?' queried the doctor.

Vezin hesitated before replying. He shuffled upon the mat.

'I must have gained time somewhere,' he said at length – 'somewhere or somehow. I certainly had a week to my credit. I can't explain it. I can only give you the fact.'

'And this happened to you last year, since when you have never been back to the place?'

'Last autumn, yes,' murmured Vezin; 'and I have never dared to go back. I think I never want to.'

'And, tell me,' asked Dr Silence at length, when he saw that the little man had evidently come to the end of his words and had nothing more to say, 'had you ever read up the subject of the old witchcraft practices during the Middle Ages, or been at all interested in the subject?'

'Never!' declared Vezin emphatically. 'I had never given a thought to such matters so far as I know –'

'Or to the question of reincarnation, perhaps?'

'Never – before my adventure; but I have since,' he replied significantly.

There was, however, something still on the man's mind that he wished to relieve himself of by confession, yet could with difficulty bring himself to mention; and it was only after the sympathetic tactfulness of the doctor had provided numerous openings that he at length availed himself of one of them, and stammered that he would like to show him the marks he still had on his neck where, he said, the girl had touched him with her anointed hands.

He took off his collar after infinite fumbling hesitation, and lowered his shirt a little for the doctor to see. And there, on the surface of the skin, lay a faint reddish line across the shoulder and extending a little way down the back towards the spine. It certainly indicated exactly the position an arm might have taken in the act of embracing. And on the other side of the neck, slightly higher up, was a similar mark, though not quite so clearly defined.

'That was where she held me that night on the ramparts,' he whispered, a strange light coming and going in his eyes.

It was some weeks later when I again found occasion to consult John Silence concerning another extraordinary case that had come under my notice, and we fell to discussing Vezin's story. Since hearing it, the doctor had made investigations on his own account, and one of his secretaries had discovered that Vezin's ancestors had actually lived for generations in the very town where the adventure came to him. Two of them, both women, had been tried and convicted as witches, and had been burned alive at the stake. Moreover, it had not been difficult to prove that the very inn where Vezin stayed was built about 1700 upon the spot where the funeral pyres stood and the executions took place. The town was a sort of headquarters for all the sorcerers and witches of the entire region, and after conviction they were burnt there literally by scores.

'It seems strange,' continued the doctor, 'that Vezin should have remained ignorant of all this; but, on the other hand, it was not the kind of history that successive generations would have been anxious to keep alive, or to repeat to their children. Therefore I am inclined to think he still knows nothing about it.

'The whole adventure seems to have been a very vivid revival of the memories of an earlier life, caused by coming directly into contact with the living forces still intense enough to hang about the place, and, by a most singular chance too, with the very souls who had taken part with him in the events of that particular life. For the mother and daughter who impressed him so strangely must have been leading actors, with himself, in the scenes and practices of witchcraft which at that period dominated the imaginations of the whole country.

'One has only to read the histories of the times to know that these witches claimed the power of transforming themselves into various animals, both for the purposes of disguise and also to convey themselves swiftly to the scenes of their imaginary orgies. Lycanthropy, or the power to change themselves into wolves, was everywhere believed in, and the ability to transform themselves into cats by rubbing their bodies with a special salve or ointment provided by Satan himself, found equal credence. The witchcraft trials abound in evidences of such universal beliefs.'

Dr Silence quoted chapter and verse from many writers on the subject, and showed how every detail of Vezin's adventure had a basis in the practices of those dark days.

'But that the entire affair took place subjectively in the man's own consciousness, I have no doubt,' he went on, in reply to my questions; 'for my secretary, who has been to the town to investigate, discovered his signature in the visitors' book, and proved by it that he had arrived on September 8th, and left suddenly without paying his bill. He left two days later, and they still were in possession of his dirty brown bag and some tourist clothes. I paid a few francs in settlement of his debt, and have sent his luggage on to him. The daughter was absent from home, but the proprietress, a large woman very much as he described her, told my secretary that he had seemed a very strange, absent-minded kind of gentleman, and after his disappearance she had feared for a long time that he had met with a violent end in the neighbouring forest where he used to roam about alone.

'I should like to have obtained a personal interview with the daughter so as to ascertain how much was subjective and how much actually took place with her as Vezin told it. For her dread of fire and the sight of burning must, of course, have been the intuitive memory of her former painful death at the stake, and have thus explained why he fancied more than once that he saw her through smoke and flame.'

'And that mark on his skin, for instance?' I inquired.

'Merely the marks produced by hysterical brooding,' he replied, 'like the stigmata of the *religieuses,* and the bruises which appear on the bodies of hypnotised subjects who have been told to expect them. This is very common and easily explained. Only it seems curious that these marks should have remained so long in Vezin's case. Usually they disappear quickly.'

'Obviously he is still thinking about it all, brooding, and living it all over again,' I ventured.

'Probably. And this makes me fear that the end of his trouble is not yet. We shall hear of him again. It is a case, alas! I can do little to alleviate.'

Dr Silence spoke gravely and with sadness in his voice.

'And what do you make of the Frenchman in the train?' I asked further – 'the man who warned him against the place, *à cause du sommeil et à cause des chats?* Surely a very singular incident?'

'A *very* singular incident indeed,' he made answer slowly, 'and one I can only explain on the basis of a highly improbable coincidence –'

'Namely?'

'That the man was one who had himself stayed in the town and undergone there a similar experience. I should like to find this man and ask him. But the crystal is useless here, for I have no slightest clue to go upon, and I can only conclude that some singular psychic affinity, some force still active in his being out of the same past life, drew him thus to the personality of Vezin, and enabled him to fear what might happen to him, and thus to warn him as he did.

'Yes,' he presently continued, half talking to himself, 'I suspect in this case that Vezin was swept into the vortex of forces arising out of the intense activities of a past life, and that he lived over again a scene in which he had often played a leading part centuries before. For strong actions set up forces that are so slow to exhaust themselves, they may be said in a sense never to die. In this case they were not vital enough to render the illusion complete, so that the little man found himself caught in a very distressing confusion of the present and the past; yet he was sufficiently sensitive to recognise that it was true, and to fight against the degradation of returning, even in memory, to a former and lower state of development.

'Ah yes!' he continued, crossing the floor to gaze at the darkening sky, and seemingly quite oblivious of my presence, 'subliminal up-rushes of memory like this can be exceedingly painful, and sometimes exceedingly dangerous. I only trust that this gentle soul may soon escape from this obsession of a passionate and tempestuous past. But I doubt it, I doubt it.'

His voice was hushed with sadness as he spoke, and when he turned back into the room again there was an expression of profound yearning upon his face, the yearning of a soul whose desire to help is sometimes greater than his power.